NIGHT SKIES

OVER

VALHALLOW

a fantasy novel for grown-ups

about life, love, magic,

and the way things might seem to be

by Dan Osarchuk

Written by Dan Osarchuk

Cover picture by Traci Meek

Cover design and formatting by Rachel Bostwick

Special thanks to Ben, Bruce, Craig, and others, who gave me so many years of great gaming.

Special thanks too to Kolbe Ann and to Mom for helping me to further refine this work.

Thanks also to Josh for his advice on helping me to get this work published.

Lyrics on p.50 by Michael Osarchuk (Dad)

Please note that this is a work of fantasy fiction and no characters, places, or situations in this book are intended to represent actual, real-life people, places, or situations, though the themes that they represent certainly might be.

TABLE OF CONTENTS

PART 1

Chapter 1

Gore

The thing's stinking breath still lingered in the cold mountain air. Pine forest loomed overhead as a solidly-built man, dressed all in black, examined the ground. Bloodstains and hoofprints littered the earth. His wide-brimmed hat concealed his eyes from the broken sunlight that streamed down from above, his long trench coat, gloves, and tall boots deflecting the wintry chill from the earth below.

Looking to and fro, he saw the path of disturbance that had been made when it had entered and left this place. It would seem that, like no normal beast, these things took time to become accustomed to their cursed ways. He loaded another bolt into his crossbow, a special one.

As he rose, the scent of fresh pine filled his senses, spoiled somewhat still as the thing's breath dissipated, leaving only a strange animalistic musk. It was unmistakable; he could probably follow this thing with his eyes closed. Checking his crossbow, he advanced into the wilderness, ready to kill the abomination. As he followed its trail, memories came to him: burned-out homes, slain livestock, terrified villagers, and... the *bodies*. The "Man-beast": that is what they called it. Little did they know...

Night Skies Over Valhallow

The forest grew denser. Out of the corner of his eye, Oborren thought he saw something move. Whipping around, he trained his weapon on the spot, but saw only trees. The pungent scent was stronger - the beast had recently been here. A noise, a snap of something in the forest. Was it the *thing*? He leaned low and scanned around, one hand's finger on the trigger, the other on his long knife. One could never be too careful. He waited, practiced, determined, ready...

But nothing. All quiet, as a cold breeze echoed through the woods, threatening to lose the scent. And the hoofprints were harder to spot here as well. The ground was frozen harder, making tracking this beast more challenging. The hunter continued then, following the trail as best he could. A few more bends and he noted that he was losing elevation; the trail was going generally downward now. A sound of moving water up ahead made him concerned: if the beast crossed it well before him, then he could lose the trail for sure.

The path grew darker as the tree canopy overhead grew heavy. It grew colder too, though Oborren wasn't sure if it was just the temperature that was dropping. He now felt like he was being watched. He subtly glanced left and right, as he continued to point his weapon down, keeping his pace steady. It was almost as if the trail was terraced here, leading like some sort of natural staircase to the river passing below. Each step was about a 4' drop, roughly five steps in all.

Just perfect, Oborren thought, that thing could be hiding anywhere.

Shouldering his crossbow, Oborren rechecked his gear and made the first jump. WHOOSH... then the impact of solid earth beneath his boots. He quickly whipped out his long knife, expecting the thing to leap out at him from one of the hidden corners of the terrace. But there was nothing.

2

He repeated the process four more times to the trail's base. Each time, expecting an attack; each time finding nothing.

He continued following the trail, his legs and feet still aching from navigating the steps. He could now see the river up ahead. The vegetation grew thicker and the sound and scent of moving water made him prick up his ears.

The river spanned at least 20' across, though it was only 4' deep at most, if his estimation could be trusted. The ground here felt softer too, perhaps being warmed by the current, and he saw a wild assortment of hoof tracks going in various directions. Where the heck was the thing going?

He ventured a squat to look at the tracks more closely, knowing full well that he would be exposing himself to an easy attack, if that thing was still even around. To his dismay, there were no blood stains- he had hoped his shot would have at least wounded this thing, if not allowed it to be more easily tracked. But that was not the way with most of the unnatural things he hunted. Such beings could only be killed in certain ways and were otherwise damnably resistant to other forms of attack. That's what made him a hunter.

He could still remember when Pa had shown him a *different thing* in the cellar. Gods, how it stunk! And unfortunately, it wasn't *really* dead, of course. And yet Pa had chained it up all the same for young Oborren to practice on it, to learn how to overcome his fears and how to fight and *kill* such things. He still hadn't forgotten how relieved he was when Pa finally destroyed that thing's head- the only way for it to truly die. That was his first lesson in destroying the unnatural, nasty things that most would never want to believe in, let alone face.

And yet what of such dangers of this world? Perhaps it wasn't entirely a *bad* thing to have real monsters to fight. For certain, they were terrifying and awful to behold, but they did make humans seem better by comparison. Oborren mused that this thing's victims were no saints themselves, yet now they seemed more saint-like because they *were* its victims.

Perhaps parents were treating their children a little better today, knowing that this thing is around. Or husbands and wives might forgive one another a little more quickly, rather than play the blame game. Perhaps neighbors might watch out for each other a little more. Perhaps brothers might...

Oborren choked back a wave of sorrow at his careless memory. Not a good idea to dwell on such things, especially during a hunt. A sudden snapping sound finally broke him out of his reverie, back into the moment. He realized that his legs were aching since he had been crouching this whole time. Panic began to set in as he picked up the thing's scent again. It must be close; he pulled his flail from his side.

Suddenly, something leaped from the brush. It was upon him! He yelled as a fawn dashed out from the thick foliage. That was not his prey! He laughed at himself and stretched his muscles as he looked for the trail again. The rushing of the river masked any other sounds. Maybe the man-beast was afraid to cross the water?

Oborren looked around for a new position. If he could expect this beast to think like an animal, or even think like a man, then that would be something. But he couldn't. It would seem that it acted erratically, like as if under some madness. Or perhaps it was Oborren who was under some spell? At times, he felt like he was nearly upon the fiend, ready to end it. At others, the creature was nowhere to be seen. What madness affected this creature, or caused it to affect him?

At that moment, seemingly out of nowhere, a pair of sharp teeth missed Oborren's jugular by less than an inch. He tried to duck out of the way, but it was too late: the thing's humanoid body barreled him down under its heavy weight. Instinctively, Oborren drew his blade with his free hand and plunged it into one the beast's hairy legs as he fell. It screamed in fury, stinking breath

4

adding to the already pungent stench of its bestial nature. He rolled away just in time, avoiding what looked like a cloven hoof thrust at his face.

Regaining his footing, Oborren desperately tried to steady himself and look for another weapon. The beast roared as it got back to its feet, ripping his long knife from its thigh and hurling it into the brush. Standing over 7' tall, the creature had the head and legs of a stag and the body of a large, muscular, not-clad-enough human. To his dismay, Oborren could see his crossbow lying behind the thing. It glared at him, lowered its antlered head and made ready to charge. His body poised, Oborren waited for it, and then it happened. He accidentally locked eyes with the thing, and saw what he dreaded: human eyes.

It brayed and charged. Oborren leaped out of the way at the last second, allowing its momentum to carry it further passed him. He rolled over, sprang up, and dashed for his crossbow. The stagman roared in fury. Oborren's shaking hand picked up the weapon, only to have the special bolt already loaded in it fall out as he ducked out of the way, nearly having his head knocked off by a huge branch wielded by the stagman! Thinking quickly, he grabbed some earth, made a distracting motion with his other hand, and then threw it into the creature's eyes. The stagman screamed in even greater rage, seemingly temporarily blinded now, but even angrier than before.

Nearly stumbling, Oborren grabbed his bolt and sprinted back up the hill, away from the river, to put some distance between him and the beast. Thankfully, the creature remained close to where he left it and had only begun to stumble to the river's edge. Whether it was a random act or some remaining human faculty to wash out its eyes, Oborren knew not, but he was glad nonetheless. The hunter took careful aim, his wide-brimmed hat shading his eye as he targeted the stagman's chest. With a click, the trigger released.

The bolt shot through the air, landing true into the stagman. A good hit! Oborren allowed his body to relax a little as he awaited the thing's death. *Birchwood for a staghead, to return its gentle demise*, as the hunter's saying goes- the only true way to really kill such a monstrosity. He watched as the bolt's black feathers fluttered in the wind, shaft now lodged into its chest, as the creature's just-washed human eyes lolled back. Drool came dripping out of its stag mouth, its cloven beast legs wobbled, and it fell.

Quiet came to the hunter who only now had realized how hard his heart had been beating during the encounter. Not wanting to take any chances, Oborren retrieved his long knife, stalked up to the stagman, and plunged it into its gut. No response from the thing, just the oozing of vital humors, which were too much like that of a human's for him to watch. Oborren would let out a sigh of relief, but his increasing sorrow was becoming too great. He backed away, not wanting to tarry too long too near the beast, making sure to keep his eyes away from its face. The looming pines around him stared down, the river's current still flowing: did they notice this battle between man and beast? How many such battles had they seen before? Or did they even notice?

Arcadian, he thought, an Arcadian Atavar. He nearly sobbed as he grabbed the journal out of his pack. Grabbing quill and ink to identify the prey, record the kill, and hopefully get his mind off his grief. *Beast in form only of head and legs.* Yes, Arcadian, he decided. Minoan would have been just a beast head, Antediluvian would be bipedal beast all over... A tear streamed down his face. St... Stag Arcadian Atavar, ss... slain by a bolt of birch, on the 2nd day of the full moon, in December, the 413th year After Lights Out, in the Wild Lands of Gore, due northwest of Middlechest.

There. It was done. Identified and recorded. Now the beast was no more and this hunt was over. Man had defeated beast, defeated monster... or at least, so he would hope.

What led folk to dabble in such ways as this, to become a monster? Yes, this could certainly be a hard world, but trafficking with unclean spirits? Why? Why would someone think that such a horrible transformation could help them?

Memories of happier times began to creep from Oborren's mind...

"Why?!?!" he shouted at the silent forest.

No response came.

Who would be foolish enough to don a stag's head and pray to become a monster? To engage in unclean, horrid rituals to make the mask a reality? That this monster had caused such damage did not bother Oborren as much; that someone would *choose to become* such a monster... did.

Death is guaranteed in this life, but what life have we chosen to live?

He glanced over at the inert form lying near the river bank. Who could possibly choose that?

He knew he'd have to bury the thing and scatter its ashes in the river just to make sure. And he knew he didn't want to, especially if he had to see its eyes again.

They reminded him too much of his own.

Chapter 2

Stephania

It had been a good run for Kolveig. He had avoided the dread Dukes of Madisonburg, the Goblins of Daphnaburg, Frankish Nationalists in Narquay, Zombies in Monjaksen, Magicrats in Caelum Mount, Fascists in Mauriatown, and even the Vikings of Strass Hill. It had been a good run. Always the champion of the Working Man... er... Person, Kolveig had made it his mission to point out the Oppression of the Ruling Classes every chance he got.

Granted, that often got him beaten and jailed, but it was worth it! He knew those stupid Bourgeoisie Lords learned a lesson or two when he would walk right up to them, knock off their stupid hats, and then deride their failure to live up to the Code of Karl! He had also enjoyed posting *non-anonymous* rants to the various Message Board Trees in those localities. Most of the common folk did not seem to respond, but he knew that he was getting through to them nevertheless.

Ah, Karl. The Anti-Imperious Deity himself. Kolveig was a follower of him in the purest form. While the Bolsheviks of Helltowne might *say* that they stood up for the Working Man/ Person, having a 140 hour work week would suggest otherwise, even if they called it 'Glorious'!

Night Skies Over Valhallow

"What did they know of Committees? Or of Power to the People? Bah! They had to be counter-revolutionaries! They had to be.... OUCH!!" Kolveig's thoughts were interrupted by a stern, but not unattractive woman striking him forcefully with a horsewhip.

"Silence, boy!" she commanded.

Kolveig bit back his outrage. The Elimination of All Gender Distinction was certainly a noble goal, but this 'matriarchy' as practiced in Stephania was no answer. He had arrived in this strange town only yesterday. As a matter of course, he then proceeded to their most obvious Opiate of the Masses, their 'Yonitarian Church', remaining cleverly quiet until he was in an area of Greatest Possible Effect: their Inner Sanctum.

He smiled to himself. Kolveig loved certain words... and he hated certain others; that's what made him a Karlist. And that's why if someone ever transcribed all of the Enlightened Declarations he ever said, both the words he liked and the ones he hated, they would all begin with Capital Letters, even if they weren't proper nouns. It was the *ideology* behind those words that mattered most to him, rather than their *actual meanings*. Most other fundamentalists in the Vale would agree, though they might capitalize *other* words instead. And even still, the more intense fundamentalists might actually capitalize ALL of the letters in every word they wrote, whether Good or Bad. *Policy was the Best Honesty* in their minds, as it was in Kolveig's.

So Kolveig had, of course, attempted to Enlighten the amazons as to their failure to Eliminate Gender Inequality, as well as their additional Conspiratorial Failure to Eliminate Discrimination Against Atheists. They proceeded to then attempt the low-brow method of throwing him out. He struggled and fought, even wielding his Marxian Hammer to good effect, though the amazons fought well in return. He eventually had to flee to the Men's Lavatory to regroup. After seeing that all of the toilet seats were nailed down with dire warnings against anyone who might attempt to leave them up, he swooned at the implications and was overwhelmed by the guards, who apparently even had no respect for one attempting to claim Sanctuary Via Lavatory.

His attention now returned to the Oppression at Hand. His own hands bound to a wooden whipping pole, his standard issue Proletarian Karlist longjacket idly cast aside. The cold winter sun did nothing to ease the pain in his back.

"I'm sure there's some Stephenian Committee that I can address my grievances..."

WHHACKK! The whip responded again. The pain on Kolveig's back was unbearable now. He could feel the blood dripping down his sides, mingling with his long, black beard.

"WHAT DID YOU SAY?!?!   It's pronounced STE – PHA -- NIA!" CCRACKK! WHHACKK!

Apparently this amazon hated certain words even more than Kolveig.

As the red haze of pain overtook him, Kolveig could make out the vague image of another amazon coming forward. She looked even more stern and muscular. As he began to black out, he hoped that his death would at least help motivate others to Stand Up For Equality.

* * *

Brymanah stared at the sleeping man in her cottage. *Why did I buy him?* His back, now bandaged by her best manservant, seemed to be healing well. Torvin had served her faithfully over the years. He was given to her by the Shell Oracle herself one evening at the Yoniversal Church, but there was always the need for more manservants.

Her attention refocused on the man lying there. He stirred again.

"Good. You'll need your strength," she stated.

Night Skies Over Valhallow

Brymanah knew it was a bad idea to mistreat anyone, including men. Granted, they were certainly still inferior in her eyes: overly violent, sexual, and untrustworthy, but there was no point in causing them unnecessary suffering like some of the other amazons did. The Dames could be especially harsh and she doubted it would really please Queen Hera. Some amazonian societies were even harsher to their laborers; luckily, Stephania was more enlightened.

Brymanah knew full well how the Ancient Womyn, who would go on to found Stephania, had thrown off their male oppression to create the paradise she lived in now. No longer would womyn have to fear male aggression, sexual obsessiveness, senseless wars, destruction of the environment, poor matching of colors, and so forth. No longer. While she and her sister Hippolytes fought to keep the realm safe from invading scum, the males in Stephania cleaned the homes, fixed the dinners, and raised the children. It was perfect.

Her attention focused now on the man she had saved. He began to stir. It was time.

Placing her wide, sharp cutlass on the mantle, she removed her leather cuirass, turning and exposing her bare back to him. She felt an uneasy excitement at being so exposed. This was the Examination and the Law for all new manservants in Stephania, and it must be done.

Kolveig rubbed his eyes and groaned as he took in his new surroundings. He got up off of the low mat he was laying on and noticed the decorations of the room: knick-knacks, paintings, and trophies- all of a military, amazonian bent. Brilliant sunshine gleamed in through a pane glass window. A cutlass was lying on the mantle, glittering in the light. It was quite sharp, and the even-more-muscular amazon he had seen before was turned away from him, her back exposed.

"What is this? Some sort of Test?" he queried.

Brymanah did not answer. She hoped now that this fool would try to attack her, so she could show him who was in charge. She was starting to find him annoying.

"Listen, this is no way to run a Society. If you want to have Gender Equality, you don't whip a Faithful Karlist unconscious and then turn your naked back at him and hope he attacks you with a sword."

"Shut up."

"What kind of insane people would think that having women dominate men might create any sort of harmony?"

"Shut up!"

"I mean really, what sort of wealth redistribution system do you have in this damn locality anyway?"

"SHUT UP!!!" Brymanah could contain her rage no longer. She spun around, grabbed the cutlass, and thrust it at him, slowing just at the last moment to only place it against his neck, rather than decapitate him.

She then noticed that he was staring at her bare chest. Pure fury arose within her now- how dare he! As the Karlist tried to explain that he couldn't help it, the amazon began to smack him senseless. After a number of hits, he was knocked to the floor.

Taking a moment to put her leather cuirass back on, Brymanah grabbed her cutlass and prepared to execute the cur- then and there. She was wrong to have saved this scum to become her manservant. It seemed that most males did not know their place after all.

Suddenly the door opened. Standing there were Poy and Jeg, two Dame acquaintances of Brymanah's. There they stood, horsewhips in hand, their tall black boots standing in stark contrast to the vivid blue sky outside.

"You are summoned to the Church, sister. The Oracle requires your immediate presence. "

Brymanah turned around and made to leave. She glanced at Kolveig lying on the floor.

"Don't worry, sister," the Dames chided, "we'll take good care of him until you get back."

Looking up meekly at the two not-unattractive, curvaceous, leather-clad amazons staring down at him, Kolveig mused that there were worse forms of torture to endure.

* * *

More brilliant winter sunshine beamed upon the Ancient Church of Yonitarian Yoniversalism. Legend had it, that at the time of Lights Out, the Founding Mothers of Stephania had met to hammer out their new society at this very place. Here it still stood and well-maintained at that, though it was said that the stables often had some organizational problems.

A unit of Hippolytes stood guard outside: plumed Grecian helms, iron breastplates, bracers, greaves, roundshields, and long spears all glittering in the light. They saluted Brymanah in amazonian fashion, their purple capes fluttering in the cold breeze. They were the warrior-guardians of Stephania, the Dames were to keep the males in line, and the Matrons were to enrich society. Being a Hippolyte of course, Brymanah assumed that she was being called because of an external threat to the realm.

Entering the great doors of the Church, she could not help but be in awe of the many Goddess statues displayed. So many wonderful facets of the Feminine! All Goddesses were honored in Stephania: from Artemis to Skadi as Maiden, from Aphrodite to Freya as Mother, and from Hecate to Hel as Crone, but most especially of all- Queen Hera herself. What better patron than the Queen of the Gods to watch over the greatest Queendom of all the Vale?

Brymanah walked forward towards the Inner Sanctuary, her sense of reverence rising, two Heran Priestesses standing on either side, dressed in white robes, hoods drawn over their faces. The glittering amethyst holy symbols of the Goddess hung from their necks. They nodded, granting the amazon entry. The towering ceiling stood over her: interlocking rafters, exquisitely carved, suggesting the movements of the Yoniverse, a testament to both the marvels of the Ancients and the dedication of the amazons who have carried on after them.

It was even said that revenants of certain Ancients still dwelt in the dustier corners of the Church, that their touch might test the faithful, when the comfort of the sun's rays had fallen. But Brymanah found it better to ignore such things.

Upon a great dais sat the Oracle herself on a surprisingly simple wooden throne. She was surrounded by priestesses, which Brymanah knew were skilled in combat, as well as spiritual matters. The lone Hippolyte approached and knelt before the Oracle.

The gregarious woman on the throne smiled at her. The Shell Oracle was no ordinary amazon. Not only was she of course gifted with great powers of divination, but she seemed to also be comfortable in all sorts of matters, whether they met with what was deemed appropriate for amazons or not. As was the case with most enlightened individuals, they never quite fit-in with their own societies, but those societies were wise to follow their counsel nonetheless. Stephania was one such society.

Brymanah gazed at the great woman, shawl in her lap, her blue eyes still youthful as they glittered and smiled at her through her dark brown curls.

"Thanks for coming, Brymanah." The Oracle looked into the stand before her. As her name suggested, it was full of sand, for Shell was rumored to have come from the shores of Atalantias to the east, where she brought the magnificent divining shells with

15

her. Used with the sand, it was all part of her divination rite, though Brymanah suspected she didn't really need them, no matter how exotic they might be in the Vale.

The Oracle was always so affable. Her magnanimous personality would often attract seekers far and wide. Even males would endure the harshness and suspicions of the amazons in order to seek her counsel and pleasant demeanor. Brymanah and certain other amazons showed their complete loyalty to her regardless. Perhaps that was why she was the one chosen to be summoned, rather than another Hippolyte?

"I've seen strange things happening in the Vale lately, Brymanah. Some of our sisters to the north, near the Hold of Kern, have started to worship a strange goddess, the Bee Queen. Not only have their minds been twisted, but apparently their bodies may have been, well..."

Brymanah shuddered at the thought. Stories of mutation were terrible enough, but to have it happen to some of her amazon sisters? Worse yet, most cases of mutation were not immediately obvious...

"And similar things have been happening in the Lands of Men, as well."

At this, all the assembled Goddess Priestesses fell silent. Many were actively indifferent to the plight of men, but then again, they did hold their Oracle in the highest regard.

"This is why I'd like you to go to Calvary, Brymanah. There is village there ruled by a womyn, a friend of mine named Agnetha. We have agreed that this New Strangeness, this Insolitus Novus, must be investigated. Venture to Valhallow with all due haste."

Brymanah nodded. This journey would probably be long and fraught with peril. She smiled as she thought of the perfect manservant to bring along with her.

Chapter 3

The Cult of R'ti

Halfdan knew that he could have a negative effect on people, but this went beyond even his usual predilection for social awkwardness. He glanced over the scroll that he had just received. Good Lord, more pronouncements from 'On High', and this time of an even more sinister slant, now directed squarely at him.

'Halfdan of Valhallow,

We have been watching you, cur. We have had a number of complaints about your behavior from certain informed individuals. You have been called to answer for your Crimes of Emotional Openness at 3 on the next day of the full moon. You are specifically allowed no counsel at this meeting, as if we would deign to entertain any such foolish mercy upon your damnable soul! You are also reminded that Tutors-Under-Review, which your foul self now most certainly is, are not permitted to express your feelings in the Schoolhouse in any way or shall thereby suffer the Branding or worse.

In addition, you are sure to not make your Yearly Required Growth now and we hereby command you to stop conversing with any other tutors in non-sanctioned matters in the meantime, <u>or else</u>!

Signed,

Ealynn and Richard, High-Monitors of the Holy Proclamation of R'ti

Halfdan gulped back his fear. If he lost his position as a tutor, how could he possibly provide for little Larnen and Kelne? He was surely doomed. His mind struggled to remember a helpful quote from Nissar or Robert or anyone. Nothing came to mind. Perhaps he had angered reality itself this time by delving too deeply into *the question?*

This world seemed so strange that in order to survive, to gain the necessary coin to provide for oneself and one's family, one had to suffer through so many things that one did not want to do. Does the raven toil? Does the yew worry about its next meal? Doubtful. It would seem that it was only in the world of mankind that this madness persisted. And a Schoolhouse certainly did not need to be so stressful, no matter how much the Faithful of R'ti would otherwise claim.

Who knew what he had done to anger them this time? He knew he was socially awkward. Others often looked at him askance around the Schoolhouse for he had been without wife for many a year. Still, the people of his new home in Calvary had seemed accepting enough, no obvious jibes, thanks perhaps to his meager talent toward hermitage. He often wondered though what life would have been like if his wife and he had remained together, but that was something he knew he needed to let go of... perhaps someday.

The Schoolhouse had been another matter. Here he was, one of the few male tutors left, too short and weak to teach at the Academy, too educated to accept a lesser post at some tavern, food-house, or merchant's floppery. The Schoolhouse work had been

18

good for many a year. Halfdan was never much for pointless toil, of course, but he did see the value in helping others and in exploring the meanings and relevancies of books and letters, helping young minds to open to the possibilities that old minds could convey. And having time to spend with Larnen and Kelne over the years was another benefit of his employ. How would he do that now? What of Larnen? What of Kelne?

First it began with a few tutors relating some strange philosophies from their farther travels. Then the High-Monitors, those at the County Castle, began to espouse R'ti Doctrine. Then a few of the School Monitors, those charged with supervising tutors at the Schoolhouse level, began to take up its worship. After that, the changes really began! Whose fault was it if a pupil failed an examination: the pupil's or their tutor's? Once the Official Answer automatically always became the latter, most tutors who could leave began to do so and the loss of so many free-thinking tutors over the years had become noticeable. Halfdan wasn't sure, but at some point, outside influences had joined in the chorus, demanding that the pupils be 'better instructed', as if the tutors were not always doing their best to make that very thing happen!

But that was not good enough apparently. In fact, year after year, it was *never* good enough. Each year, there was always some new Improved Initiative in order to improve Annua Incrementum: an exponential and irrational constant increase in pupil examination scores. What was the worst? Could it have been the insulting vignettes that the tutors were forced to act out periodically to prove some point of R'ti Doctrine? Or the 'Wear a Clown Costume to School Day'?

A new group of Monitors had been recently assigned by the Monitor Director himself: Mme. Carve as Head Monitor, with her Assistant Monitors Ms. Hollowspoke and Mr. Beauly. They took the crusade of Annua Incrementum to a whole new level with scurrilous Observances for tutors who didn't write the precise Approved Words or didn't speak in the exact Appropriate Voice & Tone when lecturing a class in especially the Correct Pattern. It seemed that they were out for blood- for tutors like Halfdan in particular.

* * *

Pupils sprinted down the marbled halls, screaming and shoving to another classroom, while tutors seemed too afraid to chastise them for fear of the wrath of the School Monitors and their High-Monitor overseers. Until recently, such dangerous behavior was never tolerated. Now, with the school firmly in the grasp of R'ti, it was permitted, since it didn't directly affect Annua Incrementum and it reduced the tutors' authority.

Halfdan's attention was drawn to a particular pair of pupils arguing over a book nearby. He rose and noticed the resistance arising within him, for it seemed that they had begun to tear apart the unabridged dictionary- one of Halfdan's favorites. Biting back the natural response to naughty pupils, Halfdan opined, "Perhaps the two of you could work this out for your Mutual Satisfaction for the Greater Benefit of All?"

Halfdan hated quoting R'ti nonsense, but it had kept the Monitors appeased (at least until the recent scroll-warnings, of course) and really, he knew that expressing one's vexation while still under its spell was often unwise. He too didn't want adults to yell when he was himself a child. Perhaps some strange, forgotten wish had somehow come true for him, after all?

A hidden like for what we don't; otherwise, our experience won't.

The larger child, Benus, looked at Halfdan and smirked. "How about you just shut yer trap, Mr. Halfdan?"

"How about... I don't." Halfdan looked straight into the child's eyes, seeing his mischievous grin slowly vanish. The child looked away, and a wave of sadness passed over the tutor. Was it this child's fault that he was so rude? The Cult would certainly not think so: it was his parent's, or his tutor's, or the town's fault, or whoever. But Halfdan realized that it was the Cult that made it

20

worse, for pupils naturally needed some discipline to mature properly, but the Cult only meted out discipline to tutors.

The pupils walked away and Halfdan carefully returned the somewhat damaged dictionary to its resting stand. The library's sage, Mrs. Fermione, approached him.

"Hope you're doing okay, Mr. Halfdan," she said. She always seemed so kind and supportive, Halfdan thought, perhaps not everyone in this place has fallen under the spell of the Cult yet.

"I am, thank you, Mrs. Fermione. How—" Halfdan cut himself off. With the recent scroll-warning against him, he didn't know who he could trust. Still, he risked engaging in a little non-sanctioned communication, "How... have you been?"

"Fine," she replied. "Some new books shall be arriving from Madisonburg today. The merchants met with some mishap on the way, so I'll have to clean all of the blood off them!" She smiled.

Halfdan couldn't tell if she was joking or simply making light of a morbid situation. It was funny nonetheless. Not wanting to press his luck with any more unsanctioned conversation though, Halfdan ventured a little chuckle, smiled, and began the trek back to his office.

Venturing through the marbled halls, he wondered if the Ancients had ever experienced the same problems as he.

As he approached one particular alcove, his pace quickened. Something bothered him about that place: the Room of Remediation was within. Outside, hung a R'ti plaque, emphasizing this year's Three 'L"s:

Labor for Tutors (ever-increasing)
Loyalty to the Monitors and to R'ti, above all else
Lasting Innovation- Everlasting Change

Night Skies Over Valhallow

Beyond the foolish R'ti rhetoric, something nasty was behind it. Something dark and brooding, a horror felt in the silence akin to waking to some dreadful presence. One that could be all too real...

He rounded the corner to his room, only to see another tutor sobbing in the hallway. It was Mrs. Geltryce. Halfdan wondered if this was some sort of Cult trick: a trap to get him into further trouble. The words of Eckhart came to him and he realized that he *had been lost in some future nightmare, perhaps one that would never be, but one that was surely now, as long as he held it.*

Breathing deeply, staying present, Halfdan approached Mrs. Geltryce.

"Are you alright?"

"No, my Observance was horrible today. A pupil was attempting to climb out the window, I yelled for him to stay inside, and the Monitor yelled at me for trying to Impinge Upon the Child's Freedom Of Expression."

"I'm sorry, I think that..."

Another Monitor, Mr. Beauly, walked by at that moment, frowned, and scribbled something on his notepad. Halfdan attempted a small joke, but the Monitor only walked on, making a "Tsk... tsk" sound. Few Cultists had a sense of humor.

He then went back into his office to write a Memorandum of Tutor Failure. By Odin, thought Halfdan, this can't be good.

It could be that it was a trap set by the Monitors after all, but Mrs. Geltryce did seem really unsettled. Realizing her Breach of Tutor Conduct (Discussing Non-educational Matters with a Tutor-under-review), she wiped her eyes and went back into her room. Pupils were screaming, running around the room having mock battles. Mrs. Geltryce quickly got them under control, even raising her voice to do so.

Dan Osarchuk

I wonder how she does it, thought Halfdan. R'ti certainly seems to have it out for *some* tutors, myself included. Was Geltryce also on the chopping block?

As Halfdan's awareness over the years had grown, he realized that the R'ti was part of something larger. A Greater Cult, perhaps made up of Multiple Cults, all with the purpose of remaking the world in a strange, utopian way. Halfdan had always considered himself to be a good person- he cared for people in general- perhaps too much. But what the Cult espoused seemed warped and deceptive, the stuff of demonism or worse. To make people act in such a way against their nature seemed so... unnatural... to him. He wondered how people fell under its spell.

It seemed that the Cult also took special aim at him for being a man and, more importantly, for not fully embracing their teachings. In fact, Halfdan only paid lip-service to their upsetting dictums and had actually embraced very little. He had hoped for a change for the better as the years went on, but the collapse in Schoolhouse rationality only seemed to get worse.

They had claimed that Walstock and the surrounding settlements would amount to nothing if the pupils did not achieve their Annua Incrementum. What that growth was and how it was measured was unsurprisingly determined by the upper hierarchy of R'ti. They knew best apparently.

There were Committees for the Discussion of R'ti Policy, where tutors would supposedly offer their input, but these were a farce. No independent ideas were ever allowed there. Those tutors who wanted to engender themselves into the Enlightened's good graces could only parrot back what the School Monitors and High-Monitors declared as Legitimate Education. All else was Heresy.

Halfdan wondered at how the other tutors were feeling from the pressure. Mrs. Geltryce was not the first tutor he had seen or heard of crying in the halls this year. Mrs. Candun, another tutor, had related to him her many troubles beginning in the fall, even her clashes *with* the School Monitors. She was a brave woman, standing up to the scalding scream-sessions that she was *made* to endure by the Head Monitor herself. The Monitors even began to pit tutor against tutor, encouraging spying and denigration. It was becoming a competition to get into the Monitors' good graces- a trait shared by most Cult hierarchies.

Then it dawned on him.

It must have been a meeting he went to at the beginning of the year, a meeting of like-minded tutors who wanted to stop R'ti's strangling control over the Schoolhouse. Could it have been that which had started this firestorm against him? It *did* seem like they really held him in disfavor this year. In years past, the Monitors had been more supportive and friendly- but not this year!

Halfdan had little further time to ponder the viciousness of regime change, for another tutor had just arrived to drop off a small brigade of 30 pupils. Halfdan hoped that they were ready to learn more of the Mysteries from his aging mind, but the grins on many of their faces suggested otherwise. He sighed as they sprinted into the overly warm room, intermittently climbing under their desks to test his resolve and then soon ask him if they could leave for the lavatory. No chance of getting some help from the Monitors now, he mused.

But this was the way of pupils, was it not? Only a special few would really enrapture themselves in a lesson's grandeur. It was the case now, as it was at the beginning of Lights Out. It was even the case most likely before, during the Time of the Ancients and even for the ancients before them. Some pupils wished to learn and some didn't. The tutor would then teach as best he (or she) could and it was up to the pupils to succeed.

What was different now was that it was *entirely* the tutor's responsibility to make his (or her) pupils succeed. And it was the Monitor's job to punish the tutors if they didn't, or if they simply weren't Faithful Followers of R'ti...

24

Chapter 4

Valhallow

Most adventures begin in a tavern. The Meadhall of Agnetha was no different. Alive with activity, the drink free-flowing, the people chattering, the many wooden carvings of Norse myth and reality looked on. Set in the sleepy hamlet of Valhallow, one of a federation of five towns that made up the domain of Calvary, it was a good mix of rural sensibility and natural beauty. Some of the ancestors of the village folk had even been rumored to have descended from the mountains centuries ago, even from very far-off Minas-Ninona via some portal, it was said. They were, for the most part, fair of feature and fair of grace: nimble of limb and mild-mannered, unless the situation demanded action of course. Framed by the scenic Appchans to the west, wild George's Forest to the north, cosmopolitan seat of intrigue Walstock to the east, and the jovial Brick Villa of Little Folk to the south, Valhallow could be the perfect place to begin an adventure, to set forth into the wide world and explore all that Providence was deign to offer.

Alas though, adventure had *come to* Valhallow, for strange tidings had been heard from other lands not so far away. Adventuring strangers have arrived here, passing through the finely-carved wooden frames of the place where Lady Agnetha held council and entertained visitors from both near and afar. It was said that a Strangeness had been arising in the land: strangely-colored lights seen at night, an increase in the activity and bizarreness of cults, and now, the arrival of these three strangers.

From the far north came Oborren, a hunter of unnatural things. Dressed in his black trenchcoat and a wide-brimmed hat, the solidly-built man sported tanned skin and black hair in a ponytail. His uniqueness was further demonstrated by a vividly colored rainbow neck tie, perhaps as vividly colored as the lights recently seen at night. He had come from Gore. Rumor had it that some beasts might even walk as men there, though to solve such debate, Oborren would not comment. His worn flail, long knife, and crossbow at his side suggested that he did indeed come from a very dangerous place at least.

From nearer north came Brymanah, an amazon warrior. Her brown, Olympian hair hung about her strong shoulders. She was dressed athletically in amazon fashion, so as to better show off her great strength; the local men did not know what to make of her. She was obviously female, albeit quite muscular, and yet lacked any feminine charm or social grace. Brymanah bore a very sharp cutlass and appeared very willing to use it on any man who might look at her askance. She was from Stephania after all, where it was the custom for only women to fight and for men to serve.

And last was Kolveig, from the south, Madisonburg perhaps, though he had arrived with Brymanah, and was apparently under her dominion. A large black beard complimented by his olive drab clothing, red star insignia, and hammer and sickle arms showed him as one the eccentric Karlists who still dwelt in the Vale. His faith used to be in the better-known Skadi apparently, the Lady of the Mountains, until he claimed to have seen the light, and changed his patron to Karl. There was no shortage of strange cults and traditions in the Vale, especially in Madisonburg, and now such an emissary sat amongst the locals in the hall.

After the meal was served, Lady Agnetha interrupted the bustle to lead the folk in prayer. Though many followed different patrons, most saw Lord God as above them all, seeing various deities more as potent saints or even philosophical denominations, rather than as completely separate religious convictions in their own right. Here, Odin and Freya were most venerated, generally seen as the best path to leading a godly life, though others were followed as well. During the benediction, Kolveig glanced over at a slender, graying, clean-shaven man, a bit out of place amongst the locals, seated with two children during the prayer. His name was Halfdan. He wore a simple green cloak and was apparently Odinnicly trained, which gave him an odd air with mortals, an austere lifestyle, and an introspective mien.

"We welcome our honored guests to our humble Meadhall," stated the Lady in her melodic voice as she smiled. Her eyes lingered on Halfdan for a moment.

Both Oborren and Kolveig blushed at her stunning beauty: shimmering blonde hair, like plated gold, vivid blue eyes, fair skin, and her curvaceous, yet supple form. It was hard not to. It was rumored that she already was betrothed to a certain man in secret, though who it was, no one seemed to know for sure.

Oborren rose. "We are the ones who are honored, M'lady, to be the guests of such a majestic queen as yourself with such highly reputable folk as your subjects."

Both Agnetha and the assembled locals smiled at this. The hunter was apparently an eloquent speaker.

"You've come at an auspicious time. Strange portents are on the rise, causing some measure of fear to drift even into our little corner of the Vale. We are quite glad that our calls for assistance have been answered," stated the Lady.

"As are we," replied Oborren.

Night Skies Over Valhallow

"We have found one amongst our noble citizens who is not as he seems. At the risk of spoiling your meal, I will refrain from discussing the specifics until later. Suffice it to say, he may no longer be considered *normal.* We would be in your debt if you were to examine him and give us more guidance based on the wisdom of your travels. We would be even more in your debt if you were to investigate as to why he has been *changed* so."

Despite the dour news, the rest of the meal passed well. Roast pheasant (a local delicacy) and lean beef were the choice for main course, garnished with roast potatoes, stewed green beans, and country rice. The food was quite fresh and well cooked, as was the local custom, but also free of the many salts and spices that Kolveig and Brymanah were accustomed to. Mead flowed freely there as well, of course, bringing a pleasant honeyed aroma and golden color to the calm merriment of the gathered folk.

Sunlight danced upon the many rafters above, kept fresh with a clean scent from the chill outside and the occasional wafting of smoke from the merriment within. Oborren got to know Kolveig and Brymanah better there, conversing about their adventures and sharing a common bond of being honored strangers in this quaint meadhall tucked away in this 'little corner of the Vale.' As they had moments of quiet during their feast, their eyes would rest upon the exotic carvings replete throughout the place: etchings of runes, gods, heroes, monsters, and mortal men and women. Such a scene sparkled the eye and triggered the imagination. The three found it comforting that others had embarked on great expeditions before, such as they themselves were making ready to do, and were at least immortalized on some carving or room painting somewhere, whether they had succeeded on that expedition or not.

The merriment died down as two of Agnetha's oversized guards entered the Hall with a deranged, jabbering man. He was dressed in local manner and had a common-looking countenance to the rest, though it was there that the similarities ended.

"Oi- yeah! Oi-yeah! 187% growth to- deah! Hip! Hip! Hip! Hip..."

The party stared at the madman. Kolveig ventured a condolence to the distressed Proletarian, "...hooray?"

"BWHEWKLHASDKSGDUK STJHHKTHF!!!!!!!!!!!!!!!!!!!!!!!!"

28

The madman screamed and started thrashing about. The guards were barely able to control him and avoid nasty bites from his drooling mouth.

"NO HOORAY TODAY! NO HOORAY TODAY! NO HOORAY TODAY!" He rocked back and forth as he screamed. The guards, apparently having gone through this before, left him on the floor of the dais to roll before Agnetha's throne.

The assembled townsfolk sat quietly, embarrassed at the man's antics in front of their honored guests. Halfdan's boy made a strange sound, as well, though attention remained on the deranged man. Agnetha grew pale, sadness filling her eyes. Brymanah punched Kolveig for antagonizing him in the first place.

"How long has he been like this?" ventured Oborren.

"For three weeks now," said a woman, slowly rising from the townsfolk. Judging by her age and concern, he guessed she was his wife or sister. Her pale blue eyes showed that she too had been crying. She nervously adjusted her bonnet that skillfully held her flaxen blonde hair as she approached the throne and the madman. "He had just returned from the north, Mauriatown, I think."

Oborren turned his attention back to the madman, who was now mumbling something unintelligible to himself. The graying man, Halfdan, also rose, his accompanying children still voraciously eating their meals.

"He sometimes worked at the Schoolhouse," stated Halfdan. "He was a replacement tutor, one who would work with the pupils when their regular tutor was ill or with child."

At this, the assembled folk sighed knowingly. Few would doubt that working at that place for long would drive one completely mad, especially under the current regime.

Apparently, even the madman was listening, for he started to become increasingly agitated.

"NO I DO NOT NEED IMPROVEMENT NO I DO NOT NEED IMPROVEMENT NO I DO NOT NEED IMPROVEMENT NO I DO NOT NEED IMPROVEMENT!!!!" with the last, he let out a long shriek, sending chills down the spines of those assembled. Brymanah walked up and smacked him.

Lady Agnetha, the woman, and Halfdan all stared at the amazon's sudden aggression.

Kolveig chided, "That's what you're supposed to do when someone's hysterical."

They all stared at Kolveig.

"She's very good at smacking."

Agnetha turned her attention to Oborren. "What do you make of this, hunter?"

Oborren got out his pack and took out a number of exotic objects: a pendulum, some sticks of incense, and a mirror. He chanted and intoned for a few minutes, walking around the madman while studying the pendulum. Kolveig could barely hold back a chuckle as Oborren quietly wrote notes in his book, absorbed in his work, as the assembled village folk looked on in awe. Even the madman quietly watched Oborren's ceremony- it did seem to be quite impressive.

Soon Oborren lit the incense and started chanting again. Kolveig couldn't make out the words; they were probably just Nonsense or some other Opiate of the Masses. Oborren then walked around the madman again, looking at him through his special mirror. The room suddenly began to grow dark for a time, as if the sun was hiding behind some cloud. Strangely enough, as Oborren finished his incantations, the room grew bright with sunlight again.

At this, all turned their attention back to Oborren.

"Well, he does not seem to be *currently* possessed, but I wouldn't rule out that he had been at some point. All sorts of malevolent entities could be the culprit when someone's mind has been distorted to such extent."

"That's helpful," chided Kolveig.

Oborren went to shush him, but was interrupted by Halfdan.

"Then we must find out where he was affected. I work at the Schoolhouse, so I can check thereto."

Oborren let out a sigh of relief, few would want to go to the Schoolhouse, he was glad the tutor had volunteered.

"Then it looks like we'll be traveling to Mauriatown, we can leave on the morrow," stated Oborren.

"Until then" added Agnetha, "you shall continue to be my honored guests."

She motioned to the flagons of mead, fine foods, and attractive serving maidens.

Kolveig smiled: perhaps this Localized Capitalist Exploitation Center wasn't so bad after all.

Chapter 5

Patmos

A cold sun awakened the slumbering lay-abouts in the Meadhall. Brymanah groaned for a manservant to bring her libation, though none came, of course. Kolveig chuckled that her latest prima donna mood must be due to her losing a wrestling match with one of the local half-giants last night. As he was about to add an especially suggestive remark about said wrestling, one of Agnetha's handmaidens entered with a tray full of toasted breads, cheese, sausages, and mead.

Kolveig's eyes lit up at the handmaiden's lovely form, while Brymanah scowled at seeing a female being put to such menial a task. Oborren ruefully chewed upon a piece of toast and stared at the cleric and amazon. This will be quite an expedition, he thought, and it was unclear how these two would behave in the field. Still, Fate had seemed to bring them all together, and it did little good to argue with Fate. Word of a knowledgeable sage in nearby Patmos was heartening, yet Oborren had never heard of him through his hunter contacts. What help he would be against this Insolitus Novus was unknown.

As they finished their meal, Agnetha and a few of her guards entered the hall, her shimmering platinum hair noticeably enhancing the illumination present therein--so illuminating in fact, that Kolveig was even distracted from sweet-talking the handmaiden.

"We have been honored by your stay. What else can we do for you before you depart?"

Nice and Norse of them, Oborren thought, polite and to the point. Kolveig began to motion suggestively at the handmaiden until Brymanah slapped his hand down.

Taking his cue, Oborren rose and bowed to the noblewoman. "We are in your debt, M'lady. We shall now be on our way."

They exited the hall, each saying their goodbyes in their own manner, leaving the humble woodbeams and memories for now.

The dazzling sun shimmered on the fallen snow, a brilliant white. The fresh air with a slight hint of cedars and burning wood awakened their senses. A cold breeze was blowing in from the west, riding down from the distant Appchans, which stood as dark blue bulwarks against the great beyond. Enticing valleys of snow in the distance lay nestled therein. The snow underfoot crunched beneath their feet as they descended past the longhouses at Valhollow. The village folk waved at them as they passed by, some faces remembered from the previous night's feasting, some not.

The hill began to level off as the party ventured onward. Even here, some last few longhouses stood, poised upon two large hills to either side overhead. It was here too that a number of Valhollan huscarls stood sentinel, strangely vigilant despite this being such an ostensibly peaceful land. Their stern gazes peeked through their ocular helms, flaxen beards belying any emotion, spears planted at the ready.

Soon the party reached the road. Taking the lead, Oborren led them up another long hill, flanked by farmland to the left and forest to the right. Suddenly, something erupted from the trees, but it was only a pheasant. Its hooting calls echoed on the road below.

Dan Osarchuk

Though it was mid-morning in a settled land of Men, the party still remained alert. None of them were strangers to peril.

As they descended the hill, a number of cottages could be seen spread out amongst the way. Calvary was surprisingly settled for being so rural. Their attention turned to the path into Patmos, the Kings Way. Soon upon this road though, they noticed a strange cabin set back about a quarter mile from the Way. It was painted vivid orange and magenta, and sweet-smelling smoke arose from its chimney. Who would know what strange folk might dwell there? It was often best to avoid such types.

As they travelled further, the road became lined with oaks and pines, blocking some of the cold wind, making it a little warmer. Brymanah noticed a strange fellow looking at them up ahead, leaning against a tree. He had a beaten yellow hat, a bright red jacket, a blond ponytail, and was clean-shaven. A wide grin was upon his face, as he leaned down to take a bite of something that looked like a pastry wrapped in a handkerchief. His paunch belly suggested he indeed did have a sweet tooth.

"Welcome travelers," he said, "what brings your necks to these woods?"

"Oh, we're just on our way to Patmos," replied Oborren, who had already calmly begun reaching for his dagger. One could never be too careful, especially around oddly dressed strangers.

"Well, hope you enjoy your stay." The odd stranger smiled and began to whistle a tune, one that seemed almost too cheery.

Brymanah's eyes darted back and forth, looking for signs of an ambush. Ignoring her, Kolveig strolled up to the stranger and began to make small-talk. He was whistling cheerily, after all.

"You know, stranger, I used to pray out in that grove yonder." Kolveig pointed to a circle of cedar trees to the left. His eyes betrayed some secret misfortune that he had witnessed, years prior perhaps.

35

"And now?" queried the stranger.

"I don't."

The stranger smiled and then laughed. Brymanah was already behind him, her cutlass held up for a killing blow. Paying her no notice, the stranger tipped his hat to them and began walking down the Kings Way. Of course, he was heading for the garishly painted cabin, whistling his nonsensical tune.

"What a weird male!" Brymanah exclaimed.

"At least you didn't summarily execute him," Kolveig chided.

Brymanah was weighing the benefits of *summarily executing Kolveig* when the party rounded the corner and beheld Patmos. The hamlet spanned a small valley that held a number of residences, all in a different sort of architectural style than Valhallow. Columns could be seen supporting the front overhangs of the houses with a number of tiled roofs, giving it a more Olympian flavor than the general Norseness of the other hamlets in Calvary.

Some children walked by, leading a few beef cattle and chickens out to pasture. The sun glinted off their wagons, giving a classic air to the procession. The party recognized them as Halfdan's children.

"Do you know where Mettec's house is, little girl?" asked Oborren.

"Yes, it's right down the hill, second on the left."

He thanked her and she went back to explaining to her quiet brother about the stealthy ways of unicorns.

Upon finding Mettec's house, it appeared that some members of his family were outside, clearing snow from the rootcellar doors. The party greeted them and they were shown inside. The cozy home still retained much of the old style of the Ancients. Gone were their amazing entertainments, but the remaining split-foyer was now an antique curiosity, harkening back to what was thought to be better times when hot and cool air elementals could be summoned by the master of the house at will to provide comfort to those inside.

A middle-aged, tall, balding man in non-descript garb stood at the top of the stairs and greeted the party. He welcomed them into his study, as his amiable wife brought in mugs of hot cider and sweetcakes.

"We seek the cause of the Insolitus Novus, a New Strangeness, Mettec. Perhaps in the area of Mauriatown- can you help us?" Oborren seemed to quickly be becoming the party spokesman.

Mettec paused for a few moments, the sweet scents of food and drink wafting on the air, as he rubbed his stubbly chin and pondered.

"Your best bet is to try the caves east of Mauriatown. There have been sightings of unusual things in that area: swirling, multi-colored lights at night, oversized insects, and the like."

He shuffled through some papers and pulled out a rolled parchment. He opened it to reveal a surprisingly detailed map- a rarity in these days. Oborren hoped it would also be surprisingly accurate too. Mettec pointed to a spot on the map with one of his long fingers.

"How can you be so sure that we can trust rumors?" asked Brymanah.

"Because," began Mettec, "I have seen the lights myself." He gestured over to a nearby window, facing north. Opening a closet, he pulled out an intricate looking device. A long metal tube was held upon a tripod, cleverly repaired. It looked like it came from the elder days: it was made of *plast*, as well as various types of metal. At the side of the device, near where the tripod met the tube, a number of metal dials could be found, assumedly for adjustment.

Mettec motioned for Oborren to come take a look. Gazing through the tube, it seemed that Mettec had ingeniously modified a gazing tube to be able to see even greater distances than most, even focusing past foliage and cloud cover. Amazing.

While the map and gazing tube may have been impressive, the party felt a slight chill at the mention of Mauriatown. Kolveig was especially concerned, since they were quite hostile to those of his Pro-Proletariat persuasion. In addition, they wore cowls, kept gnomes as slaves, and seemed fanatically loyal to their Leader-obviously some sort of Right Wing Extremists.

Afterwards, the party chatted with Mettec and his wife, speaking of comings and goings, the ways of the world, and the weather this season. Once they finished their food and drink, they thanked the couple, and went to leave some silver pieces in thanks, but the couple would not accept them.

"It looks like you may need all the coin you have to buy your way through the gates of Mauriatown," Mettec joked. The party laughed nervously and bid them good day.

On the way down the path, Oborren left a few coins in their message box regardless. It was good to help such a helpful family.

Back on the Kings Way in Patmos, the party began to ruminate over their next step. It seemed certain that the hills outside of Mauriatown would be their best lead, but walking *into* Mauriatown would be no small matter. Brymanah glanced down the steep road and noticed a sign depicting a bow and arrow. She sprinted off as the party cautiously followed, not sure what the amazon was up to.

They soon came to the homeshop of Aeschenia the Bowyer. A roundish, almost glorified tent hut, it was surprisingly comfortable and warm inside despite the outer chill. The shopkeep herself seemed friendly, of medium size and athletic build, with long, brown curly hair. She spoke of her nearby hometown of Walstock as Brymanah examined her 'workwomanship'. It looked like her

38

bows were all well-put together: fine cedar wood frames, deer antler reinforcements, and worked leather straps. The arrows seemed quite straight and well-fletched.

Brymanah decided that this would be the perfect place to commission a strength-bow: one with a harder draw, but an even more powerful release. Smiling, Aeschenia began to take measurements of Brymanah's height and reach, as well having her lift sample weights to judge the new bow's specifications.

Kolveig snickered in the back, whispering to Oborren, "I'm not sure if she likes this because it's a *woman* who's so skilled at making bows or if she just likes showing off her muscles." Noticing their whispers, Brymanah glared.

After Aeschenia's measurements were finished, she informed Brymanah that it would take a few days to complete. Brymanah thanked her and left a deposit of coin for the bowyer. The party left, not before Kolveig had a chance to wink at the woman.

Chapter 6

The Clearing Node

Halfdan looked upon the clear stars shining over the treetops in the night sky. The Node drew all around him, a circle of trees holding an inner circle of snow-capped ground within. It was here that he could relax, to clear his mind from the day's perturbations, to become one with the peace that seemed ever-present, yet beyond a mortal's usual grasp, at least when one mistook one's thoughts for reality.

Despite the Scolding-scroll a few days ago and the very unnerving Inquisition with the High-Monitors that lay ahead, the current day had been relatively good. No major misfortune passed with the Schoolhouse pupils, the other tutors, or even the Monitors- all seemed fairly quiet. He had of course enjoyed his evening time with his own children, and though Larnen would often keep him busy with his Spectrum Disorder, Kelne had been her usual self, helpful as ever. Cooking them supper in his longhouse, playing games of *civi-chess*, watching the *dell-scope*, going for walks, and reading stories to them, it filled his day with a sense of family and purpose. He certainly missed them when they were with their mother, but he knew he needed some time to bring more peace and patience to his mind, if nothing but to be a better father.

He always looked forward to seeing them again the next day regardless.

This evening, he had mused on his way back from dropping them off at their grandsires' house about how his life had turned out the way it did. Little did he know as a child himself, far off in Seavilla (which lay beyond even forbidding Metros) so many years ago, that he would be living alone a good part of his time.

In those early days, Halfdan was certain he would become an adventurer. He spent much of his childhood reading and imagining stories portrayed by toy knights and painted dragons, but things did not work out that way. He had in fact felt like he had ended up in another world entirely, but few would believe him.

Instead, he had finally gone to University in Southbyrg at the beach, to study in the ways of tutorship and sagecraft. It was there that he had met a beautiful and amazing woman, fallen in love, and enjoyed a romantic happiness that he could never quite seem to recapture in this life. In those days he had felt so free, boundless opportunities seemed to avail him and yet so little required, at least as much as could be said for a young man in the New Dark Ages.

Of what the Ancients had described as the Old Dark Ages, few texts remain, but that this was a new era of that old pattern, few could deny. When Rome fell, when that great empire had collapsed, peace, science, and prosperity went with it, which apparently took centuries to recover. The same seemed to hold true for Amercia. Many now had their own theory on what triggered the most recent Dark Age, but most agreed that it had resulted in the Ancients losing their lines of power and the failure of their metal *drive-chariots* somehow. For at first it was simply termed 'Lights Out,' fittingly enough to begin a new dark age. It was said that great war and famine befell the land in those days, that millions cried out in fear.

And yet, like all great storms, this one passed, but left major changes in its wake nonetheless. Most returned to the Old Ways,

Dan Osarchuk

to a time before switch and button, pedal and key were the main grantors of sustenance and succor. The people and the land grew hale once more, engendering themselves to the cultures of their pre-industrial ancestors, though most now bowed knee to new masters, who were otherwise free to forge their own, smaller kingdoms: unique and unfranchised from the rest. God was once again worshipped in more archaic ways, sometimes under other, older names or as His Name Alone, though the orthodoxy and tenets of those of a spiritual bent would vary wildly from place to place. It was also said that even miracles began to return once again to the land, though some might claim they were merely fortuitous coincidence, while others would say such miracles never left.

The old terrors of World Death, Mass War, Race Extinction, and Police State seemed to have then become defunct, but rumors of new Terrors began to arise. Though many still claim that it was simply the intoxication of cave vapors, strange, diverse creatures, peoples, and worse were said to dwell below the ground, where no sunray might find purchase, nor may any starlight or moonlight be known. For it seemed that the New became Old and the Old became New. The old stories of nightmare beings rose again: horrid beasts that sought to dine upon man, creatures of the night, nightmarish races of half-men, users of dark magic, or even fell spirits of tainted purpose.

Whether Halfdan believed these tales or not, he was not sure. Perhaps they were indeed all just the work of breathing too much cave air or of a New World that could not now so easily abolish the night with technomancy. But he had wished to seek them out in his younger days nonetheless, even venturing *around the bend*, for they were too tempting to pass. Even now, such things certainly were more compelling and meaningful than the foolish nonsense he was commanded to recite by the Cult at the Schoolhouse.

But many dangers of this New Age seemed altogether too real. Above ground, bandits were not unknown, nor were wild animals, including those of nearly monstrous size though they were luckily rare in as safe a place as Calvary.

Other places were *not* as safe, and even the local rulers could not be altogether trusted, especially the more eccentric ones. Some communities in the Vale were quite eccentric in fact. Regardless, it was wise for men and women to travel armed, and preferably in groups, especially when entering into other domains.

So here he was in one of the safer realms of the Vale. His wife and he had both journeyed to the stunning Shenbyrg Vale almost a decade and a half ago. It had seemed safer than other realms of Amercia at the time, and the mountains and valleys, forests and fields were ever-beautiful as they remain today. They had been happy for a short time, both serving as tutors in their own manner, seemingly welcomed by the locals. And yet, it was not to be: they drifted apart, had argued on many an occasion, and then finally parted ways. He sometimes wondered if coming to the Vale had been a mistake. They had seemed to fare much better those few years in Southbyrg and Seavilla, when they were together.

Still, Valhallow remained a breathtaking corner of the Vale. He found one of the less prestigious longhouses to live in, but it still was nicely made, with a good amount of land to boot. The architecture was a bit eccentric, with large windows placed on the side nearest the neighbor's house. Halfdan did love to look at the sky, including from the comfort of his own longhouse, so the large windows could be a boon, but he also worried at times over his history of problems with folk in general and neighbors in particular. Most of his neighbors seemed friendly enough, though it was rare for him to find others that he could truly find dear friendship with these days. It had seemed easier to do so back beyond Metros in his younger days.

Was it because he was not born in the Vale? He had known a number of friends for a time who had entered into the Vale, only to leave a few years later. Strange. Or was it now that he was a bachelor living amongst whole families? Valhallow was a very peaceful place, but certainly not the type of place to *meet love*. Or was it because of Larnen's bouts of madness with his Spectrum? His mother and he had even wondered if the poor lad was possessed when he was younger, but it was not the case: his periodic fits of rageful screaming, destruction of things, mischievous pilfering, and even harming of himself or even others, was apparently the work of some exceptional imbalance in the humors of his mind. Perhaps Halfdan was different too, just like his son was different, though not as obviously so.

What was it in this world that made this seeming misfortune befall a man such as Halfdan? Was it simply fated to be or some sort of karmic reckoning that he had triggered instead? Or that he felt he was from another world? Or was it many reasons? Or none? Perhaps his very run-in with the thuggish tenant Kilroy next door this past summer had triggered his very problems at the Schoolhouse? It was impossible to really know, *for who really knows why anything really happens anyway?*

So much had happened to Halfdan over the last decade or so: terrifying mental trials followed by a generally greater sense of peacefulness, that perhaps this was all simply God's will. It never ceased to amaze him how this world, *his* world apparently, could seem so strange to him. If this was all that there really was, then how could he possibly feel that way? Was it really: *row, row, row your boat?*

Halfdan's mind finally slipped from its reverie. I could be lost forever in my thoughts, he realized, perhaps that's what this life really is?

The rising of the moon signaled it was time speak with his mentor. Valhallow looked so beautiful tonight, the silver-blue light shining across the snowy ground, shining bright, but softly, like a phosphorescent lake set amongst the mountain views. Longhouses of the villagefolk framed by candlelights in their windows, a large stand of pines stood quiet sentinel to the north.

Night Skies Over Valhallow

Returning his gaze back into the Node, Halfdan closed his eyes, tuning his consciousness to a far-off land to the southwest, where great red-rock stones still held the energies of countless generations who had come to visit, both in-person and in the manner of Halfdan's undertaking. Perhaps some would think this to be magic or imagination, he thought. It could be hard to tell the difference: they both had 'magi' in them. Even the Science and Machines of the Ancients could have been called the same.

As his mind began to clear, waiting, he soon sensed the presence of his mentor. She had helped him a great deal over the last year, showing him the ways of allowing things to resolve of their own accord, since perhaps we are indeed *not the doer.*

They spoke for some time, Halfdan relating his concerns and his mentor simply listened. During his pauses, she helped him find and drop the emotional obstructions in his chest that seemed to be triggered by his life worries, but in fact could actually be the triggers of such worries, it would seem. Working with her not only helped Halfdan with *the question,* but also helped him to let go of many of the perturbations that would arise due to life's many vicissitudes.

It never ceased to amaze him how *one's actual worries were really so unreal,* possibly the work of imagination alone, *and yet one's feelings about one's worries were in fact much more palpable.* For example, a feeling of sadness could be said to be more real and evident than that which one might apparently be sad about. It was there *in the feelings* that suffering lay and he was forever in her debt for helping him to be free of them.

At the end of their chat, Halfdan wished his mentor well and returned to his reverie in the clearing. His mind cleared too and melded with the silence. No thought came for a time, only joy, for having no thoughts *was* joy itself.

Halfdan remembered the other teachers who had helped him over the years, such as Guido the Guide, who had shown him the way to dive into one's feelings in order to dissolve them- a great boon. He had even sat with the Shell Oracle in Stephania. Her deep meditations and magnanimous ways had greatly impressed him. It also helped that he could actually physically sit with her and others, sensing the peace beyond all human comprehension, where others seemed in fact as extensions of one's heart.

All this was the way of Odin, the way of Insight. The quiet, simple path that could be sought at any time and used to remove the eye (the I), in order to reach the deepest understanding.

After a while longer, he turned back to his longhouse. The moon had shifted, casting shadows upon the inner ring of snow, a cold wind rustling through the branches. The peace of the place often made it difficult to leave. He mused for a moment about the way of things and the way of this world. Then he knelt, prayed, turned, and left.

Halfdan had originally begun to pursue this inner search so as to find a blonde woman that he had dreamt of since a tender age. Courtship had never been his strong suit though. Understandably, most women found his frail form, over- sensitivity, and social awkwardness to be unappealing- the latter flaw was even codified in Official R'ti record now. But though the inner search never did seem to yield the blonde mate, his true companion, it did seem to bring him to something else: a more consistent sense of peace that made him less averse, less pained, and a bit easier to converse with on the average, or so it would seem.

* * *

Lying in his bed, Halfdan gazed out the large window into the night sky. Fears of the next day at the Schoolhouse and the Inquisition began to activate his thoughts again. They could flutter around him like a swarm at times, creating such a cloud that he might easily mistake it for reality. Then he remembered how the Ancients used to watch acted plays through their Viewing Screens, and he wondered if this life was akin to that.

Night Skies Over Valhallow

Is it all just a dream?
A picture projected onto a screen?

Halfdan knew not what the next day would hold. He knew not how to prevent himself from facing hardship, or hate, or misfortune, or disaster. Much as he might try, he could not prepare for everything, could not hold back the strands of Fate from striking him, or even strangling him or the ones he cared about. He could not hide in his longhouse forever, hoping to never offend another, to never be misunderstood, to be protected as if in some womb.

And he *did* know that this life was dreamlike, if not just a dream itself. And he did know that letting go and being who one really is always seemed the wisest course and the most direct path to inner peace. And that God always seemed to be with him, too, no matter what.

As he drifted off to sleep, an old song that his father used to play for him, from another life it seemed, entered his mind.

Young boy in the mirror
Tell me what do you see?
Young boy in the mirror
Tell me what do you hear...

Rich man, poor man, gunman, thief
I can't see it in the glass
Perhaps a glass of one of each
Will help us understand?

Chapter 7

Mauriatown

Emerging from the still-verdant hills of Calvary, the party ventured forth on the Mighty One trail. Once used by the Ancients with their *drive-chariots* to go incredible speeds, the Trail now consisted of two simple, parallel roads, which everything from ox cart to brigand might make their way upon, whether heading north or south. It is said that the old magic of the Ancients could still be felt there, so folks continued to travel on the eastern side when going north, and the western side when going south. It was said to be simply faster than walking other trails. And more often than not, that truth held firm.

Oborren took in the rolling hills, woodlands, and farms. He never tired of the serenity of the Vale: the stunning vistas, the quaint pastoralism, even in wintertime. Little did the generally innocent Vale folk know of the dangers that awaited below them. Little did they know how little earth stood between them and the realm of living nightmare. The clear blue winter sky hung overhead, making such fears seem impossible.

His attention refocused on the toll ahead. The party would soon be entering Mauriatown, a place that didn't take too kindly to strangers. Oborren had only recently traveled this way for the meeting in Calvary. The Maurians had given him little trouble then, but a repeat of that was never a certainty. He wondered how they would take to the neo-Marxist and the amazon- he assumed that they must have avoided the place on their own trip to Calvary.

The party arrived at the toll shortly thereafter. The scene seemed a classic example of order attempting to sort out disorder. There were many travelers, wearing a variety of garb, contrasted amongst the uniformed ranks of Maurians. Most of the latter wore the archetypical grey uniform and cap, cut in military fashion. The Grey Shirts were the most numerous of Maurian soldiers, typically armed only with daggers and billie clubs. Somewhat less numerous were those in blue, slightly armored with stahlhelms and breastplates. Full soldiers, unlike the more paramilitary Greys, these Blue Shirts also wore balaclavas, apparently to evoke a greater air of mystery and fear. They had better weapons, as well: crossbows and short swords hung ready at their sides. The finest soldiers of course were the Black Hats, the elite soldiers of Mauriatown, looking much like the police officers of yesteryear in full dress uniform. Each one was given a finely crafted broad sword, signed by the Hooded Leader himself, as well as one-handed, superbly-crafted repeating crossbows that were deadly efficient.

Even 'soldier' was not perhaps the best term for all these groups, for that would suggest something different than a citizen of Mauria. But no, all citizens of Mauria were Soldiers, at least of some type, so as to better serve the Leader. All non-citizens were either Visitors or Slaves.

A multitude of banners featuring the Leader himself flapped in the gentle breeze as the party and other travelers waited in line. Such a cult of personality: 'M' symbols were everywhere, found upon building, flag, and minion alike. Depictions of the Leader too had him dressed in military fashion, always with his great hood covering all but his eyes, though the color of his hood and uniform would vary, perhaps to pay homage to (and maintain support from) the Grey, Blue, and Black- clad castes of Maurian society. It was said that the caste system did help to maintain loyalty to the Leader, and when that failed, he could always use his secret police.

The right-wing display of pageantry was almost too much for Kolveig. Oborren and Brymanah could barely keep him quiet as he muttered such phrases as, "Bourgeoisie Tyrants!" and "Oh, now I see who has the Ownership of Production!" and especially "why doesn't the Proletariat Rise Up against these FASCISTS?!?!"

Oborren was just about to remind Kolveig of the many *left-wing* tyrants he had known in the Vale, when Brymanah shushed them both. They were now staring at four Grey Shirts, two Blue Shirts, and one Black Hat. Oborren prayed that they hadn't heard Kolveig's "Fascists" comment.

"Anything to declare?" asked one of the Grey Shirts. Another was looking at the party, while the other two seemed bored. The Blue Shirts stared silently at attention. The Black Hat smiled at them, as Kolveig fought back his outrage- he certainly felt like *he* had something to declare!

"No, sir," replied Oborren, "we were planning on heading to the Twice Journeyed Tavern, if that would be alr-"

"That would be acceptable," interrupted the Black Hat. The first Grey Shirt gave them each a small scroll, complete with the laws and glories of Mauriatown and a 24-hour visa stay.

The party moved on, as Brymanah interrupted Kolveig's forthcoming comment with a concealed jab to his rib.

They quickly moved off the Trail, heading east in the direction of the Tavern.

"Who do they think they are?!" exploded Kolveig finally. "Harassing Honest Working People like us with their stupid uniforms and their STUPID writs! And did you see how he INTERRUPTED YOU, OBORREN?!?! Huh?!?! HUH!?! I have half a mind to start a Revolution in this place, AS KARL IS MY WITNESS!"

51

Night Skies Over Valhallow

"Maybe they were looking for capitalists?" chided Brymanah.

Kolveig's face turned bright red and he looked like he was nearly ready to vomit.

* * *

The party ventured deeper into the realm, noticing evidence of a great deal of lima bean cultivation, the staple crop of Mauriatown. Many gnomish slaves were still out in the fields this cold afternoon, repairing greenhouses that had been damaged by frost, hauling compost in wheelbarrows, and tending to the winter cover crops. Their short stature suggested how well-suited they were for the tasks, despite their most likely performing said tasks against their will.

Oborren and Brymanah could barely steer Kolveig away from performing a Revolution then and there.

Soon the country became hillier and clouds began to roll in. The blue sky that had accompanied them since setting out from Valhallow that morning was quickly departing, darkening their moods, and bringing the scent of impending new snows upon the air. Doing his best to navigate to the Tavern while avoiding the roads (and a likely Kolveig-induced incident thereto), Oborren left Brymanah to keep her eyes on the cleric. He continued to mumble to himself about something regarding Oppressed Workers.

Just then, the eerie sound of singing children's voices rose on the wind. In the darkening sky, their firebrands could be seen glimmering from around the corner. The three party members quickly leapt off to the side to hide in some brush just as the procession began to march by. Roughly two score children, perhaps ranging in ages from 7 through 14, walked by, all dressed in uniforms. They were singing a patriotic song, with one adult Black Hat leading in the front and one in the rear.

"Death to the enemies of the Leader! Death to the enemies of Mauria! Death to all who oppose us! We can't wait to kill ya!"

52

Dan Osarchuk

On and on they chanted their morbidly patriotic marching song as they walked by, apparently taking no notice of the party. Brymanah was relieved that they were pinned down in the bushes: not only did it help to avoid detection, but it made it easier to strangle Kolveig if he tried anything stupid.

As the last of the Leader Scouts marched by, Brymanah relaxed her guard. Luckily, it only seemed like Kolveig was praying.... praying!?!? Before she knew it, Brymanah and Oborren were held fast, unable to move. Stinking magic! Kolveig would be wise to kill her now because if he didn't, he would have wished he had when this spell wore off and she got through with him!

The cleric stood up and brushed himself off. This was the Last Straw! Tormenting travelers and gnomes was one thing, but Corrupting Children with Right-Wing Patriotic Rhetoric was another!

He stalked behind the rear Black Hat, his face burning so hot that he didn't realize that his target was a shapely woman.

Oborren and Brymanah looked on helplessly, still unable to move thanks to the cleric's spell. The gentle left-wing patriotic songs playing in their heads confirmed that the enchantment was the work of Kolveig, as if it had not been obvious enough.

The cleric slowly began to pull out his Marxian hammer, when suddenly, the Black Hat spun around and faced him.

Their eyes met.

She was a stunning beauty to behold: deep blue eyes and raven black hair; fair, chiseled features. There was something else about her too that prevented the cleric from thinking clearly.

Kolveig stammered, "I.. I..."

"Are you just going to stand their holding your hammer?" She smiled at him.

53

He laughed nervously. She winked and went on her way. His last thought was that perhaps Mauriatown wasn't such a bad place after all. His comrades, now free of his spell, grabbed Kolveig and hauled him to the tavern, taking extra efforts to be rough with him.

* * *

The Twice-Journeyed Tavern was a welcome change for the party from the rest of Mauriatown. Granted that while Maurian flags and banners of The Hooded Leader abounded on the outside, inside it seemed more the norm for the Vale. Apart from a few Maurian soldiers, folks could be seen from all over the region: Walstock, Caelum Mount, Strass Hill, Fairfacts Lordship, and even some from Calvary, as well.

After they were seated, Oborren began to subtly move about the room to collect some information. He wasn't exactly sure where the place was that Mettec had mentioned earlier that day, plus it was always a good idea to pick up a little extra muscle, or *meat-shields,* before heading into a dungeon-like situation.

As Oborren mingled, Brymanah stared at Kolveig. He had nearly gotten them killed back there, but he currently didn't seem to notice. The idiot cleric still looked hopelessly love-struck. Perhaps it will help him to finally shut his mouth, at least for a while, thought the amazon. Men did need a good woman to keep them in line. Perhaps it took a Maurian one to fix Kolveig.

Soon after, Oborren returned and discussed what he had learned. "According to one of the Blue Shirts, multi-colored lights could sometimes be seen coming from a cleft in the hills, not far from here, due northeast."

Brymanah was already deep into her roast venison and ale and Kolveig had still been smiling dreamily, his food and drink barely touched, but they now gave him their full attention. Oborren made a wry look, turned and pointed to a table across the tavern. Seated there were two odd-looking individuals: one male, one female, both with fairly innocent looks on their faces, marking them as excellent prospective henchmen.

The man was quite large, even more so than Brymanah. He had a battle axe resting on the table, sported a mullet, wore crude overalls, and wasn't wearing a shirt, making him a probable barbarian. Still, he was at least wearing some form of pants. The female was smaller and quite slender, with vivid green eyes, remarkable red hair, and dressed in exotic-looking robes and boots. The party could only guess at what she could do.

Oborren motioned them over and they introduced themselves as Gorm of Everlur and Cherries of George's Forest. The party introduced themselves and debated a price with the newcomers.

"One gold coin per day, plus half-shares of any treasure taken," stated Brymanah.

The female smiled and nodded. The barbarian looked to be confused, attempting to count something on his fingers.

"Something wrong?" asked Oborren.

"Me not know what half-share means!" declared Gorm.

"It means half a share."

Gorm stared blankly for a moment.

"Half a what???"

"Share."

"Fine. Me share. Then me have more beer!" Gorm gave a great smile, which was missing a number of teeth, handed his mug over to Kolveig, and then downed Oborren's flagon in one mighty gulp. Brymanah rolled her eyes.

Now this should be fun, thought Kolveig.

Chapter 8

Into the Warren

A pinkish dawn greeted the still sleepy trio as their new comrades waited for them outside the tavern. Upon Oborren's advice, they had all turned in fairly early last night in order to get a head start for the day's journey. It had taken nearly a half hour of repeated explaining for Cherries to finally convey to Gorm the necessity to stop trying to force other bar patrons to "share" last night. Apparently it worked, though the barbarian still kept talking about it in his sleep.

"What do you do when you're not adventuring?" joked Kolveig.

"Hairstylist," replied Gorm in a matter-of-fact manner, as he proudly stroked his mullet.

Great, just what we need: a *barber-barbarian*, thought Oborren.

The five soon ventured into the hinterlands of Mauriatown, leaving behind most signs of civilization except for an isolated farmhouse or two. The land here was hilly, interspersed with open fields and denser woodlands. After about an hour of hiking, the clouds above began to break, casting warm rays of light down from the azure openings above. Soon, the party came to a stream. They forded it easily, for it was only a foot deep at most. A number of pines grew there, enjoying the moist earth.

Cherries leaned down to get a drink of water, smiling as her red strands fell over her face. Oborren had to admit that she was beautiful. Her lithe features, the way her hair color complimented her eyes, her mysterious robes, her tall, red boots.

"Are you a magi?" he inquired.

"Of course!" she replied smilingly.

"It's good to have you with us."

"It's good to be here!"

Oborren fought back a blush as he grinned, trying to distract himself with the surroundings. The rich scent of the pines wafted down as he listened to the current of the stream. Brymanah was stretching out her muscular legs, as Gorm stared at them without the least degree of discretion, his eyes bulging and his mouth wide open. Strangely, Brymanah didn't admonish him.

Kolveig looked at the sky, noticing how a bright blue patch looked just like that Black Hat maiden's eyes. Perhaps she too was really a Marxist, seeking to bring down the Fascists from within? No one that beautiful could really be so right-wing, he thought.

After dining on some rations, it was time for the party to continue their journey. Traveling onward for a time longer, they could make out the hills that the Blue Shirt in the Tavern had mentioned to them the night before. The trail led into a thick growth of brush. Suddenly, they spotted bloodstains on the grassy ground. The party drew their weapons, ready for trouble. Oborren kneeled and checked for tracks. Lo and behold, a number of small, humanoid footprints could be seen, coming upon a single pair of normal-sized ones. Only the small tracks led away in the direction of the hills, with one large groove of something being dragged behind perhaps, as well. It did not look good.

Dan Osarchuk

Moving deliberately now, the party cleared the brush and, following the sinister trail, soon looked upon a cave entrance. It stood starkly in the hillside, framed by the winter morning sky. The cave was still held in shadow, most likely due to its westward orientation. Outside stood two short individuals: quite ugly, burnt orange-skinned humanoids with oversized noses. They each held a short spear at attention; primitive-looking weapons, but sharp and apparently capable. They wore a mish-mash of light armor and bore small wooden shields. Strangely enough, each creature also had a badly-constructed fake beard on its face.

Oborren stalked up, flanked by Brymanah. His crossbow out and notched, her cutlass glinting in the morning sun. The creatures, only noticing the two just before they were nearly upon them, stated in broken Amercian, "You.. not... allowed... here! We... are... gnomes!"

Gorm looked at Kolveig perplexed. Perhaps there was some sort of misunderstanding?

In an instant, Oborren's crossbow launched a bolt into one of the creature's eyes. The other's head rolled off, cut clean by Brymanah's blade. As the party advanced into the cave, Cherries took sympathy on Gorm and pulled off one of the creature's fake beards, demonstrating the ruse. Gorm made an angry face and nodded, he would be wise against these diabolically clever creatures in the future!

The party readied themselves to enter the cave. One never knew what would happen once one entered the underworld. Any sort of horrible thing could be down there, sheltered from sky, sunlight, and human incredulity. But there was also the promise of great treasures to be had, not to mention clues as to what was causing the Insolitus Novus. They quickly checked their gear and entered, not wanting to give up too much of the element of surprise.

The cave entrance chamber had exits to the left and the right. It appeared naturally formed, but the tunnels beyond appeared well-worked, looking more like carved stone hallways than natural shafts. Though the original masons seemed to be well-skilled, the place did not seem to be currently well-maintained. Dung and garbage leant an unpleasant odor to the area, as well as another blood stain, found on the passage to the left.

"What were those things?" Kolveig asked Oborren.

"Goblins."

The party readied themselves in response to the news. Most expected as such, but to hear Oborren confirm what they were facing only made them more concerned. Though small, goblins could be quite vicious and cunning, especially in large numbers.

The passage was about 10' wide, allowing them to walk two abreast comfortably. Oborren and Brymanah took the front, with Cherries in the middle, since she lacked any armor. Gorm and Kolveig took the back. Cherries's lantern lit the hallway well, though Oborren had her cover it somewhat to prevent them from being too easily spotted. Goblins often lived in the dark, along with many other nasty things of the underworld, and would easily notice illumination.

Venturing on, they saw another room up ahead. Oborren and Brymanah split left and right as they entered a large chamber, roughly 40' wide and 60' deep. Detailed murals covered the far wall, pastoral scenes of gnomes happily casting off the chains of Maurian enslavement and donning their otherwise ubiquitous pointed hats (which are, of course, banned in Mauriatown to prevent any sense of gnomish ethnic pride). In the center of the room, what once must have been a statue of some important gnomish hero or deity, was now converted in a most gruesome manner. Bones, branches, earth, excrement and gore had changed the shape of the statue's head to some sort of reptilian monstrosity, which had also been garishly painted to boot. Brymanah wondered at how such nasty creatures could have such bad taste.

Dan Osarchuk

Cherries's lantern flickered, sending strange shadows around the seemingly empty chamber. The party split-up to investigate the room. Kolveig examined the murals on the wall, judging the gnomes to be good artists of Proletarian Liberation. Brymanah stalked to the far left corner, so as to better watch the room they were in as well as the hall from which they came for any danger. Cherries began to chant and, as he looked back, Kolveig was a little startled to notice her eyes glow blue. She appeared to be scanning the room for something. It was rare to see such obvious displays of magic on the surface world, but the eldritch manifestations that were now occurring showed that they had indeed entered the underworld.

Gorm stared at the statue suspiciously. Perhaps it really concealed a gnome? These goblins were tricky!

And at the far end, Oborren found a stone altar over which an unfortunate human's body lay. It had been badly mutilated.

"I guess we found our victim," the hunter stated.

"Brilliant deduction," goaded Kolveig.

Oborren grimaced at the comment as he looked over the altar, trying to recollect the names of the various goblin deities and ways of shooting irritating clerics in the arm. The altar looked like it used to have some other use; perhaps it was simply an overturned stone table on bricks. That was the goblin way. They, like most humanoids, could build little and instead relied on looting human folk to stock their lairs and have some measure of civilization. The sacrifice was also fairly typical for goblins: killed and then the body was mutilated, or even worse, in reverse order. What sick little things they were.

At that moment, the tenor of the room suddenly changed. The party glanced over to look at Brymanah, who had her new strength bow out, an arrow ready. They quickly moved into defensive positions, though Gorm still felt like that statue was staring at him.

Suddenly, a large number of yipping, short, burnt orange-skinned humanoids came rushing into the room. With their overly long arms, the nasty things held wooden planks with rusty iron nails sticking out of them. Goblins! And those with burnt orange hides were known to be especially bloodthirsty and superstitious!

The sound of battle rang out as the goblins engaged the party. Brymanah's strength bow and Oborren's crossbow both found their mark, slaying one through the throat and another through an eye. Steeling himself, Kolveig issued forth a mighty swing with his hammer, smashing one goblin clean through the chest, then followed up on another with his sickle. Cherries uttered strange words, echoing against the walls in strange ways, as bolts of multi-colored light issued forth from her hands, striking three goblins dead. And yet still more came. At least that got Gorm's full attention: he was still struggling to not keep an eye on that statue!

More goblins rushed into the room, a dozen at least. Kolveig smashed another with his hammer, only to be sucker-stabbed in the leg by one with a rusty blade. Cherries vanished from sight just before three more could tackle her; the evil grins on their faces vanishing into a state of terrified amazement. As they stood dumbfounded, Brymanah drew her cutlass and hacked into them. Oborren yelled to Gorm to get into the fight.

"But what about the statue?"

"But nothing! FIGHT! Or... are you too SCARED?"

It was risky taunting a barbarian, but it was a risk that Oborren had to take.

A pile of goblins had now begun to smother Kolveig, biting off his ear, kicking his stomach, and drooling on his beard. The neo-Marxist was nearly overwhelmed. Brymanah had her hands full, alternately chopping off goblin heads and kicking them in vulnerable spots. And Cherries was nowhere to be seen.

Perhaps they should have hired more henchmen?

And where was that damnable barbarian?! Oborren glanced over and saw him absent-mindedly strangling a goblin with one hand, while he was pointing menacingly at the statue with the other.

"What's the matter, Gorm?" he chided. "Afraid these goblins might make fun of your SKILLS AS A BARBER?"

"WHAT!?!? ME KILLLLLLL!!!!!"

The room went silent at the sound of the barbarian's booming voice. His face turned bright red, one eye nearly popped out of his face while the other sunk in deeply to a squint. Drool ran rampant down his enraged face.

"BHHWAAHHH!!!!!!!!!!!!!!!"

Oborren and Brymanah ducked as the now apparently insane barbarian sprinted around the room, screaming and chopping goblins nearly in half with his great axe. It was all they could do to stay out of his way or risk getting their own heads lopped off. The barbarian luckily still had the presence of mind to pull the goblin pile off of Kolveig, rather than just chopping into it, though the barely conscious Kolveig probably didn't notice. Goblins flew through the air now, tossed by the raging barbarian, squeaking as their bodies broke against the ceiling, furniture, and muralled walls.

With no goblins left to kill, Gorm stared viciously at Oborren. His rage was not yet at an end.

"Hey Gorm: did that statue just move?"

Chapter 9

Tutor Meeting

Halfdan hurried to the library, feeling a chill run down his spine as he made sure to avoid the Room of Remediation. Yelling and crying could be heard from within. Halfdan shivered. If it had been a pupil crying, that would have been one thing. In decades past, pupils were even paddled for misbehavior. That must have been nasty for such youngsters. Now it was a *tutor* crying in the Room. Halfdan shuddered at the thought. It certainly was a far cry from the days of Mr. Corse.

Oh, how the pendulum swings and the seeming misfortune it brings.

Nearly out of breath, Halfdan made it over the threshold of the library, just before one of the Assistant Monitors, Ms. Hollowspoke, began recording any tutors who were late. She glared at the room, feverishly looking down at her pad to record any errant tutors. Afterwards, she would write Memorandums of Tutor Failure to put in their files.

This was a Mandatory R'ti Schoolhouse Required Meeting! All Meetings were Mandatory *and* Required (in case there was any doubt). Sometimes, Halfdan wondered at what truly being treated like a 'professional' would really be like.

Night Skies Over Valhallow

The Hounds of Guardianship were also there: local men that were brought in ostensibly to help with pupil discipline. But since 'pupil discipline' was a forbidden concept in the eyes of R'ti, they really were there to keep an eye on the tutors. A number stood at the back of the room, their white tunics and golden badges of smiling hounds clearly visible. No smiles were on their own faces though. It never hurt to have a bunch of goons around apparently.

The Head Monitor then stood up and surveyed the assembled tutors. No one spoke. In past administrations, the tutors had been more jovial and may have taken a minute to quiet down, but now no one dared to talk or look away when Mme. Carve spoke. Halfdan glanced around and could sense the tension in the air.

He also noticed a small band assembled on the far side of the room. The performers each held different musical instruments: one with a drum, another with a lute, and another with a guitar. Each one was of course wearing the compensatory clown costumes and make-up, adding to the grim, warped, false sense of joviality in the room.

Suddenly, Mme. Carve began to sway around and sing as the clown band began to play a very dramatic, slow tune. The tutors stared on, too mortified to react.

"You are all such great tutors..." she sang, " ...we are all so in your debt! We can't do this without you... ...but no you can't leave just yet!"

The staff looked on as she finished capering about. Thankfully, the performance soon ended. Everyone clapped politely. Halfdan had learned that the Ancient Communists would shoot the first person who stopped clapping after one of Stalin's speeches. The Monitors and the Hounds were watching the tutors for the same. The only difference now was that the Political Religion was R'ti in this case, rather than Bolshevism, and that the punishment for lack of adoration was termination from one's livelihood, rather than an actual firing squad.

Regaining her composure, Mme. Carve began her speech to the assembled tutors.

"Our schoolhouse is FAILING! Not every pupil in this school is showing *Exponential Annua Incrementum*! How can that be? Because... we... have... FAILED! But 'failure' is not in my vocabulary, so I won't use that word anymore. Instead, we have to learn to make a... *a Strategic Withdrawal from Our Old Ways*. We have to make a SWOOW. That means we need you, our wonderful tutors to give 187% to your pupils- 179% just won't cut it anymore! I hold myself accountable and I hold you accountable, so that you can hold me accountable, so that I can hold you accountable AGAIN!"

"We are the WORST schoolhouse in the Vale and I will find out why! We have all these other schoolhouses to compete with nowadays! It's not just Mauriatown and Caelum Mount anymore! No! We have to compete with schoolhouses from Middlechest all the way to Madisonburg nowadays. We now live in a *Vale-lu-lar* society. And what we used to do in the past now just won't cut it!"

"All Lesson Scripts will now be checked daily and *re-checked* to make sure that we are encouraging EXPONENTIAL learning in EVERY SINGLE PUPIL, NO MATTER WHAT! If your 7- year olds can't learn Calculus, then that's not because they're too young, it's BECAUSE YOU NEED TO BECOME A BETTER TUTOR! If your 9-year olds can't recite the 1100 Varied Dichotomies of Cortas the Great BY HEART, then you have failed again! We have to put our BEST PRACTICES into place to foster pupil learning! The EXAMINATIONS are coming! We must make sure our pupils are ready! And that's YOUR job!"

"That is why we need more nights for pupils to be at schoolhouse with their tutors! All staff are now REQUIRED to attend the following Group Fitness evenings..."

Mme. Carve read off a list of dates. Halfdan tried not to groan when he heard them. How many hours a day did they wish him to labor? He *had* liked this profession, because it had given him reasonable requirements so he could also spend time with his *own* progeny, especially since Larnen faced so many challenges. Seeing the blank stares on the faces of the other tutors, he wondered: *do you want to live in fear and be unhappy or do you want to be free?*

"We, of course, HAVE A MISSION to encourage parents to spend more time with their progeny, in the school setting, of course... And it would be best if you NOT notify parents of any upcoming events for their progeny at the Schoolhouse that they might, ahem, object to..."

At this point, Halfdan spoke up. He couldn't contain his outrage at R'ti's contempt for parent's wishes, no matter how much it might irritate Carve.

"Wouldn't it be better to let parents know what's going on during their progeny's day? Don't we have a responsibility to do that?"

Carve stared at him condescendingly. "Only parents who have something to hide would worry about such things."

Now she was channeling the Demon Lord C'ps, it seemed.

Translation: "R'ti Monitors know what's best for your children. And if you don't play along, then watch out!"

"...and, you better remember: the Group Fitness evenings are <u>Mandatory</u>!"

The key approach of any totalitarian regime is to remove the freedom of its subjects to question Declarations from On High. Period. Otherwise, they might question the rationale behind the edicts. For instance, if the Group Fitness evenings were really that helpful, then they wouldn't *need to* make their attendance Mandatory.

Freedom. That would be nice. For a man to be able to do what he wanted to do, when he wanted to do it, as long as it didn't really

68

harm another. Halfdan had experienced that during a few times in his life. Contrary to what the R'ti totalitarians might think, when he was in that free state, he only wished everyone else the best. It also occurred to him why Fitness for Tutors was now part of the R'ti agenda: totalitarians want to control *every* part of their subjects' lives, unlike simple authoritarians.

"...We have ABSOLUTELY NO IDEA what challenges our pupils will face in the future, or even what type of professions they will have. That's why we need to start preparing NOW for the tasks that we know NOTHING about! For our PUPIL'S sakes..."

Something in the far corner of the room caught Halfdan's eye. God, anything to take his attention off the rantings of this madwoman...

"...so now, we're going to show that we're giving MORE than our VERY best to our pupils by reciting all the Wonderful Celebrations in our Lives!" beamed Carve.

Wonderful Celebrations meant ways for tutors to ingratiate themselves to the Monitors by boasting of their achievements, though it sometimes backfired. Mentioning any problems with the Required Approved Words, Correct Voice, et al., would be sure to wind the tutor's up in Hollowspoke's book, rather than in Carve's good graces.

The former continued to note any tutors who weren't paying full attention on her notepad. Mr. Beauly kept a friendly smile on his face.

Halfdan glanced over at the clown performers as subtly as he could, trying to avoid being seen by Ms. Hollowspoke and having his name written onto the Pad of Remedial Memorandum. Something was *off* about them. He had sensed a darkness, almost energetic, around the performers before. He had at first just assumed it was his depression at being forced to sit through yet another meeting. Now the darkness *around* them was gone, but their clown *eyes* were very dark. *Completely* dark. As if clowns weren't creepy enough. This couldn't be good.

"...In closing, I wanted to let you know, that all of us at the Schoolhouse are in for a Special Treat! We have a new Performance Observer coming to visit us in a few days. He, of course, is well-versed in our sacred ways of R'ti! He and some of the other Count's Monitors could enter your classroom at <u>any</u> <u>time</u>. But don't worry! They're just there to evaluate whether you're doing an acceptable job or not! Why would you worry about that? And to keep this fun, we will continue to refrain from telling you exactly what an acceptable job is..."

Halfdan could see that many of the tutors tried to smile, but the burgeoning frowns on their lips belied their concerns. Understandably so: Carve was known to scream at tutors for nearly a half hour, without letting them leave the room, so debating her would have been quite unwise.

Even complaining to the Monitor Director himself did no good, it would seem. He would feign concern when questioned, but would take no discernable action. He was most certainly well aware of what was occurring and may have actually been quietly encouraging Carve's viciousness. After all, the Schoolhouse was pronounced to be FAILING. Something had to be done... right?

The problem was, nobody had any idea what that was. Year after year, some new Initiative was taken, and yet Exponential Annua Incrementum could not be attained. Strangely enough, even though the Examinations kept increasing in difficulty, the pupils' scores kept falling! Of course, the tutors were to blame.

The meeting began to break up and Halfdan remembered to avoid any Unprofessional Conversation. For certain, the *favored* tutors were essentially allowed to discuss whatever they wanted. But as an *unfavored,* Male Tutor-Under-Review, it was best if he just kept his mouth shut.

Dan Osarchuk

Halfdan wandered as nonchalantly as he could over to the clown band. Apart from being dolled up in heinous make-up and garish clothing, they seemed fairly normal now. He could not detect any darkness around them or in their eyes. He smiled at them meekly and glanced around at the books nearby. One in particular caught his eye: <u>The Chromatic Cat Consumes the Vital Humors of His Tutor</u>.

In this bizarre book, wholly approved by the R'ti censors of course, the Chromatic Cat goes to a schoolhouse. He appears as one of the freakishly demented drawings from Sir Comkorn, an author of pupil's books. Aside from the inane ramblings and ridiculous poems as found in most of Sir Comkorn's books (that included many made-up words just to make the sentences rhyme), this one in particular gave him chills.

After a schoohouse breakfast of sugared toast, sweetest juice, and malted sausage, the Chromatic Cat throws his fork at one of the tutors, because she told him it was time to go to study. A Monitor comes in, Ms. Sunshine, punches the tutor in the stomach and gives the Chromatic Cat a gold star for Asserting His Educational Independence.

The Chromatic Cat then trots to his classroom and gives a high-five to his friends, Roger Rouse and Louis Louse, some other garish monstrosities. After some inane rhyming about the shortcomings of tutors and how it's their fault that the schoolhouse was failing, the Cat runs into the classroom, barreling over a number of tables. His classroom tutor tells him it's time to take his seat, so the dementedly sadistic Cat smashes him in the head with a chair. The whole class laughs.

Later on in the day, the Cat engages in even more outrageous behavior and eventually convinces one of the Monitors to kill his tutor and eat him for lunch. It even makes special mention of all the food groups that the tutor's body would comprise.

Luckily, it wasn't this bad in the *real* Schoolhouse, but this was the type of entertainment many of the pupils enjoyed, and it would show in their disrespect for their tutors. That the blame for all of society's ills was a *Lack of Proper Education by Tutors,* rather than simply being character flaws in some members of society, was the cornerstone of the Cult of R'ti. It was true in all other forms of totalitarianism throughout the ages, as well, though the scapegoat might be different.

Halfdan returned the book to the shelf and saw that it was amongst other books penned by Sir Comkorn. One in particular caught his eye, an older one that must have been around for years. It was also about the Chromatic Cat- this one being: <u>The Chromatic Cat Goes for a Walk</u>. Strangely enough, this version had a similar plot to the first one, but involved none of the violence towards tutors, nor any R'ti propaganda. Instead, it just had inane rhyming for no particular reason.

On a whim, he glanced on the inside back cover of the book and examined all the names of those who had borrowed it. The adjacent dates stretched back almost 30 years. One name was repeated a number of times, the pupil had also apparently repeated quite a few grades, since his time span of borrowings was nearly 10 years: Billy Berray.

Halfdan went over to the card file and looked up his name; it had wrung a bell. The file showed that he had been a library patron at the Schoohouse from ALO 383-393, indeed for 10 years, while most pupils finished in six. He went back to the Sir Comkorn section and noticed that Billy had checked out quite a number of other books from that author, and for multiple times.

Becoming curious, Halfdan then looked at the old Pupil Directories for those years: hand-written tomes which mentioned pupils' achievements and excerpts by pupils who were ready to graduate to the Academy. After searching for a few minutes, he found only one written by Billy:

Dan Osarchuk

"Tutors suck! So long IDIOTS!" –Billy

Billy Berray was a local legend. About twenty years ago, as an adolescent, he had wandered off into the woods, never to be seen again. Variations of the legend differed on what had happened to him next, but a number of deaths were involved.

A chill ran down Halfdan's spine. It was the same feeling he had when he had sensed the darkness around the clowns.

He then noticed that Ms. Hollowspoke was glaring at him and writing something on her pad. Halfdan realized that it was time to go.

Chapter 10

The Terrors Below

Trying to staunch the blood from the goblin's bite wound on his ear, Kolveig surveyed the situation. Was Oborren just toying with the currently more-deranged-than-normal barbarian? He glanced over at the statue and smiled. The ruse appeared to have prevented the barbarian from attacking any party members so far. Gorm was now sprinting over to the thing, its crude reptilian head shaking, probably due to the big man running towards it. What it used to be a statue of, Kolveig could not tell. Hopefully the barbarian would soon remove its head and....wait: did that thing *really* just move?

To Kolveig's horror, he realized that one of the statue's massive stone arms had just shifted to engage the charging barbarian. Not just that, but it seemed that its entire body was animate now. The thing is alive! No- it can't be! Some mechanical trick perhaps? Cave gas? Such things were not poss...

Kolveig's inner dialogue was interrupted as Gorm's oversized body was hurled at him, the barbarian's still-raging red face and fluttering mullet coming at the cleric at great speed. He, Oborren, and Brymanah ducked quickly, narrowly avoiding being squashed by their own party member.

This wasn't good, Kolveig surmised. If the goblin statue could toss the party's muscle like that....

"RRRRRRAAAARRRRRAAAAAHHH!!!!!!!!!!!!!!!!!!!!!!!!!!!!!!!!"

If it was possible, Gorm became even angrier.

Bruised and bloodied, the barbarian launched himself at the statue, bashing aside its thick stone arms in order to grasp it in a great bear hug. He then proceeded to head-butt it repeatedly, which had the vicious circle effect of making him even more angry and disoriented, which made him want to head-butt the statue even more.

To make matters worse, goblins began to rush into the room again, perhaps emboldened by the statue's attack. This time though, Brymanah had had enough of these little scoundrels. She resolutely grabbed a decapitated goblin head in one hand, her cutlass in another, screamed, and charged the burnt-orange skinned humanoids. She slashed a hook-nosed one right across the neck and thrust the decapitated head into the face of another that was holding a spear. It screamed, panicking its fellows, the lot of them fleeing out of the room. Brymanah pursued, a look of bloodlust in her eyes.

"Great, now we have split the party," said Oborren.

Not sure which way to go himself, Oborren shoved Kolveig in the direction that Brymanah charged, while he headed back to the statue. It must be a golem, he thought, a statue animated by some sort of elemental spirit within. It seemed like a nasty one too, because its makeshift reptilian mouth was now closing over the barbarian's semi-aware, still gyrating, profusely bleeding head. He couldn't decide what was more disturbing: the rusty nails and knives that the goblins had used for its teeth or the fact that since its mouth was closing, part of the original gnome statue's face could be seen, smiling with seemingly innocent glee, as it prepared to decapitate the barbarian.

76

Dan Osarchuk

Who knows what horrors one will find when one ventures underground?

* * *

Brymanah sprinted down the passageway, slaying goblins as they fled, the thrill of the kill within her. Death! She continued passed the entrance where the party had first entered the warren. Heading down the other passageway now, she ducked to narrowly avoid some sort of nasty goblin trap. Black ichor dripped from the spear that thrust from the wall. That these little, mannish monsters would use traps and poison on her only enraged Brymanah further!

Rounding a corner, she came to a huge cavern, perhaps some 60' wide and twice that deep. A large group of goblins had gathered there, numbering roughly 30 or so, with crude spears, nailed clubs, and rusty knives readied. They seemed surprisingly brave in the face of the amazon warrior. Perhaps they really were that stupid.

As she prepared to advance on the orange goblin regiment, a hideous roar echoed from the back of the cavern. The goblins began to scream and caper about, though they seemed more excited than terrified. Brymanah prepared herself for whatever horror approached. The goblin regiment noticed her reaction and smiled wickedly back at her, murderous lust in their beady eyes.

* * *

Reacting quickly, Oborren grabbed a stout table leg that had been broken when Gorm had thrown a goblin aside during the first assault. Pushing with all his might, he was able to wedge it in-between the golem's teeth and Gorm's bleeding mullet, narrowly saving the barbarian from a very painful lobotomy. The statue turned its misshapen head at Oborren then; its dead eyes suggesting some malevolent intelligence within. As it pried the table leg from its mouth, Oborren dutifully pulled the now comatose barbarian away from the golem, making sure to stay out of the thing's grasp.

Night Skies Over Valhallow

As Gorm moaned, Oborren's mind raced for a way to kill this thing. That was just the problem though: how? Golems were specifically designed to be nigh-unstoppable. Even magic could do little against them directly.

Speaking of magic, what had happened to Cherries? Had she suffered some form of mishap when she had cast a spell? Such things were unfortunately fairly common for those who did not take the time to couch their effects in the seeming-plausibility of happenstance or, at least, patience. Or had she simply turned invisible and fled? Such things were unfortunately *also* fairly common amongst henchmen.

His train of thought was interrupted by the golem stalking towards him. Its icy malevolence grew more palpable in the air. Bloody headprints from the barbarian littered its stony form. Oborren feebly pointed his crossbow at the thing, knowing full well that such an attack would be useless against it. As he said what he thought were his final prayers to the Northern Gods of Middlechest, he noticed a greenish-black stream of nastiness dripping from the golem's mouth. Had it been wounded?

* * *

Back in the huge cavern, Kolveig paused a moment to stop the bleeding from his ear. Those Bourgeoisie rascals! Any such creatures that would attempt to steal any of his body parts in such a manner must certainly be working for some sort of latent Capitalist!

He focused his attention on his ear. Brymanah and the goblins seemed to all be distracted by *something large* moving at the far end of the cavern, so he risked some obvious magic. He simply didn't have the time to fool around with bandages and the like. Praying to Karl, he felt the reddish energy passing through his hand into the wound, knitting the broken tissue and compelling his immune system to redouble its efforts in the name of Socialism-or else!

Dan Osarchuk

A short distance from the cleric, Brymanah attempted to get out of that *large something's* way, but was too late. Some enormous beetle had grabbed her, stabbing into her ankle with one of its many legs! It roared as it readied a vicious bite, its huge antenna spanning forth from a triangular head. The goblins clapped and screamed as this fifteen foot long monstrosity prepared to kill the intruder. Then they would do nasty-nasty things to her body! Its mandibles dripped acid onto the cave floor, a potent stink of sulfur as the stone beneath began to dissolve.

Brymanah had heard of such things. Apparently the Ancients had been invaded by tiny versions of such creatures from a far-off land during the last few years before Lights Out. Of course, as the creatures had found their way underground, they had become mutated into virulently carnivorous, much, much larger versions over the centuries...

"This is one Proletariat that you will not harvest body parts from—Corporeal Capitalist!" Kolveig screamed as he rushed into the room, hurling his hammer at the giant beetle's head. It shrieked as the hammer connected, cracking part of its carapace, yellowish ooze leaking out.

The goblins stood dumbfounded at this surprising attack on the beast. Fighting back the urge to chastise the bloated apparent insectoid Capitalist further, Kolveig rushed passed them and helped Brymanah back to her feet. The two limped out of the cavern, heading towards the rest of the party. The strange stink intensified.

* * *

Oborren desperately dodged another of the golem's slams. The animate statue had cleverly backed him into a corner, giving him few other places to go. Gorm still lay comatose on the other side of the room. Not bad, thought Oborren ironically, we've only entered one room of this warren and I seem to be the only party member left standing. Perhaps I should....

Night Skies Over Valhallow

Just then, the golem got in a surprise slam, knocking Oborren back with incredible force. It was akin to being hit by a small mountain. Oborren wondered at how the barbarian had stood against the thing for so long.

Suddenly, Kolveig and Brymanah rushed back into the room, fear in their eyes. In his delirious state, Oborren actually thought that they were afraid for him, since the golem had both arms raised over its head, ready to smash the life out of him.

Another crash settled the matter. It was the giant beetle attempting to rush into the room! It was still squealing from Kolveig's wounding. Oborren had no idea how something so big could have made it this far down that hallway. Such creatures had an almost magical talent for getting into places despite their size, but it seemed it had gotten its shield-like body stuck in the entrance to the statue room they were in nonetheless. Its caustic mandibles dripped on the floor, dissolving what it touched. A horrible stench filled the room as its alien eyes stared at them.

Moving quickly, Oborren dove passed the momentarily distracted golem towards Gorm's prostrate body. Grabbing the barbarian's great axe, he backed towards the giant beetle, nearly being overwhelmed by its terrible stink and screeching.

Kolveig and Brymanah rushed over to Gorm and pulled him to the wall near the beetle too, making sure to avoid its mandibles. The muted sounds of irate goblins could be heard on the other side of the beetle while in-between its shrieks, its corpulent mass fully blocking the doorway.

The golem lumbered forward, its makeshift reptilian face barely covering the cherub-like smiling gnome head beneath. It seemed to particularly dislike Oborren, for it made right for him, as Kolveig applied some bandages and healing salve to Gorm's many wounds.

The golem moved in for the kill. Just as it was ready to make a second try at pummeling him, Oborren ducked, drew back Gorm's axe, and swung with all his might. The stinking beetle's head came clean off, stifling its screams, and causing a torrent of stinking acid to pour onto the golem. It stared silently as its body started to dissolve. Oborren leapt away in pain as splatters of acid fell on him as well. Soon the golem was destroyed, goblin additions, gnome base and all. And a large stinking chamber was left from the beetle's decapitated body, fully blocking the goblins from entering the room. Their indignant cries could still be heard on the other side, still somewhat muffled.

* * *

With the two horrors defeated, the party took a moment to catch their breath and search the room. Kolveig was able to miraculously help Gorm come back to his senses, though he gave all the credit to his deity, Karl, of course. Brymanah and Oborren searched and came up with around 40 silver pieces from the many slain goblins in the room. Not a bad haul. The coins were a mix of those minted in Mauriatown, Walstock, and even Helltowne interestingly enough. Kolveig took a particular interest in the latter, after he had finished with Gorm and heard Oborren mumbling to himself. Brymanah traded places with him, strangely taking to comforting the now recovering Gorm.

"Bolsheviks! My how they've corrupted the true meaning of Karl!" exclaimed Kolveig, as he held up some of the Helltowne coins.

"No one cares," retorted Oborren.

"You're just unhappy because you've thus far failed to see the light of Pure Karlism!"

Just as Oborren was about to point out how Kolveig wasn't "pure" himself, he noticed the pedestal that the golem had been standing on. It looked to have some sort of circular door set in the stone.

"Looks like we've found a way out after all."

Night Skies Over Valhallow

Oborren, Kolveig, Gorm, and Brymanah all stared at the hatch. True, it was a way out, but it was also a way *down*.

Chapter 11

The Halls of Madness

Getting through the hatch was surprisingly easy work, especially after Cherries rematerialized just in the nick of time to assist its opening with a spell. The well-crafted, stone door was obviously not of goblin make, and its lack of graffiti suggested that they didn't even know it was there beneath the statue. It did seem a little *too* clean though, despite its apparent age. Whether it was by good sealing or by some other craft or circumstance, it was unclear. Still, it was a way out of the room rather than through the giant stink beetle carcass and goblins beyond.

When Cherries had reappeared, she offered little explanation as to where she had gone. In fact, she claimed to actually have been gone for no time at all. The party wondered at her inane explanation and watched her suspiciously, wondering if she was a liar, a coward, or even just crazy. Such things were not unheard of amongst magi; to delve into the occult arts certainly would risk one's sanity, even more so than the clerical followers of divinities. Her constant giggling in response to their pointed questions did not help much either.

Nevertheless, her opening spell proved to be much more effective than Gorm's newly repaired cranium, which he had offered to use as an improvised battering ram for the situation. Beyond the 10' diameter portal, metal rungs were set into a smooth, tan stone tube, forming a ladder leading down. Before Oborren could organize the party into some sort of rational marching order though, Gorm impulsively leaped into the hole, not bothering to steady himself on the rungs. The rest of the party wasn't sure whether to laugh or cry at his antics.

As there was no immediate thud or screams of pain, Brymanah looked down and saw that the hulking barbarian had caught himself on the ladder, roughly 20' down. She smiled furtively. Oborren took a torch, gave a "Look out below" and tossed it down. Bouncing off of the clueless barbarian's mulleted head, it continued further, revealing that the passage was nearly 50' deep.

The outraged cries of the goblins on the other side of the giant beetle's carcass grew louder. A deep banging sound also suggested that they were hitting it with some sort of large, heavy object, perhaps using a battering ram of their own.

"Time to go." The rest of the party responded to Oborren's prodding and followed Gorm down the ladder, one by one.

"Is our fearless leader going to lead from the back?" heckled Kolveig.

"Someone has to close the hatch," Oborren retorted.

Kolveig rolled his eyes and descended. Oborren took one last look around and closed the hatch behind them. The only light now emanated from below, from the fallen torch, burning feebly, as he began the long climb down.

* * *

A mild cave scent greeted the party at the landing. They glanced around in the flickering light of the additional torches now lit. Arched ceilings, roughly 12' high at the apex with well-fitted stone bricks descending down to the walls and floor below could be seen.

Semi-precious stones were set into the walls at regular intervals. Oborren whispered to himself as he noted the workmanship.

"Gnome-made, probably." The oversized architecture of the gnomes was only surpassed by that of the dwarves, which would have had closer to 40' tall walls. It appeared that they had dropped into an intersection.

Cherries began to chant and the party immediately began to back up. Kolveig caught one of the words: 'Calator'. He whispered its meaning to the rest of the party: 'Servant'. Being a Karlist, he was quite familiar with a wide variety of terms of class distinction in different languages.

There was no telling how magic would behave down here, though Oborren was beginning to believe that it didn't need as much restriction to work. He had never seen an *obvious* monster in someone's home or in a town in broad daylight, but he had certainly seen them in the wilderness, at night, as well as in many places below ground. Was there some relationship between obvious magic and obvious monsters? He guessed they would find out soon enough, if and when this 'servant' arrived.

Cherries completed her chanting with a crescendo and the torches abruptly blew out. An uncanny silence filled the hallway. Brymanah and Kolveig scrambled to relight their torches. Something seemed to move at the end of the hall, but continued gazing in that direction revealed nothing.

"What have you done?" questioned Brymanah, her breath bated.

"Simply getting us some help!" replied Cherries. She smiled cheerfully at the frowning amazon. The latter did not seem impressed.

"Perhaps you should ask the party before working magic next time!" scolded Oborren.

Cherries looked at him sheepishly and made as if she was going to cry.

Seeing the upcoming possible calamity of an upset magi, Kolveig, hammer in one hand, torch in the other, led the party forth. Gorm took up the rear, fighting back some tears of his own: that Oborren sure could be scary, he thought.

* * *

The party ventured further into the halls, and though the halls were wide, the sense of being underground began to compress upon them. No sign of Cherries's 'servant' could be seen thus far. Still, she did not seem the least concerned about it which made the rest of the party even more concerned. It was wise to keep an extra eye on overly happy people, especially when underground.

Kolveig had the party halt with his upraised hand. A series of doors stood before them, five in all: two on each side of the hall and one at the end. All appeared oaken and reinforced with brass pinions and pull-rings. The finely carved lintels above them and empty wall sconces seemed to be the only other adornments visible. Each door had a different colored gem set above.

Cherries immediately made to open the door closest to her on the left. Brymanah slapped her hand away before she could touch it. Gorm imitated, doing the same on his side, so Oborren slapped his hand away, as well.

"Ahhhh.... henchmen..."

Kolveig snickered at Oborren's remark as he examined the doorways. He was no thief, but he did have a working knowledge of how various Unenlightened Capitalist Hoarders might keep their treasure from Honest Workers such as himself. Seeing no concealed tripwires, catches, or pressure plates, he invited Gorm to open the first door on the left.

Dan Osarchuk

The rest of the party stood well back as the large barbarian made to pull the door open. Much to their surprise, it seemed to move of its own accord. Another rumored trademark of gnomish construction was the use of various mechanisms and gizmos. Apparently this was the case here: at the first contact with Gorm's meaty fist, the door opened outward with a whirring sound being heard. This did not stop Gorm from trying to hurry the process by pulling on the door with all his might, of course.

Inside spanned a medium-sized room, roughly 20' wide and 40' deep. Its gray stone walls were highlighted by a bright orange trim where the walls met the ceiling. In the center of one wall was a strange rectangular bas relief. Oborren was no expert on gnomish design, but this emblem certainly seemed magical. The curling weaves of the bas relief seemed to confound the senses and confuse the soul. It was almost as if they were moving...

"My eyes hurt!" exclaimed Gorm.

"Try closing them and checking out the room," offered Kolveig. He was a skilled Motivator of the Working Class, after all.

With no one's conscience becoming sufficiently motivated enough to intervene, the hulking barbarian blundered blithely into the room. Poor Gorm stumbled about for a minute, his long, thick arms outstretched, a look of painful concentration on his meaty face.

With the barbarian's eyes still squeezed shut, Kolveig offered, "Try going that way."

"Huh?"

"That way," Kolveig pointed in a random direction, knowing full well that the barbarian couldn't see which way he was pointing. The cleric felt that it was sometimes good to Test the Proletariat, to keep them resolute.

Night Skies Over Valhallow

"Enough!" Brymanah smacked Kolveig aside and entered the room. She approached Gorm and got him to relax a bit, showing a surprising degree of gentleness.

Seeing that neither of them had died yet from some hidden monster, deadly trap, or other calamity, the rest of the party entered the room.

The strange bas relief continued to curve and swirl before their eyes. The room also felt unpleasantly warm. Suddenly, most of the party began to wretch and stumble around dizzily. The only ones who did not seem so affected were Cherries and, of course, Gorm, since his eyes were still closed very tightly, as he continued to try to go "that way."

What manner of sorcery could this be, Cherries thought. That was the mystery and mystery was the way of magic! To explain one's spells to another was to risk their dissolution through disbelief, or so her Master used to say. The Ancients had called those who used sleight of hand 'magicians'... true magi of this age were not entirely different, even though they could do way cooler things!

She did know a spell that would notice the presence of magic in the area. With some elaboration on her part, she could adjust it to notice *traps*. They *were* both forms of *noticing*, after all.

Cherries just *loved* elaborating- almost as much as she *loved* shopping for shoes. She glanced down at her gorgeous cherry-brown thigh-highs. Everything of hers needed to have at least something to do with cherries, even her hair was that color! But her boots still had some gore on them from that giant beetle thing. It would be such a pain to clean it off...

But back to the spell! Some magi didn't like to elaborate, but Cherries certainly did! Those silly-nillies thought it *was too dangerous*. Hrmph! More like *more fun* in her book! Now, if she could just adjust her finishing words slightly....

Dan Osarchuk

Oborren, Kolveig, and Brymanah found enough strength during their retching to panic as they noticed Cherries casting another spell.

A brief flash of light filled the room and Cherries' eyes seemed to take on a vivid red hue. She stared at the bas relief and giggled. Oborren nearly vomited again as she pranced back out into the hall and started opening all the remaining doors, singing some nonsensical song.

Well, at least we'll be put out of our misery soon, he thought.

Instead though, no horrible monsters or other calamities came out of the rooms. They all appeared identical to the room they first entered except that the bas reliefs were somewhat different and each trim was another color. Oborren also noticed that the trim in each room matched the gem above each door that led to the room. Being a hunter, he was good at noticing such things. Cherries gasped as she seemed to notice the same about the rooms.

"A puzzle!" she exclaimed. She jumped up and down, clapping.

Oborren had to admit that he liked puzzles too and, by all the Gods of Gore, his head was beginning to clear.

* * *

Despite Brymanah's objections, Kolveig soon had Gorm scout out the other rooms, just to make sure that Gorm didn't feel left out. Oborren was surprised that Brymanah seemed to care so much about the barbarian: he had thought that amazons hated men. After a few more minutes of blind stumbling, the party guessed that the rest of the rooms were safe to enter, or at least safe for Gorm to enter.

Starting at the left door that they had first entered, going around clockwise, the trim and gem colors for each room were: bright orange, gray, gold, green, and blue, ending on the first door on the right. Each room otherwise appeared empty, except for a strange bas relief that would defy description. Each room also had a sensation to it- not too overpowering as long as all the other doors were open, but palpable nonetheless: warm, breezy, bright, stuffy, and moist.

Even stranger, each party member went to investigate each room separately, breaking the Cardinal Rule of adventuring: Never Split the Party. Gorm returned to the room with bright orange trim, Cherries in the gray one, Kolveig in the golden one, Brymanah in the green one...

"Oh why not?" said Oborren to himself as he trotted over to the blue one, "What's the worst that could happen?"

Strangely, nothing did... at first.

Though most later regretted it, they then followed Cherries advice:

"On the count of 3, let's all touch the bas-reliefs at the same time!"

"1... 2..."

Brymanah glanced over at Gorm across the hall. The over-anxious fellow was touching the relief over and over again, not even close to waiting until the count of...

"3!"

Silence. For a moment, it seemed as if they had tempted Fate and yet avoided calamity.

But then a whirring sound could be heard. At first, it was barely perceptible, then it grew louder and louder.

Slowly at first, but then gaining speed, the rooms began to spin around of their own accord. Before the party members could rush out into the hallway, the spinning had increased to such speed that they were thrust back into the rooms, pinned against the walls! It seemed as if the whole series of rooms were spinning in unison with the hallway as the fulcrum.

As the spinning accelerated, multicolored hues of light began to emerge and mingle in the center of the hallway. Finally, a deep BOOM resounded and the spinning slowed.

The disoriented and nauseated party started to regain their bearings, stumbling back out into the hallway, only to notice that someone *else* was standing there. A little man, a gnome perhaps, with bright, rainbow-colored eyes, hair, and beard. They glowed with the light reminiscent of the spinning. He smiled at them.

Only Cherries smiled back.

Chapter 12

Averaphne

The rising, jeweled moon shown over the frosty cedar woodlands. Halfdan pulled his heavy cloak and wool hat closer to him to ward off the chill. He knew he shouldn't be out here this time of night. Though it had been a hard day, it seemed he had survived the latest Inquisition with the High-Monitors of R'ti, and currently maintained his position as a tutor at the Schoolhouse.

The recent troubles there had only amplified his endemic sense of paranoia. *If I could be accused of something that ridiculous, why not something else?*

It was a poisonous thought, he knew. That sense of fear would never end, for being afraid of fear or being afraid of letting one's guard down was only self-perpetuating- it could be nothing else. And as long as he identified so much with his body and his life story, he would continually suffer, it was inevitable.

So why was he here in this cold clearing on a winter night? Halfdan obviously had not had female companionship for quite a while. He had not been able to find that right *someone*. Halfdan had always dreamt of a certain woman since he was of a very young age, a blonde woman with a particular countenance, whose *presence* felt a certain way. In the dreams, it would feel as if they were *soulmates*, meant to be together, connecting perfectly on every level. The sense of her was like coming home, as if they had never been separated in the first place, since they were already one.

But it had never happened. No manner of soothsayer or guide was able to bring him to her. They would all offer either overly optimistic pleasantries, such as "you will meet in another year or two" or hopelessly empty predictions, like "you'll meet when the time is right." Unfortunately though, that time never seemed to come.

Instead, he was out in the woods to see the nymphs. Many warned about meeting such fey or spirits of place. Of course, they were beautiful, *painfully* so. But one never knew what type one might run in to. That such beings could change to any pleasing shape to fulfill a man's desires was well known. This was one of the problems with nymphs. Mortal women couldn't usually alter their physical forms on a whim, so men who fell into the graces of a nymph found it hard to settle for all but the most beautiful of mortal maidens again. And of course, those most beautiful of mortal maidens were often betrothed to only the most capable and powerful of mortal men- qualities that Halfdan lacked.

It was also well-known that men who dallied with nymphs might not even return from their otherworldly abodes at all! Such sirens, another division amongst nymphs, were said to lead men to their deaths, but more often it was actually the man who chose to leave the vicissitudes of this mortal world behind to join their new nymphly paramour. Whether it was a realm of whimsy and wonder or quintessential vivacity, the man was lost nonetheless.

Was this why so many sought the nymphs? Beyond their obviously shapely forms, enticing aromas, and honey-soaked voices for which no man could tire, there was the allure of the unworldly. Why toil and suffer in the fields, or bend knee to some cruel lord, or labor away in some God-forsaken Schoolhouse, when one could lose oneself in such ostensibly better realms of pleasure, excitement, and pastime? Perhaps one should ask why more men didn't do that very thing.

Halfdan's thoughts were interrupted by the snapping of a branch. He glanced over and smiled, but paid special mind to keep his eyes on the snowy ground. There he saw a beautiful female foot, perhaps the most beautiful he had ever seen. She must have snapped the branch to play with him- no fey or nature spirit would ever have been detected so unless they wished it, at least in normal circumstances. Her honeyed voice rang warmly in the cold night air.

"What brings you to my humble abode on such a cold winter's night, Halfdan?"

Every tendon in his body longed to turn and gaze upon her beatific form, but he successfully held back the urge. If he did so but once, all would be lost. He might lose contact with her completely and feel as if he was only *imagining* her presence. Or he might instead be whisked away to the paradise of her *real* abode, losing contact with those who he cared for in this world for evermore. He was not yet ready to take that risk.

Almost as if reading his mind, as most spirits are wont to do, the nymph took on a slightly cajoling and yet no less intoxicating tone.

"Come on, Halfdan, you know you wish to gaze upon me and find your fitting release."

"I do," he replied eventually, "but I'm here tonight for guidance, rather than for your indelible pleasures."

He could sense her smile. There, in the full moonlight, his slender body bowing, she shifted, her irresistible scent wafting upon the air, making the winter night more *magical.*

"I would be happy to guide you, to whatever it is that you desire," she replied suggestively.

Halfdan also smiled; the nymph's charms were verbal as well. Quite clever too, he noticed that she had moved so that he could see her shadow in the moonlight: lithe, yet voluptuous; free, yet mysterious, buxom and inviting. He felt the chill air leave him as well, perhaps from her magic or simply the increase in his blood pressure from her standing so close. He fought back another urge to gaze at her face. He knew that it would perfect, exactly what he desired. She was a nymph after all; there was no companion more pleasant for a man to enjoy.

Another might have seen nothing or perhaps just taken this unclad beauty to be some sodden tart. Such was the way of supernal things on the surface world: they could be hard to discern from fancy; easy to explain away as just one's wild imagination, even when such an encounter was actually unfolding.

But those who actually realized that they were encountering a fey or spirit of place risked great peril as well as reward. For such beings were said to be able to work magic with a whim, unlike the required spoken words and occult formulae of mortal wizards and witches or the devotion of clerics. Theirs was the province of the otherworldly, so much so that those who crossed them ran as much of a risk of being lost in some strange land as being blessed by some amazing wonder.

All fey followed strange rules, but what they were and how a mortal was to come out the better from them was never certain. And spirits of place, the *landvaettir* of the Norse and the *genii loci* of the Olympians, simply reflected the potency of life. It was impossible to tell which type this nymph actually was or if she could even be truly defined by such limited mortal concepts.

Regaining his composure, Halfdan continued, "I seek information, my dear. Information about what's happening at the Schoolhouse and my best approach thereto."

He could sense her shift in position. The depths of her consciousness were palpable now. He ventured another request.

96

Dan Osarchuk

"And I would love to hear your name."

Halfdan was no shaman, but he did know some things about spirits. It was risky to ask such a thing of them. To know their name would be a hold over them. Of course, they'd never admit to their *real* name, but any sort of name that they'd use for themselves would hold power nonetheless. Such reasonings might understandably come to an Odinnic who spent much time alone and in quiet contemplation, such as Halfdan.

But he trusted to this very fact, for he was not seeking a siren tonight, but a muse. Such a nymph was less interested in luring men from the world with their pleasures and more interested in helping men to engage the world and enjoy its many expressions. He had heard that such a nymph dwelt in these woods. He hoped that he was right.

"Averaphne," she said with honeyed voice and his spirits rose.

Halfdan smiled again, it seemed that he had much more luck with spirit women than with mortal women. He began the trek back, keeping his mind clear as he could and his heart open. He sensed her presence follow him. He wasn't sure if it was the nymph doing it or if it was his own rambunctious mind, but suggestive images of Averaphne would flicker into his imagination. He trudged on though. Warmed by her presence and his own open heart, the stars twinkled in the cold, inky darkness overhead, like some Northern Spectacle.

* * *

The moonlight shown on Halfdan's longhouse, lighting the place in a surreal, heavenly silver-blue glow. He could sense that Averaphne was still with him, but he dared not look back to check. Despite his rising sense of excitement, he remembered that doing so now would either make him entirely smitten with her, bereft of all sense, or in fact scare her off, dispelling the entire task of his going to the woods, for an unbeliever's eyes made quick work of fantasies, even at night.

His house door creaked as he let himself in to a simple wooden room, a small fire still burning feebly in the corner stove. No cold wind followed him, as was wont to do on other nights when he walked alone, to gaze at the stars and treetops before slipping off to slumber. No, she followed him. He could sense her presence and almost smell her radiance now: something akin to vanilla, mixed with flowers, sensuality, and joy. His quiet mind allowed the magic of the moment to overtake him, as he gently shut the door, mindful that she would have time to enter first.

He stood there smiling again, put a few more logs on the fire and ventured off to bed. Firewood was a welcome commodity these cold days and nights. It was said that the Ancients own magical heating sources grew too rare, as well. Was that their undoing? At least in the present era, sources of warmth could still be grown: a blessing from God, or fortune, or even with the help of fey or nature spirits perhaps.

Excitement filled his body, for she was nearby. Perhaps she really was a muse, for the excitement was pleasant, not overwhelming. He changed into his nightwear and was surprised to actually see her there for a moment, smiling as the moonlight beamed through the window. Averaphne's curvaceous form sat on his bed, her intoxicating scent filling the air. A nightgown covered her voluptuous body, giving off a sense of more classic beauty than that of craven abandon.

Memory flickered in Halfdan's mind.

Gazing into Averaphne's face, a face that reflected his true desire, Halfdan could see that woman that he had always dreamt about, even at a young age. He nearly cried as her flaxen hair flowed around her shoulders, showing as a silver-blue river in the light.

"Let me tuck you in, Halfdan."

98

He thanked God for this moment and was amazed that she was still visible. Such things were rare, to actually *see* the supernatural of the world. Unless one was below the surface, deep in the wilderness, enlightened, or quite inebriated in some way, such things often remained invisible. Those who claimed to *see* ghosts, demons, angels, or other spirits, usually often only *felt* their presences, rather than truly observing them. This time was different. He felt her near him, and it felt perfect, complete, as if he was really home again. But he could *see* her too: her deep azure eyes gazing at him, her smooth gentle hands caressing his head, and the weight of her body embracing him.

And yet, he knew that it was not real, and that Averaphne was not his soulmate. He opened up his arms and smiled at her. She smiled back knowingly. Oh, how he longed for it to actually be her! But both knew it was not. He did love Averaphne with his very being, how could he not? But there was another, a certain mortal woman, who Halfdan hoped and prayed to meet again someday.

* * *

The first rays of morning light beamed through his window. In a moment, the dark, sad desperation came upon Halfdan again, as he realized that it was the start of another workday. Though he tried to fight them, the thoughts of the awaiting lunacy, hectic ways, and belittlements at the Schoolhouse were too overwhelming. The thoughts and the fighting of them went hand in hand.

As he arose and made himself ready and dressed, he glanced back at his bed and could still see the impression where Averaphne had lain by him the night before. Her scent was still in the air. He looked within at his dark feelings and let them arise and leave.

What good did it do to lock dark feelings in with yet more darkness?

He felt emboldened now after her visit. Perhaps he was still a slave to the Monitors, who could command and belittle him all they wished? Perhaps more vicious, false accusations would meet him this day? Perhaps today he would meet with disaster...

But he knew that God would be there too. And that same love that he had held with Averaphne last night had come from within his own heart. For it could be said that the heart was the projector onto this screen of life. And the more open, the brighter and lighter the image would appear to be.

At that moment, a memory came to Halfdan, a memory not of this life; a memory of a man and a blonde woman in a distant land, yet all very familiar, of them walking through the woods, hand-in-hand, love in their hearts, being in their stride. They looked upon each other and Halfdan knew it was *her* and she had that same look in her eyes as she gazed at *him*. The woods seemed to be their home, their *special place* to be together, the link perhaps that held their many romances together, through many lives, throughout the ages. Words could not truly describe the bond they felt.

What else could compare with that?

And yet, it was not to last. For on that very day, Halfdan could remember a shot, some projectile striking his love in the belly. Shocked, he desperately clung to hold her... trying to staunch the blood... her pale face still smiling... loving him still... knowing how devastated he will be without her... and yet happy to still be in his arms....

That loss Halfdan still carried to this day. He loyally tended to it, without even always realizing it, as a tribute to her, to his lost love of a life past.

What else could one do for true love?

Chapter 13

Little Man from a Can

The strange gnome with the incredibly rainbow-colored glowing hair and beard began to chant. Surmising his intent, Brymanah and Gorm rushed him in an effort to disrupt his spell by dashing his brains out upon the far wall. Not good: with a wave of his hand, the two were thrust back as if by an invisible force, slamming into their own wall. Oborren attempted a stealthy crossbow shot at that moment, but his bolt simply dissolved when it came in contact with the gnome's neck.

"He's too powerful!" warned the hunter.

Either distracted or not hearing him, Cherries attempted a spell. She'd need something powerful to deal with this crazy-looking guy! Blasts of cherry-hued vivid light, complete with formed energetic cherries on the front, burst forth from her fingertips. Few in the party had ever seen such an obvious display of eldritch arcanum before, let alone from a party member!

Alas, the magic cherry missiles dissipated harmlessly too when they came in contact with the gnome.

He smiled faintly, maddening multi-chromatic light scintillating in his eyes- a New Strangeness indeed.

Night Skies Over Valhallow

The gnome raised his arms to complete his incantation. His booming voice seemed not of this world, nor one befitting such a small body.

Kolveig strode forward, hammer in hand. He began his chastisement:

"Who are you to be taking such an Individualized Path? Don't you know that it's only through Collective Action that any sort of Positive Improvement can be made?"

The rainbow gnome stared at the Karlist cleric. For a moment, his scintillating eyes began to clear and he swooned with memory...

* * *

Tepson had thought it was a good idea to come in to work that day. At first, he was surprised that they were still open, since most of the rest of the government was closed, but then again, it was his department's job to be open in emergencies such as these. Leaving his family behind had been very hard that morning, because he knew things were bad: riots, explosions, and talk of worse things, even in such a seemingly bucolic place as the Valley. Law and order had broken down throughout most of the country and it wasn't safe to travel. Still, he knew there wasn't much he could do for them at home: perhaps he could help set things right at work, so that his family would be safe in the long run?

That hope soon dissipated upon his arrival. Most of the staff had either fled or taken to walling themselves off, using the complex as their own, private little survival retreats. He couldn't say that he blamed them, the complex was well stocked: food, water, toiletries- even firearms, ammunition, and medicine- any prepper's dream. That wasn't how Tepson was built though. He was a man of duty, or at least, he would never give up on his family. After a bitter argument with a number of his remaining co-workers, they scuffled, and old Tepson got tossed into a deserted area of the complex. He was a small person, after all.

102

Dan Osarchuk

He had never been a fan of Political Correctness, but certainly didn't appreciate being picked on because he was a midget. He personally found the term 'little person' insulting, because of its inherent condescension, but being one did seem to help him land his job. And all those years of ridicule from bigger people really helped to sharpen his mind and his wit. Plus, he was an excellent biologist, if he did say so himself.

After some rummaging around, he stumbled upon a hidden door and found one of the secret areas that were often rumored to be in government facilities. Down a number of halls he had wandered, until one door in particular caught his eye. Entering a passcode that he had 'noticed' a superior typing once, the metal door slid open. Inside were all sorts of strange equipment, including a large vial with a swirling, multicolored light in it. The strange thing even had some sort of weird cartoon cat embossed on the side. Tearing his eyes away, he also noticed a very large, bigger person-sized metal cylinder with a variety of tubes and dials hooked up to it.

A great BOOMING sound at the other end of the complex signaled that something was up. Perhaps his former co-workers had decided that there might not be enough supplies for all of them after all? Or perhaps someone else had realized how poorly guarded the complex now was and had decided on claiming the supplies for themselves? In either case, he didn't stand much of a chance if he went back that way- the only way out- and the only area with supplies, he woefully conceded.

His eyes turned to the great metal cylinder. 'CRYOGENIC CHAMBER' it read. He was familiar with such a device, even though it was supposed to be classified TOP SECRET and, beginning to shed tears now, he climbed in. He set the controls to awaken him in just one week- that should be enough for things to calm down at the complex. He would miss his family, but would also be no good to them dead. He sat on the interior chair as the sounds of commotion drew closer to the room he was in.

Just one week, then whatever whackos that were here now would either have killed each other or left. Just one week, and then he could walk back home and help his family. Maybe there would even be some supplies left over. Just one week...

He gasped as the Chamber's door swung shut and the temperature began to drop rapidly. He looked through the plate glass window as it began to fill with frost, those strange chromatic lights still shimmering from the vial he had seen upon entering, shimmering through the eyes of the crazy cat that stared at him, so strange...

* * *

The rainbow gnome shook his head and regained his chromatic-induced composure. He smiled fiercely this time. Completing the incantation, a great rushing sound emanated from the rooms with differently colored trims. To the party's horror, strange beings of pure elements began to emerge from the bas reliefs in the rooms: one of fire, one of wind, one of earth, and one of water. Nothing seemed to emerge from the golden light room, nothing yet anyway.

The gnome seems to be possessed by something, Oborren thought. His mind raced for any hunter's tale of *rainbow eyes*. None came to mind. The party turned to face the elementals entering the hallway.

Nearly unstoppable, elementals were beings comprised completely of energy, or pure matter, in the case of the earthen one. Unless some special way to defeat them was at hand, Oborren doubted that the party had any chance of even damaging these beings, let alone destroying them.

That fact seemed to be lost on Gorm and Brymanah. The warriors each rushed an elemental. Though the barbarian and the amazon were both large, the elementals were even larger, looming over them at over 9' in height! Gorm fought the earthen one; Brymanah, the one made of fire.

With a mighty swing, Gorm launched his great axe into the thing, embedding it in its mass of rock and soil. It stared at him unmoved and then swatted him away with little effort. Brymanah nearly dropped her cutlass from her hand as she swung at hers, her face contorted in pain and rage from her burns, as the fiery thing countered.

This did not look promising, Kolveig realized. He shot a look at the gnome, who was now levitating about 3' off the ground. It was time to bring the Wrath of Karl down upon him again!

"So! Exploiting Working... um... 'Things'... with Your Capitalist Slavery again? It *is* a sign of all Tyrants to have others perform their Labor for them, even if they ARE using elementals!"

The rainbow gnome stared at the cleric again. His face began to show a little emotion, twisting slightly in contempt.

But more memories began to flood over the gnome, reminding him of his former life. Walking in the fields outside his home. A life with a wife and children, happily together, with none of this... craziness... within him. This... strange... CHROMATIC LIGHT! In a moment, the scintillating force left him. The elementals vanished, his eyes, hair, and beard turned normal. The gnome collapsed to the ground.

* * *

It took a while for the little man to come around. The party had spent the time when he was unconscious first tying him up, then discussing various ways to torture him, then arguing about the best ways to torture him, then agreeing to loot his body, then arguing over the loot, then nearly coming to blows over the allocation of the loot when he finally woke up. They didn't find much on him, only some strange rectangular device that could fit in one's hand and his strange clothing. They assumed that all of it was magical, since the gnome had been glowing rainbow colors, tossing their two strongest members around magically, summoning elementals, and levitating off the ground less than an hour before. At least they had left his undergarments on.

Shaking his head, the little man stared at Brymanah, who had won the drawing for being the first to be allowed to torture him. Her burned arms and hands, cracked and weeping, loomed over his head, as she pointed her cutlass down at his soft tissue. She smiled wickedly and glared into his eyes.

"Hold on!" said the little man. "Who are you people? I must get back to my family!"

Though his accent was strange, the party moaned disappointedly when he began to speak. Perhaps they couldn't torture him now?

"What do you mean: 'family'?" questioned Oborren.

"I mean: 'my family, the ones back in in Maurytown'".

The hunter mused over this. He glanced at Brymanah and shook his head. She reluctantly lowered her cutlass.

Tepson looked around the hall; obvious bewilderment and concern filling his voice.

"Where am I?" he asked.

Most of the party lowered their heads in disappointment, as they realized that they would probably not get to torture him after all.

* * *

After some more debate, the party decided upon the entering the fifth room, the golden light room, since no elemental had emerged from there.

"I think Gorm and I should go back," said Cherries. "Fighting goblins is one thing, but elementals are just freaky!"

Oborren, Brymanah, and Kolveig looked at her inquisitively.

"And that gnome is.... scary!" whispered Gorm. He grew pale and pointed repeatedly at Tepson, making sure the rest of the party knew who he was talking about.

"I understand you're afraid, but we must find that presence that was possessing him," explained Oborren. "It could be what's behind this Insolitus Novus."

Cherries smiled at Oborren disarmingly. Brymanah stared at Gorm; it looked like she was about to cry, but she choked whatever feelings she had and embraced the big guy. Gorm giggled and embraced her back.

Kolveig noticed, not because he was ogling her body of course, that Cherries was making arcane gestures and little motes of pinkish light were floating around Oborren. Oborren just smiled and reached for his coin purse. What harm was there in the hirelings getting a little extra bonus for their efforts, thought Kolveig. He knew they would run into each other again. Let the Workers Earn Their Just Due. And if they got it by manipulating the hunter with an enchantment, then so much the better!

The hulking barbarian and the lithe sorceress then bid the rest "adieu" and ventured back from whence the party came. Most of those remaining wished to see them again.

Tepson then let out a, "Ho! What have we here?" amidst a clicking sound and a secret door opened. Oborren, Kolveig, and Brymanah followed him down the darkened stairs beyond.

Chapter 14

The Bridge

Based on what he could gather from his new traveling companions, the world above had changed radically. How on earth could he cope with those changes now? In the past, everything was at a touch of a button; everything was easily accessible and lit. But now, Tepson reckoned that they were in the midst of one, centuries-long power failure that had turned things... *medieval.* What had happened to him during his long sleep, he could not tell, nor why he had slept so long. What had happened to his family? Perhaps no one was meant to witness such things, even such a substantial midget like himself. Based on what the hunter could tell him, the cryogenic chamber that Tepson was in must have seriously malfunctioned.

He looked around and took in his new surroundings. The austere place had an aura of majesty without presumption, oldness without decay. Oborren had described it as a place of ancient relics, lost from the elder days. Hah! Elder days indeed! These so-called 'Ancients" would have been nothing more than mere twinkles in the eyes of their great-grandparents, who Tepson himself might have seen in passing as small children in his day! What could these mystics possibly teach that Tepson didn't already know?

Night Skies Over Valhallow

Adjusting the pack that Kolveig had "Redistributed" for him, Tepson had to admit that his companions did seem to possess some skill in spelunking- if that is indeed what one would call what they were doing. Worked deer leather straps, padded with what would be wool, he assumed, it held the load well: hard tack and pork jerky rations, hemp rope with a cleverly worked grappling hook, spare torches, and of course, water. They even gave him a pickhammer to use as a weapon. And they did seem to know how to use their weapons, especially the 'amazon'. With his thirst beginning to diminish, Tepson placed the stopper back on his water flask.

Brymanah stared at some of the strange bas-reliefs etched upon the walls. This place was thankfully different than the Halls of Madness that had nearly destroyed them earlier, for the glyphs of these carvings did not seem to move of their own accord. With her cutlass, she lightly pinged the ancient stone, having imaginary arguments in her head with the austere-looking men pictographed therein.

"I think it will be an easy victory for you," Kolveig chided. "Who could compete with such an unstoppable war-maiden as yourself?"

Brymanah grimaced at the cleric's insolence. She hated the Karlist less when he had been her man-servant back in Stephania. Now thoughts of turning *him* into a carving began to take on a new strength!

Sensing a noticeable, feminine increase in aggression in the air, Oborren quickly ventured into the next chamber, though he would have liked to have spent more time examining the one he had been in. Who knew what secrets could be gleaned from such a place? Ever since they had descended the darkened stairs, the halls had taken on an even greater aura of mystery. Perhaps he could examine the previous areas more thoroughly at a later time, but it was now time to explore the rest of this place, to see if they could find that chromatic disturbance that had earlier possessed their new gnome friend. He hoped that the Ancients were not overly jealous in their guardianship of these halls. That disturbance could be the clue they were looking for in determining what the Insolitus Novus actually was.

* * *

The party soon emerged into another chamber. The halls they passed on the way held the same bas-relief pictograms: austere men (with no women present, much to Brymanah's chagrin and Kolveig's amusement at her chagrin) staring back at the passers-by, enigmatic looks on their serene faces. Perhaps they were some sect of ancient Odinnics?

This new chamber was noticeably different though. Roughly 60' in diameter, it featured a pond that filled most of the room, complete with an antique wooden bridge to cross to the far landing. A plaque outside the room depicted melting clocks and ascetics tying down the moon, sun, and stars with ropes.

Brymanah entered the room and eyed the bridge suspiciously. "What makes us choose this one, hunter?" They had passed an intersection earlier. She stared at Oborren, her stern face starting to set his nerves on edge, not to mention his concerns with going anywhere *near* a subterranean body of water.

Still, his thirst for knowledge drove him to choke back his fear of dark water. He replied, "Because I say so. Can you accept that?"

Brymanah looked away angrily and put one of her sandaled feet onto the bridge. She looked back at her party, passingly expecting one of them to volunteer to go first. Of course, she had no takers. *Men*, she thought.

The ancient bridge boards creaked underneath. That it had no railings did not worry her half as much as the dark water below, inscrutably deep. She braced herself and stepped a little faster now, her less-than-courageous companions inching forward as well, still a safe distance behind her. To her surprise, she began to make out a familiar word taking form, painted on the bridge at her feet. "P-A-S-", she began to spell it aloud to the group.

Surprised, Oborren guessed she couldn't read Ancient, and yet there it was, plain as day, in Amercian no less: 'PAST'.

As Brymanah read the words on the bridge, Oborren mused. Kolveig noticed slight ripples arising in the water below. He looked at Tepson wistfully. At least he was a smaller, more vulnerable target, perhaps more tempting to whatever horrible thing or things lurked within.

"Karl save me..." he muttered.

Strangely, Tepson realized that he too could read the word painted on the bridge. He would be shocked if language in the Valley hadn't changed too during the many centuries that he slept. How could this be?

As the group neared the apex, a noticeable silver painted border could be seen on the bridge, after which a wooden pedestal was placed. Something different was also painted on the bridge's floorboards here, as well.

Why couldn't these idiots have hired a thief, thought Brymanah. Such thoughts were not common for a Womyn of Stephania to entertain, but she knew full well that some bridge in the middle of a dungeon room with mysterious water below meant trouble. Some expendable *man* should lead the way.

"What does it say?" ventured Oborren.

"Why don't you see for yourself?" she retorted.

Edging passed the silvered threshold, the hunter hesitated, unsure whether to refer to some protective spell or simply beg for some small favor from the Northern Gods. Brymanah's not-so-subtle shove across settled the matter. Barely keeping his balance, Oborren read the inscription on the floor: 'NOW'.

112

Hmmm, he thought.

The whole scene appeared so surreal to the gnome and yet strangely familiar. A vague memory of some mention he had heard in the old days was beginning to come to him, interrupted though by Kolveig's mumbled prayers about Bourgeoisie Bridge-makers and at his repeated glances at the water. Tepson could now see the disturbances himself, ripples arising.

As he was about to notify the rest of the party, Oborren read the words inscribed on the pedestal aloud: " 'Stand in the place where you have your only power.' "

Bewildered, Oborren could not comprehend how this was all written in Amercian. Perhaps some inherent magic made it legible for all to read? He would have preferred it to at least been written in Ancient, so that it would have seemed more authentic and less like a trap. What was he missing?

As Kolveig began to back away from the disturbance in the water, Tepson let out a shriek. Something big, green, and vaguely humanoid suddenly erupted from the depths, clutching onto the bridge, its seemingly blind eyes staring right at the gnome, fanged maw open in expectation. Tepson's biologist mind rushed to classify it.

Brymanah responded instantly, relieved to no longer have to endure listening to the hunter mumble to himself. Her cutlass slashed at the thing's throat, slicing open its jugular. It croaked and fell suddenly back into the water, splashing black water upon the bridge.

Still petrified, Tepson finally whispered something to the effect of, "What in blazes was that thing?"

Kolveig, taking a more pragmatic approach, ran up to the apex where Oborren was still standing. "What does the DAMN bridge say!?!?" he screeched.

"Well, we may have bigger problems than that."

Kolveig stared in terror as he waited for the hunter to continue.

"The creature looked like a troll and it most is certainly...," Oborren paused, eyeing the dark pond below.

Kolveig interrupted: "What?!"

"It's probably not-"

"Not what?!?!"

"Dead."

"NOT DEAD?!?!?!?!"

"No."

Pulling himself together, Tepson hurried up to where the two men were talking. "So what do we do?"

"Fire!" Oborren exclaimed. "Use your torches to burn the thing!"

"No more figuring out riddles?" the amazon teased. Remembering the earlier puzzle, Oborren glanced at the stretch of bridge beyond. It read 'FUTURE'.

The whole party waited, staring at the water, weapons ready, torches out, sparks falling, waiting...

They didn't notice the creaking sound behind them until the very last moment. Brymanah's cry was stifled as a pair of large, green hands wrapped around her neck, attempting to throttle her. Oborren's mind raced as he considered the best place to strike. Acting quickly, he launched a crossbow bolt right into its eye, narrowly missing Brymanah. Kolveig, his fears forgotten for the moment, grabbed his Marxian hammer and brained the foul thing, shattered bone and foul ichor mixing with its tangled, wire-like hair. The troll shrieked, as Tepson added his aid by smashing it in the kneecap.

The wounded beast and Brymanah swayed and then pitched over into the unknown depths below. Oborren attempted to grab them but couldn't hold onto the troll's slimy hide. With a splash, the two were down in the pond. Tepson shuddered at all the germs that Brymanah must now be exposed to.

Thinking quickly, or perhaps not thinking at all, Tepson himself launched into the water after them. "Now he must have really lost it," muttered Kolveig.

Down in the dark, watery depths, Brymanah struggled against the foul troll. Though she knew it was sorely wounded, the monster was still unnaturally strong and apparently quite at home in the night waters. Struggle as she might, her toned, muscular body had little hope alone against the wicked beast. So, letting her battle-training take over, she reached up and intuitively found Oborren's bolt, still lodged in the troll's eye. With all her remaining strength, she pushed and twisted it in its ocular cavity, causing the beast to convulse. Then, with an instinctive kick to the thing's crotch (or so she hoped), Brymanah launched herself away and then burst through to the surface of the water, gasping for air. The feeble light of sputtering torches, now lain upon the bridge, illumined her allies looking down at her.

Kolveig and Oborren reacted quickly, hauling her up to the bridge, her strong, wet body now showing the toll of her recent battle. Brymanah's wounds about her neck and back were especially bad, Kolveig thought, he wasn't sure if Karl would grant so much healing to an obvious Matriarchist such as she.

As Kolveig began to call upon his faith in his deity, Oborren trained his crossbow on the dark water. He kneeled to present less of a target and a more steady shot. He also made sure to hold the bolt since he was pointing it downward. There was no telling when and where exactly the beast might emerge again. And what of

Tepson?! The poor little fellow was down there with the troll. A fairly small troll from what Oborren could see, but a troll nonetheless. Its goblinoid face, approximate 7' tall size, long, wiry limbs, claws, and wicked hair, left no room for doubt in Oborren's mind. And how were they to burn it, if it kept falling back into the water?

A momentary altering of the room's light to a more reddish-golden color and the sound of distant, almost imperceptible left-wing patriotic music broke Oborren from his reverie. He ventured a glance back at Kolveig and Brymanah and now it did not look like her wounds were nearly as bad as recently thought. His attention was quickly drawn back to the water though by another disturbance. Waves and bubbles were emanating rapidly now, something was definitely going on underneath. The three readied themselves. It occurred to Kolveig that it might be a good idea to leave the area before the troll was done feeding on Tepson.

Suddenly, something leaped out of the water.

Surprisingly, it was Tepson. His clothes were torn, but his wounds were not nearly as bad as Brymanah's had been. How the little fellow had enough momentum to clear the water with such speed, Oborren didn't know, but he was glad to take his finger off the crossbow's trigger and grasp the gnome's hand.

Brymanah, now recovered, croaked out a command to the group, "Get up to the middle, fools!"

Not having time to argue, the males heeded her, moving to the apex of the bridge, and the disturbance in the water ceased.

Oborren glanced down at the word 'NOW' underneath and mused over its relevance. Kolveig smirked, ready to mention a variety of puns in reference to the 'troll', 'power', and 'now'. Brymanah cut him off though, baring her teeth and fingering the hilt of her cutlass menacingly. There were few things that enraged her as much as the gratuitous use of puns by uppity males. The two turned to look at Tepson as he spoke.

Dan Osarchuk

"It's not dead, is it?"

No one replied. Only the dark waters stared back at them.

PART 2

Chapter 15

Mistro Tsar Huk

Halfdan felt his thighs burn as he climbed the hill. Overhead, the great, white tower loomed, its edges clearly defined by the cold, deep blue sky. He had heard that the 50' tall structure had been used in some other capacity in the elder days, but ever since he had dwelt in Calvary, it had always been the home to a mighty wizard.

It was said that those who sought the metaphysical in this world could fall into two camps: the spiritual and the occult. Though he knew the fallacy in labels, Halfdan would probably admit to being placed in the former camp. It always had seemed that the best thing in his life had been to let go and let God, to be who he really was; to follow the Path of Odin, the way of Insight and Absolution.

Odin had always appealed to Halfdan in particular, what with the study of the Runes, removing of one's 'Eye' (I), and his connection to Freya and her loving tears of gold. Later wise ones, such as Lest, Eckhart, Nissar, and Robert, added further to the Odinnic practice in the current day. Different devotees might gravitate to certain teachers, just as those who traveled different paths to God might harmonize with different divinities. Even the followers of the same divinity might have varying world-views, depending on how much orthodoxy was enforced.

Those of a spiritual persuasion might delve more into the ways of Priesthood or Mysticism, Shamanism or even the Druidic following of the Seasons and of Nature. This choice was based as much on the devotee's own strengths as on the faith of which they followed. Whatever their approach, the miracles of the clerical camp were typically more subtle, allowing happenstance to befall themselves and others more easily, to provide healing, sustenance, succor, as well as protection from that which could be deemed unsafe, unholy, or unwise.

It was within the latter camp that wizards and their ilk fell. Theirs was the way of much more blatant power, of obvious *aealae artes* made manifest. Whereas it might seem that the spiritual path would subsume one's ego, the opposite could be said to be the case with practitioners of the arcane arts. It was *their own* will that was being done, not that of a higher power. It was not unknown for magi, sorcerers, wizards, and the like to perform great feats of eldritch amazement: flying through the air, blasting foes with raw elemental magics, or even summoning strange beings to do their bidding.

Still, such phantasmagoric occurrences could certainly strain the credulity of banal onlookers in ways that the workings of the divine would not. Would an *obvious* act of magic have actually occurred, if the one so affected did not believe it to be so? Would it still be magical if it were ordinary? And how would the gods respond to those who would alter the world so vainly?

And such strains on reality would necessarily thin the ranks of those already rare individuals with such occult talent, for they would also need great luck and intelligence to avoid and survive the inevitable magical mishap that would occur. Wizards were therefore quite potent and rare indeed. Circumstance dictated that it be so.

Dan Osarchuk

The Ancients too had their own true magicians, though Science was rarely deemed as such at the time at least in public discourse. It was the full faith of that lost society that their drive-chariots would (usually) speed of their volition to their destinations with reliability or that their light-screens would organize nearly all facets of their lives: from entertainment to livelihood to frequent correspondence- all without fail. Science even had its own arcane language, its own inner teachings, and its own required formulae, just like the magic-users of this day, though the Ancient magi were able to get the populace to *believe* that such things would work more obviously. Even the latter-day teachings of Quant Theo had shown how the Ancients had even begun to codify this truth a few decades before Light's Out: that one's beliefs determined one's reality as far as one could stretch them.

It could also be said that wizards and others in this current day lacked such cooperation from common folk though. For sure, the people were certainly *terrified* of wizards, even if those being accused weren't real ones. Witch hunts had become somewhat popular again, unfortunately for those affected, like in the Old Dark Ages. Some might point out that witch hunts even continued uninterrupted from the Old Dark Ages straight into the New Dark Ages, despite the many modern marvels and so-called 'Social Advancements' of the Ancients, thanks mostly to the rise of Political Cults and their variants. But still, the overarching belief systems of the New Dark Ages did not correspond as well with the existence of obvious magic. Therefore, most wizards and the like did not have free license to attempt any magic effect that they wished to use without the threat of great misfortune.

Such spells could cause those beings from more empyrean realms to react to such prideful attempts at the world's alteration in ways far differently than practitioners of spiritual paths. For example, if a cleric were to bless his comrades in battle or pray over their wounds for speedy healing, it could be more easily said that the benevolence of Providence had occurred or that the comrades had simply gotten lucky in battle and the wounds were not as bad

123

as previously thought. On the other hand, if a sorcerer erupted bolts of flame from his own hand and then teleported twenty feet passed his enemies in the blink of an eye, it would not be so easily explained away.

Was this simply the continuation of the Ancient's Quant Theo? Or perhaps some Enchanter's obscure Attraction's Law? Most would say that it was simply ordained by the Gods and be done with it. Or that all magic required due payment to balance one's meted change with another.

Perhaps the teachings of Science never fully left the common folk? Perhaps these New Dark Ages held a different Magical Law than the Old? Whatever the case, any spellcasters who attempted such obvious magic in such obvious places could suffer from a wide range of effects, being distorted in mind or body. Even clerics might be *tested* from time to time...

It was at this juncture that Halfdan finally arrived at the guarded gates of the Tower of the Wizard, Mistro Tsar Huk.

Whether wizards specifically attempted to put on airs of intimidation or if it was simply their nature, Halfdan couldn't say. He did know that wizards and other occultists could certainly be influenced by any magical corruptions that they had and if not, would certainly work to conceal them at least.

An eccentrically dressed guardsman approached him at the gate. A mask of what looked like teeth or claws covered his face, with a similarly designed breastplate providing some measure of authority and protection. A large, encircled blue 'M' on the front rounded out the ensemble The rest of him was covered in a magenta colored cloak, lined with black- nothing could be seen of his face or eyes. Halfdan stated his business and in a refined, almost relaxed manner, the guardsman let him in.

The tower loomed above, closer now, as the silent guardsman led him to the double doors at its base. Two more large, encircled 'M"s could be seen, painted in blue, suggesting that Mistro might have a bit of a megalomaniacal disorder.

Within, Halfdan encountered another silent guard, dressed similarly to the first one yet with a cloak of yellow, who escorted him up the stairs. Portraits of a black-haired man with a long, thin moustache engaging in many acts of heroism and occult legerdemain were displayed on the way up. At the top landing, the portal opened into an opulent suite, replete with fine embellishments, attractive serving-maids, and a number of other guards with cloaks of various colors.

The scene stood in contrast to where Halfdan had trained in the past. The Odinnic way was one of minimalism and quiet: set in a simple wooden cabin, learning to drop and go beyond the many vicissitudes of the body's pains and the mind's desires. Stunning serving maidens were also present there for the devotees, but instead of bringing libations, they hit the initiates with sticks if they started to nod off or talk...

Halfdan was surprised suddenly by a booming voice with a strange accent.

"Greeetingsss. I am Mistro Tsar Huk... And you are NOT!"

The man from the many stair paintings stared at Halfdan. He was dressed in shiny blue and magenta robes, complete with a matching skullcap. A great 'M' was emblazoned on his chest. Perhaps he was a megalo...

"So! Vhat is it that you vant of my greatnesss, mere mortal?"

"Greetings, Lord Mistro. I am Halfdan of..."

"I already know who you are, cur! My mental abilitiesss had already asssesssed that! I vass assking: vhat do you vant? Do I need to vrite it down for you?"

Were all wizards this eccentric... or sibilant?

"I've become aware of an entity at the Schoolhouse where I tutor. I was wondering if you could shed some light on it?"

"Light? Light? A vool such as you vishes me to make Light?... Certainly."

"Come now, Lord Mistro, don't you think that calling me a 'fool' is overdoing it? You've just met me and can so definitely pass judgment?"

"It is not! You ARE a vool! The Great Mistro can certainly pierce a veeble mind such as yours with his Glorious Vit! You are even more a vool for believing othervissse! You, Halfdan, are a mere nanny-man of children, content to have Monitorss harasss you daily at their earliest convenience, to be imprisoned in some chamber that rages overly hot, to be compelled to tutor pupilsss thingsss that they cannot reliably comprehend, nor do they vant to comprehend, so they give you nasty staresss and chattering voices... and yet you are considered the one who has failed in the processs!"

He did have a point. But, how was Halfdan to make a living?

" 'Oh, look at me,' " Mistro imitated in a sing-song voice, " 'I am Halvdan and I am scared of my own shadow, unable to vind some other manner of employ, due to my severely lacking mental facultiesss!' "

At least his impersonation made it a little easier to understand him.

"Neverthelesss! I shall deign to inconvenience Myself once again to listen to your painful prattle, no matter how agonizing it may be."

"... Much thanks... Mistro...." Halfdan allowed himself a moment to let his mind clear.

126

"There appears to be a ghost haunting the Schoolhouse, making the Monitors extremely hostile to certain tutors, including... me."

Mistro smiled wickedly. Halfdan did not know how to take it.

"I see. And vhat makesss you think it is a ghost, my moronic vriend?"

"A young man had died some years ago and strange things have been occurring at the Schoolhouse to the types of people he disliked."

"Strange thingsss are ALVAYS occurring at that crazy place!"

"But this is different: now the Monitors are actively harrying certain tutors."

"And you blame a ghost?"

"Yes."

"A ghost."

"Yes!"

"My, my, you are a ssstupid one, my dear Halvdan... or should I say 'Halv-vit'. "

Mistro laughed maniacally at his own joke for nearly a minute.

Pulling himself together, Mistro continued, "Such thingss are certainly beyond a ghost, don't you think, my dear Halvy?"

"But what else could it be?" queried the cleric.

"Ah HA!," Mistro punctuated his remark by throwing a goblet at an assistant, "THAT isss the question!"

Mistro paused for a moment. His other assistants attempted to clean up the goblet without having another one thrown at them.

Night Skies Over Valhallow

"Are you avare of a certain night-creature-thingy that is called the Least Ovver?"

"The Least... what?" Halfdan looked confused.

"The Least Offer," added one of Mistro's assistants. He backed away quickly as Mistro shot him an imperious glare.

"That's vhat I SAID, cur!"

Halfdan had heard of it: some sinister being that would apparently prey on people, even in their own homes. He had considered it a rumor, since such things couldn't happen in civilized places...

"Silence!" perhaps Mistro really could read minds, Halfdan was sure he hadn't said anything out loud. "It CAN happen, because it DID happen! My, I become overly naussseousss in your nonsssensical presssence, my dear Halvdan! Not *all* creaturesss are *new* to this vorld. Some have remained, hidden amongsst usss, since time imm... imm... since... forever!"

Halfdan's mind raced- what could the wizard mean?

Mistro smiled sinisterly again. A chill ran down Halfdan's spine.

"Go and find this Least Ovver. He is quick vitted, yet he doess have a bit of an ego-vhat-you-know! He is vise in the vaysss of entities, and of coursse doess not take kindly to otherss encroaching upon hiss... prey."

Chapter 16

It's A Strange World

Beyond the bridge and the troll attack, the party wandered. Through rooms strange and defying reason they passed. It is said that the deeper one went underground, the stranger things got. And whether it was the work of the Insolitus Novus or some pre-existing law of the underworld, Oborren, Brymanah, Kolveig, and Tepson were beginning to see its truth.

Who would possibly fashion a trapezoidal room, replete with only a single banner and an incomprehensible inscription, followed by a hallway which contained a fountain that dispensed wine? Was it the work of some hereto unknown race? Or a known race driven mad? Or even a mad deity? Or something else entirely? It was perhaps best not to question, especially while one was caught up *in* the oddness of the underworld. Where else could the New Strangeness have come from or even gone to once again?

Amongst the wanderings of the party, time also seemed to pass strangely too: not only had they been completely underground, bereft of sun, stars, and sky, but they had not even a vague idea for how long they'd travelled. Had it been days, weeks, or even months since they had first ventured into the apparent gnome warrens with Cherries and Gorm? All they could do now was follow where Tepson thought it best. True, he was the newest member of

129

the party and had actually tried to kill them not long ago, but he once had the Strangeness within him, and was hopefully the best judge of where it might be found again.

And despite the occasional insane goblin or gnome that they ran into and had to dispatch, the beings they encountered in these depths of the earth were stranger still indeed. Creeping horrors with many eyes that only feared the touch of flame, mobile slimes and mosses that nearly devoured Tepson and did devour one of Kolveig's shoes. There was even a strikingly attractive woman who seduced Oborren for a while, until Kolveig was able to drive her off, seeing her as an obvious Bourgeois demon-harlot. Oborren seemed somewhat drained, weaker, and not really himself after receiving her kiss. Kolveig told him that was normal with women.

So it was at this juncture that the party's spirits began to lift. The path finally began to slant *up* again, giving the party hope that their quest might soon be at an end. True, they had agreed to this quest, but the reason for their not turning back at this point was more due to their fear of becoming forever lost in this underground world- they knew not whether they'd even be able to find their way back.

The out-of-place scent of sweet baked goods and sundry confectionaries soon began to waft around them. Fearing some sort of diabolical trap or subterranean disaster, Oborren leaped to the side of the passage, while Brymanah, fearing that she was hallucinating, walloped Kolveig with the side of her cutlass to test the solidity of reality.

"OUCH!" wailed the Karlist.

"Perhaps it's not a dream," replied the amazon sardonically.

Nerves would often fray when underground for too long, even moreso amongst a group of adventurers.

Snickering, Tepson sauntered down the passage. Assuming that he had finally gone mad or was simply hiding his truly evil nature

130

this entire time, the party followed, hoping that they could finish him off quickly if either or both were true.

To their partial dismay, they soon found him standing in front of a large, round wooden door. The stone threshold around it was carved with strange symbols, similar to the ones they had seen at the mystic area near the bridge, and yet this door seemed to be glowing different colors, nearly pulsating with energy. The sweet smells that they had noticed before were now wafting unmistakably from it.

"Should be pleasant enough", said the still one-shoed Kolveig, who quickly grabbed and pushed open the door.

Oborren stared at him aghast, not even knowing where to begin with all the adventuring rules he just broke.

Beyond the rainbow-colored door, eerily cheerful music piped down a long hallway of worked stone. Kolveig seemed strangely drawn to the place, so the rest of the party followed along, not wanting to lose their healer, but also not wanting to lose Kolveig's share of the treasure if he did happen to be killed horribly in this strange place.

The Karlist soon stopped ahead and the party noticed, to their increasing concern, that he had begun to sing along with the inane melody that permeated the hallway.

"La, la-la, la, laaa, la-la…. La, la-la, la, laaa, la-la…"

Brymanah moved in for the kill. She hesitated though when she saw what lay before them: a short dock with a brightly-colored rowboat, subterranean channels going straight ahead, left, and right. Brightly-colored paintings covered the walls and, of course, more of that very annoying music that the Karlist seemed to like so much. Staring at a particularly garish painting of some multi-colored, talking cat, Brymanah reasoned that slaying Kolveig then and there might not necessarily end the annoyance of this place.

Chuckling to himself, Kolveig jumped into the rowboat and looked at the party, smiling, waiting for them to join him. Seeing that they were just staring back at him, he left the Capitalists to themselves, and rowed down the channel to the left, naturally enough.

Perhaps this place is some sort of Karlist paradise, thought Oborren. It certainly seemed otherworldly.

* * *

The row was enjoyable and easy, almost as if Kolveig had been carried by some current within the canal. The stone causeway rounded overhead, with interesting pictures of happy, fey creatures smiling back at him. He especially enjoyed all the bright red colors that he could see and the lack of any apparent Class Distinction amongst the groups depicted. He soon met his destination, enjoying the wonderful melody all the way.

At another small dock, Kolveig moored the rowboat to a very large candy cane that some Comrade must have thoughtfully left behind. It looked delicious to taste, but the cleric persevered in his mission and strode up to a bright green-colored door. Opening it without a care in the world, Kolveig entered a strange new land. A deep, almost violet sky hung overhead, with cottony clouds, and a friendly yellow sun shining down upon him. He could look at it directly and it did not blind him. It actually appeared to be smiling. Jagged mountain peaks, almost translucent, framed the distance beyond. Kolveig could have taken them for candied rock. He kicked off his remaining shoe.

He strode deeper into this world, leaving only a suspended rectangle from the portal of his entrance door behind him, giggling to himself. The green grass, perfectly straight, even, and yet soft, massaged his bare feet and sang softly as he sauntered over a rolling hill. Jumping over some sort of milk chocolate stream, he saw a forest up ahead that had a puffy, flavored, cotton-like substance, instead of leaves. At the threshold of the forest, stood a

Dan Osarchuk

friendly looking house, apparently made of some cookie-like material, complete with a white frosting roof, and windows and doors made of what looked like confectionary.

Ah, thought Kolveig, a Worker's Paradise! What hardship or exploitation could be had *here*? He thanked Karl that he had taken the *left* channel.

Recovering from his reverie, Kolveig made his way to the cookie cottage. He knocked on the 'door', which was made of some sort of rounded candy cane. Strangely, no one answered.

Hmmm, thought Kolveig, perhaps I'll just have to let myself in? Everything here should be State Property, he assumed.

Finding a hidden catch on the 'door', he was able to open it and it led into a quaint series of rooms, replete with all manner of sweet-baked good and dainty. He stood in awe, gasping at the sugary bounty before him, until his attention was drawn to a room further inside, perhaps a kitchen, where he heard some commotion.

"Hello! Is anyone here?"

No response. Kolveig made his way to the back, gingerly avoiding all the sweets precariously displayed around him.

Entering the far room, the Karlist realized that it was indeed a kitchen, stocked with a huge, wood-fired oven, tables, pots, pans, utensils, and cooking ingredients, the vast majority of which were sugar-based. It looked like someone had just been working there, for Kolveig could see the yolk of what must have been a newly-cracked egg sliding into a bowl.

Suddenly, out of nowhere, something hard, blunt, and full of flour smashed into Kolveig's face! Dazed, he stumbled back into a cupboard, knocking over a number of tea cups and fancy little plates. They seemed unpleasantly Bourgeois.

He shook his head fiercely, regaining his vision only to see a smiling, demented-looking, fat elfish chef looking back at him! He held a large wooden rolling pin in his hand and had 'The Sweet Chef.' embroidered onto his white apron with what looked like a bright green button as the period. A look of murder was in his eyes, unusual for bakers of his type.

Kolveig ducked another swipe from the rolling pin and retaliated with a smash from his hammer. His strike struck true, cracking into the Sweet Chef's shoulder. To Kolveig's horror, it was not blood that spurted from the wound, but some sort of sweet jelly-like substance instead.

The Chef grimaced, wound up, and smashed Kolveig in the face once again, knocking him fully back into the next room, landing on a platter of what smelled like pumpkin pie. Kolveig did not bleed sweet jelly, of course.

Dazed even more so this time, Kolveig stammered, "So... are you... you a *sweet* chef or are you a *chef* of sweets?"

SMASH! Another mighty hit, this time knocking the poor Karlist into a gourmet cookie display.

"I... I... I... guess it's t' latt..."

SMASH, SMASH, SMASH! Repeated hits, bashing into Kolveig's face and ribs, cracking bone- Karl have mercy!

Blubbering and nearly blacking out from dizziness, the cleric grasped wildly at his tormentor. The Chef's meaty jowls curled into a rictus, his beady eyes staring at the battered Karlist like dough that was ready for a bit more heavy kneading. Kolveig's bruised hand landed on the chef's apron. Unfazed, the Chef's white hat leaned to one side, as he drew back his rolling pin for the killing blow.

At that moment, whether by luck or divine fortune, Kolveig pulled back on the small object that he had been grasping. The Chef looked on in surprise as sweet jelly burst from his apron, rushing out of the hole that Kolveig had created. He screamed in agony as more and more of his apparent vitae spurt out onto Kolveig and the floor.

Stumbling back up, Kolveig wiped his face and licked his lips: he had to admit that this victory was sweet. He looked down at his hand and gazed at the object that he had plucked from the Chef. As the fey being shuddered on the floor in its death throes, Kolveig held a bright green jellybean up to the light. It was the same color as the door through which he had entered this world. And it was also what he thought was the green button at the end of the Chef's embroidered name on his apron. It was then that Kolveig knew that the Chef was now finished... period.

* * *

Oborren, Brymanah, and Tepson watched as the little rowboat floated back to them from the channel to the left. Leaning back with his feet on the rim of the boat was Kolveig, beaming. Held between his forefinger and thumb was what looked like a bright green jellybean.

Despite his obvious serious injuries, the Karlist seemed very pleased with himself.

"Not much in the way of treasure?" teased Oborren.

"Oh no," said Kolveig fervently, nearly drooling "this is *quite* the treasure...."

Brymanah wondered if she was allowed to kill the cleric now.

The two other canal passages harkened before the party. Kolveig could barely contain himself, wanting to immediately investigate the next one. Brymanah could not decide what would be worse: waiting here, listening to this annoying music, and looking at the *annoying* paintings on the walls, or going with Kolveig and listening to his ANNOYING words and looking at the stupid look on his face!

135

Oborren weighed whether it would be more expedient to let the cleric go off on his own to get beaten severely for another jelly bean or to go and assist him. Tepson settled the matter by hopping into the boat next to Kolveig, who in turn gave him a hearty slap on the back.

The quicker we get this over with, reasoned Tepson, the quicker I could get back to the surface and get away from these crazy people.

Chapter 17

The Least Offer

By Juno, she looked so beautiful. Ever since he had put that posting up on the Message Board Tree, his life seemed to have changed for the better. Balverone had never wished to remain with just *one* lady. He found such beauty in them all that it did not seem reasonable to remain with only one. *One farmer, many fields* was certainly not a sign of devotion, he knew, but perhaps one of pragmatic realism. Of course, most would effuse him as a scoundrel for such an ungentlemanly request and manner of discourse. But yet, his fortunes seemed to have turned, for here was his chance! Inspired, he had posted a fairly suggestive notice, not unheard of these days: "Looking For a Fair Maiden *Without a Ring* to Her Name."

He knew it was risky, but he had seen far more suggestive postings on that tree before, so he reasoned: what could be the harm? There was something about a woman who didn't wish to wed that greatly appealed to him. Of course, such activities were quite forbidden according to the dominant churches in town: those of Tyr and Minerva. It was said to even be a greater Declaration throughout the Dominion that all acts of love must either *be within* or *lead directly to* the bonds of holy matrimony, *or else.*

Night Skies Over Valhallow

Why the old Commonwealth seal had been reinterpreted as being Minerva, rather than Columbia, Balverone did not exactly know. But going with the latter could have helped made his desire for an *unusual* relationship statutory, or at least, *not unstatutory*. Now even a *mention* of his interest could land a man in the gaol, whether he actually sought it or not. Whatever had happened to *Sic Semper Tyrannis*?

But the vagaries of political and religious discourse found little ground for purchase in the mind of the aroused Balverone at the moment. *Someone had replied to his posting!* A small mark was made on his notice, a very feminine looking 'X' with the initials 'GW'. He immediately went to the western side of the gazebo in the nearby park, and there, with an identical 'X', was a small envelope!

Now Balverone was not perhaps the wisest of men, for without further thought, he opened the note then and there. It was wonderfully scented and even included a picture, a self-portrait that was also quite common in correspondences such as these. He swooned at the suggestiveness of the letter, as well as the beauty of his apparent paramour.

She indicated that she now wished to meet. What a stroke of luck!

So he awaited her arrival. A waxing crescent moon arose over the barren trees, the scent of burning wood on the air. He pulled his woolen cloak closer around him as a chill wind blew. Just as the correspondence had agreed, they would meet at this very spot, the spot of her note, at the west side of the gazebo here in the park. Oh, the excitement was growing now- what a find! How could such a strikingly beautiful maiden, and with such skill at penmanship to boot, be not spoken for or not even seeking a husband? It seemed almost too good to be true.

Suddenly, a rustling in the bushes nearby... and then she emerged! Striking beauty, even more stunning than the self-portrait she had included. Auburn hair, straight and long, gracing her long, white neck, framing her finely chiseled face and strikingly green eyes. Her curvaceous form, respectfully covered, yet still visible, in a farm girl's outfit, yet free of grime and signs of drudgery. She looked at him with those piercing eyes and smiled.

"Balverone?" she queried. As if there were any doubt!

He smiled, elatedly, finally he would get some...

To his horror, her face began to change. It suddenly became more pale and man-like in the dim moonlight. And her form too began to change into that of a man. He wasn't even sure if she... er... it was wearing farm girl clothes anymore. This was not meeting he was hoping for!

"Are you surprised, Balverone? Isn't it more perversities for which you seek?"

"What?" Balverone choked. He struggled with overwhelming fear and confusion.

"Your kind," the former woman spat. "Your kind who would seek any sick perversity to slake your wanton lust."

"Now...now... hold a second," Balverone stammered, "I just wanted to meet a woman who..."

"Who what? Helps you to defy the laws of the land? Helps you to defy the laws of decency? Scum."

It occurred to Balverone now: "You wrote those letters!"

"Of course I did. What better way to lure in the likes of you?"

"But... why?" Balverone's voice was beginning to shake now as the pale stranger drew closer.

It seemed that it was a man of average height, dressed as a constable. He looked old though, and yet not; aged but well-preserved. His deep, green eyes were the only noticeable trait that remained of the woman who had been standing before him only a few minutes ago. And he was pale, dear Lord, he was pale....

The stranger stared at Balverone and smiled again. He licked his lips. Was that fangs that he could see?

Panicked, Balverone started running up the hill, attempting to put as much distance between himself and this creature as he could. Not only had his dream courtship fallen through, but his dream courtship had turned out to be a nightmare! He raced through the open woodland of the park. The quiet night sky gazed down upon him, unmoved.

Panting, he ventured a quick rest to catch his breath. The stranger was nowhere to be seen. Balverone noticed that he was sweating even in the chill night air. Perhaps he had escaped? He glanced around to make sure and then he stealthily began to make his way back to his home. He was just about to thank Juno for saving him when he heard a 'snap' off to his right.

Terrified, he started sprinting back to his house, but it was too late. The pale stranger, still dressed as a watchman, emerged from behind a tree up ahead. How did he get in front of him so quickly? Balverone tried to change direction, but before he could, the stranger rushed forward and grabbed him by the throat. His speed and strength were incredible. Balverone stood a full head taller than him and yet the stranger still lifted him up with one hand without the slightest bit of strain.

The last thing Balverone remembered of that night was those deep green eyes and a growing, fanged smile.

* * *

"Rise, accused," the wigged judge Barnaby A. Halooran loomed above those assembled in the courtroom. Ancient, paneled wood surrounded the place. A faint scent of mold and dust in the air mixed with the apparent air of final authority.

Dan Osarchuk

"The defendant stands accused of Unstatutory Acts Most Foul, including, but not limited to: Attempting to Lie with a Woman with No Intent to Marry, Repeated Solicitation of Such Immorality, and the Possession of Forbidden Demonic Texts. How does the jury find?"

The jury forewoman, an aging petite with gray hair replied, "Guilty, your honor."

Balverone burst out into tears. The star witness, Captain Tamerland, gazed at him emotionlessly with his deep, green eyes.

The judge continued, "Balverone of Walstock, I hereby sentence you to 20 years at the Walstock Gaol. May the Gods have mercy upon your soul!"

It would have been nice to have bled him dry the other night, the Captain thought. But this way, he could feed upon his terror for years to come. All he had needed to do was slip some Forbidden Demonic Texts into Balverone's bedroom for the other constables to find: those things always turned a jury.

Most would not have convicted on a simple attempt at a fling, but the Texts branded Balverone and countless others as perverted freaks. And such Brandings stayed with them for the rest of their lives. Few would even want to rise to their defense for fear of being labelled perverted freaks and become Branded themselves! It was beautiful. Mortals were such predictable sheep. And to think, he used to be one of them.

Balverone was still sobbing as he was led out of the courtroom in shackles. And he was one of the larger-sized victims to be sentenced. Oh, the exquisite terror when some smaller man gets sent off to the Gaol! Those would always either end up being a larger prisoner's plaything, simply hang themselves in utter despair, or both. The captain could almost feel his stomach grumbling. Ever since he had learned how to gain sustenance from *feelings*, instead of just blood, he could experience a smorgasbord of delights, with very little threat of being exposed himself. Delicious!

Oh, and Balverone *would* suffer. Did these mortal fools even care that he really *didn't do* anything wrong? Of course not: they get to point their fingers at a 'bad man' and feel better about their own miserable souls. Ha! If the Captain could only harness the energy of the *guilt of hypocrisy*, he would never even need to get innocent men thrown into the Gaol. There was plenty of it right here in the courtroom!

The Captain ventured a smile as he, the jury, and the other witnesses left the Courthouse. He avoided the direct sunlight, keeping to the edge of the building and then stealing away through the more shadowy alleyways. His mind ventured to the Gaol. It occurred to him that that place was even worse than Hell for those condemned: at least God chose who went *there*, not some foolish mortal sheep jury!

* * *

Night fell over the squat, brick building. Smoke rose from the nearby townhouses. To the casual passer-by, all was quiet; only an occasional constable could be seen patrolling the street outside. To Captain Tamerland though, it was an entirely different matter. Fear and frustration emanated from the place like freshly baked sweetbread. The outrage and dismay of humiliation, isolation, and worse from the inmates wafted up on the air, filling his dark heart with twisted nourishment. It was all he could do to keep walking his route outside the Gaol, fighting back the urge to scream with pleasure and sadistic delight. He often volunteered for this assignment, especially when there were *new arrivals*. It was much tastier that way.

True, not all inside were innocent. The emotions of the truly guilty were a little overly meaty to Tamerland's sensibilities. Murderers, robbers, rapists, and other mortal abusers, those who *had actually harmed* others, certainly needed to be locked up. That did not appeal to Tamerland's palate though. He far preferred the pastry sweet energy of those who were appalled and terrified for being locked up for really doing no wrong to anyone. Perhaps they had said the wrong thing to the wrong person at the wrong time or ingested some substance that was deemed unholy by those who currently held apparent moral authority?

Of course, the energy was even sweeter when those locked up were falsely imprisoned for even more heinous crimes, crimes that they themselves would see as morally repugnant. What frustration they must feel that no one would believe them! Delicious! And planting Forbidden Demonic Texts somewhere in their homes for the constables to 'find' was the Captain's favorite way. How could they possible prove their innocence then? They *were in possession of Forbidden Texts*! The bitter irony of those incarcerated became delicious icing on the cake for one such as he. Even if released, they would carry that bitter stigma for the rest of their days!

He remembered centuries ago, when the decision was made to have the state seal embossed with Columbia herself. Ha! What a joke! He and some others like him had been throwing 'the innocent' in jail whenever they could, even back then, whether it was to feed, to demonstrate a sense of moral responsibility, or because they had some valuable 'evidence' that they needed to 'confiscate'.

And it wasn't just the immortals who felt it essential to break as many eggs as possible to make a delicious societal omelet. A number of mortal constables turned a blind eye or were even complicit themselves! It looked good to make many arrests, even if those arrested never really did anything wrong.

Oh, and when they turned on the electric power everywhere, what a joy it was to feed on outraged souls to the sounds of music, especially... *disco*! The beat and strumming bass of it had reminded him of Old Anatolia and the feeding rituals he had engaged in when he had become newly 'born'. That and the cries of the victims he had thrown in with real monsters was ever a timeless pleasure.

Their horror and disgust was not that different than the castrated victims of Cybele, now that he thought of it.

And even more delectable was the fear and horror when they realized that they would never return home. Torn from their place of comfort for committing some apparent sin, it was no mistake that the Least Offer picked Balverone. His former friends and family might have even called him a *good man*, but no one would now, except possibly the other inmates that would defile him!

Tamerland couldn't hold back a chuckle now. Things never changed! Sheep juries would continue to bow to an 'almighty judge' and convict, allowing far more horrible things to befall those found guilty than anything they were accused of! And they even claimed that they were doing society a service! Hah! Perhaps mortals really were evil.

Whether it be a Lord stomping a peasant, a Supervisor firing an employee, a Bully pushing a shopkeep, or a Righteous One burning a heretic, the human world was far more cruel than the animal one. This wasn't the Mountains of Candied Rock! And it was up to ones like him, like Tamerland, to rule over all; to dine upon the sweet cream of the crop of mortal-caused suffering. Was he so wrong in helping it along a little?

Chapter 18

Of World Walking and Insulting Toys

The rowboat, now roughly 3 ½ times more laden than on Kolveig's first, solo journey, floated down the canal passage that lay straight ahead. Since Kolveig had apparently now appointed himself captain, he refused to venture *his vessel* down the passage to the right. He reasoned that since the destination at the end of the *left* passage had been so bucolic, then the passage to the *right* must be replete with the Exploitation of Workers and other Such Horrors to the Highest Degree. Ironically, his memories of the beating by the Sweet Chef had apparently been bashed out by the Sweet Chef himself.

The sing-songy music continued to play as the boat drifted down the center canal. Oborren mused over what could be hidden in the aquamarine-colored waters that gently flowed around them. Tepson wondered at the happy-looking talking flower, animal, and pixie paintings that adorned much of the walls and ceilings, as well as what narcotics the people who drew them were on. And Brymanah pondered what was the best angle to slice Kolveig's head off, since the Karlist had taken to singing along again with the incredibly irritating, apparently ever-present music.

Soon the boat came to yet another small dock, this one with ropes that looked like they were made of licorice. Kolveig immediately leaped out of the boat, shouting out a hearty "Land Ho!", while his comrades clung to the sides as it rocked violently, thanks to his hasty departure.

"KOLVEIG!" screamed the amazon. The cleric seemed too busy staring at the bright red door that led from the dock to notice her chastisement.

The party soon joined him: Tepson taking a moment to tie up the boat with the licorice rope and Oborren taking a moment to remind the murderous Brymanah that Kolveig was their only healer. With a huff, she sheathed her cutlass. For now, she would spare the cleric. She settled on just glaring at him instead.

Kolveig was still transfixed by the red door. It was *red. RED!* And after all the other wonderful things he had experienced in this place so far, sans the Sweet Chef of course, he could barely muster the will to open the door. He was just too elated.

Seeing his opportunity to open a dungeon door properly, Oborren walked up to it carefully and pulled out a round piece of slightly concave glass from his rucksack. As he looked through it, strange motes of purple light could be seen, suggesting that the glass's purpose was not simply magnification, but also some sort of magical detection. As to what sort of detection, Oborren kept it to himself. Apparently satisfied, he put his piece of glass back in his rucksack, stepped back from the door, and nodded to Kolveig that it was okay to enter.

"After you, captain."

Giddy in anticipation, Kolveig burst through the door, nearly tripping over the floorplate in his excitement. Much to his chagrin, this place did not have puffy white clouds and cotton candy forests like the land behind the green door.

Instead, this land seemed less fantastic, but more idyllic. A pleasant breeze blew upon the air, wafting up from a bucolic, deciduous forest. It seemed like early summer, so his hand instinctively went to his pocket to draw out his spin-string. Yet there was not a gnat to be seen, unlike the swarms that still troubled the Vale, so he had no need to repel them with it.

A lovely path stretched before the Karlist. The reddish bricks, edged with gray paving stones, looked newly laid and lead off into the forest. Ahh, good Proletarian Workmanship, thought the cleric.

As he sauntered off, Kolveig didn't realize that the door through which he came had closed.

* * *

"Well, he did trip and... the door closed behind him..." offered Oborren.

And try as they may, they could not get the red door to open again. In this situation especially, they really missed the magic of Cherries and the brawn of Gorm. Assuming that their socialistic comrade had finally met his end, the rest of the party reboarded the boat and let it carry them back down the channel. The sing-songy music played again, echoing against the moist stone tunnel walls. Brymanah couldn't decide if she was happy that the Karlist was gone or not.

After a few minutes, the boat returned to the chamber the party had first entered. Oborren, who was apparently the new captain of this vessel, decided to take it down the canal to the right.

"Why not? What's the worst that could happen?" Oborren said, tempting Fate.

Tepson stared at the vivid colored aquamarine waters. Unless the Valley's biome had changed radically, he reasoned, there is no way that the water here is natural. Suddenly, he was startled to see a disturbance at the spot at which he was gazing.

Night Skies Over Valhallow

Oh no, not again! The gnome was becoming worried. Half expecting another troll to erupt out of the water, he was mildly relieved to see it was the outline of a large fish. He was glad it wasn't a troll, but who knew what the heck that thing really was, if it was dwelling in this bizarre place?

* * *

Kolveig observed this so-called 'granny' attentively, adjusting his red cloak and hood. He had just debated this obvious imposter on the important distinctions of Stalin-Trotsky *yet again*, when he realized that it was futile. How on earth could some anthropomorphic wolf, dressed as a senior citizen, possibly grasp the futility of Over-Bureaucratization in order to Enable Worker Paradise? All the wolf would do was try to eat him.

And this would be the third time! Oh yes, he had found the unattended Worker's Basket upon arriving in this world, donned the cute Red Cloak, followed the path, saw the broken windows and other obvious signs of struggle, and had entered the house, which had a large sign out front: "Granny's". After debating the beast, during which time Kolveig felt he made some excellent points, it would attack. He would then slay it with a smack from his hammer and then immediately reappear back outside the house as if nothing had happened, only to go through the entire encounter again! Perhaps this time would be different?

Kolveig gestured at the granny clothing that the wolf was wearing. "What a big Misappropriation of Equitable Allocation of Resources you have!"

"The better *to exploit* you with!" replied the wolf.

Kolveig then pointed out the damaged windows, walls, and doors. "What a big Desecration of An Elder's Domicile you've made!"

"The better *to DESTROY* you with!"

148

Bloodstains on the walls stood out next, still dripping onto the floor. "And what a big Failure to Respect the Lives of the Proletariat you have!"

"THE BETTER TO REPRESS YOU WITH!" roared the wolf. It leaped from granny's bed and made to eat Kolveig, *yet again.*

* * *

What they hoped was the last door in the complex stood before the three remaining party members. It was blue. With none of them being as brash as Kolveig, they all glanced at each other to see who would touch it first.

"Since you're a short, little man, you're less likely to set off a trap," said Brymanah to Tepson.

"Since you're a big, manly woman, you're more likely to push it open," he retorted.

Fearing an intra-party brawl, Oborren hastily pulled out a short staff from his pack and touched the door in random locations, tapping it firmly. Seeing that the staff didn't explode or turn into a bouquet of flowers or something to that effect, Oborren tried the doorknob. To his surprise, it opened without killing him, driving him insane, or teleporting him to some even more upsetting part of the underworld.

Instead, the door opened into a large room, roughly 40' wide and 70' deep. It was full of all manner of children's toys: dolls, horses, soldiers, and the like, as well as their sundry toy furniture, accessories, and other paraphernalia.

Nothing seemed to be attempting to kill them at the moment, so the party fanned out to examine the room. Brymanah took the left, Tepson the right, and Oborren the center, after spiking the blue door open, of course. The sheer number of objects in the room was staggering, and yet they had an otherworldly quality, as well. Not only was the place exceedingly clean and bright, since there was not a speck of dust and all the toys looked brand new, but they also seemed to be *aware* even if they weren't moving. A large rocking horse stationed in the back of the room upon a wooden dais seemed particularly cognizant.

Brymanah looked angrily around when she ended up at a table full of toy girl dolls. She snorted: they weren't even wielding weapons or wearing armor. What sort of girl dolls were these supposed to be?

Tepson gravitated to a toy train set. Ironically enough, he was the probably the only member of the party who could have realized what it actually was. He wondered if any real trains still ran on the surface world nowadays. He pushed one of the engines around absent-mindedly.

Oborren lingered around the stairs to the dais on which the rocking horse sat. He was still baffled by how clean this place was. He experimented by putting some lint from his pocket onto the hat of a painted wooden soldier. A strange voice resonated from up the stairs.

"Oh look out now, it's the dirt patrol!"

The party immediately crouched down, looking around for where the voice came. It seemed to come from the rocking horse.

"Who said that?" queried Tepson.

"Short *and* dumb: must be a genius with the ladies!"

The party could see now that it was definitely the horse that had spoken. Its wooden mouth was moving and it even rocked a little bit.

Brymanah stalked towards the dais, cutlass ready.

"Oh look now, everybody! It's a man... no, it's a woman.... no, it's definitely an ugly...."

150

Dan Osarchuk

Brymanah's face reddened at the horse's jibe. She screamed and rushed forward. Her cutlass struck true into the horse's neck, but it only let out a fake 'neighing' sound and emitted a potent shock, causing Brymanah's hair to stand up on end and throwing her back.

"Oh my, I'm shocked by your lack of civility... and intelligence," stated the horse.

At this point, Tepson grabbed a metal caboose and hurled it at the horse. Even though it struck the horse right in the head, it only laughed with its fake jaw flapping. The attack seemed to have no other effect!

It was now Oborren's turn to move up. Seeing Brymanah's still prostrate body, he checked her pulse: she still lived. He refocused his attention on the horse. Attacking it seemed pointless, unless....

"How about you try and run after me, horse?" teased Oborren.

The horse was clearly not amused and sealed its fake mouth in a frown. Seeing that his approach might be working, Oborren continued.

"A horse and a halfling walk into a bar. What did the halfling say?

No reply came from the increasingly irate rocking horse.

"'Stupid horse: you're not allowed in a tavern!'"

Tepson even broke out laughing at the statement. At this, the horse looked outraged and noticeably began to turn red. It seemed as if steam was beginning to emerge from its wooden horse ears as it muttered angrily...

Seeing where this was going, Tepson joined in: "How can you tell if you have a useless rocking horse?"

The horse looked confused now and attempted to babble an answer. Brymanah looked like she was beginning to come around.

Not waiting for a clear response, Tepson gave the punchline: "Of *horse!*"

The rocking horse's head began to spin around in its increasing anger and frustration. The party members laughed.

And then, it seemed the horse couldn't bear it any longer- its head exploded. A blue coin flew through the air, freed from its wooden casing, landing at Brymanah's feet. She looked over at Oborren. What manner of creature was that?

As if reading her mind, Oborren replied, "Mocking Horse."

Puns were most certainly the worst.

Chapter 19

Mishap

The verdant smell of early spring wafted upon the air as the dusk sky shimmered orange and pinkish-blue. Two wanderers emerged from the hills outside of Mauriatown, one large and bulky, the other small and lithe. The two walked side-by-side, one with a brown mullet, the other with long, cherry-red hair, shining almost supernaturally in the magical time of eventide in the Vale.

Their journey back had not been as difficult as one might think- with Gorm's mighty thews and Cherries's eldritch powers, most of the remaining orange-skinned goblins cut and ran at the first sight of them. Those who didn't were simply cut down.

Both missed their former companions, but were now venturing onward. Gorm mused over the peculiarities of the various hairstyles of the Vale, while Cherries mused over the new, demonic presence that had taken residence inside her soul.

Yes, something had happened when she had elaborated her spell, *yet again*. This time though, it wasn't that her spellcasting powers got frazzled for a time, or that she fell into a light coma, or even that her mind, body, or soul was mutated to reflect her light-hearted disdain for the hard laws of reality. No, this time it was something altogether *different*.

Night Skies Over Valhallow

She might have wished that she had been whisked away to some strange new land, perhaps like her master had told her about years ago. Perhaps a place where the laws of magic weren't so restrictive. A place where one could frolic upon yellow brick roads, meet amazing new friends, and then incinerate any ninnies who might get in the way with one's raw magical artistry. Cherries giggled at the thought.

Or maybe if I had a brand new friend, she thought, like an aquatic elephant who could sing or something.

But Cherries *did* have a new friend, far more interesting than any melodic maritime pachyderm: she had *Whanna-Ghonna*, a high-ranking demon from the Court of Wanton Abandon. She smiled fiendishly at the thought of her *new friend.* The dark presence curled around her heart like a new fur coat: so warm, so naughty.

Her attention shifted to the strong body of Gorm walking before her. Unclean thoughts filled her mind and excited her senses. She would have him and it would be good.

The hulking barbarian glanced at her and showed concern at the evil grin on her face.

Perhaps there was something wrong with his mullet?

* * *

Mistro stared at his crystal ball, carefully polished by one of his faceless servants. The images within flickered in an orderly pattern, showing him his many observations of the Vale: a farmstead, the Schoolhouse, and a hall with many doors. Here he sat, observing the world like some gamemaster observing his screen.

"Vhat idiotsss!" he exclaimed finally, "Look at them with all their ssstupid livingsss about!"

Mistro was interrupted by a servant boy with blond hair. Like all of Mistro's servants, he wore a uniform with the requisite 'M' emblazoned on the chest. The boy was too young to wear a mask yet.

"VHAT SHALL I TURN YOU INTO FOR DISSSTURBING ME, BOY?"

The serving boy's face went white, "Mis.. mis.. Mister Mistro...."

"VHAT? SSSSSSSSSSSSSSSSSSSSSSSSSSSPIT IT OUT!"

"The.. the.. doorguard sent me. He says you have a special visitor."

"VELL IT'S HISSS JOB TO SSSHOW ALL VISITORSSS IN, INCLUDING THE SSSPECIAL VONESSS!"

The blond boy squeaked as he dodged the back of Mistro's hand. At least he hadn't been transmogrified.

* * *

A petite maiden with vivid red hair waited at the entryway, flanked by a hulking brute that seemed to be nursing some sort of groin injury. The door guard glanced at the pair nervously; even his tooth-lined mask and magenta hooded cloak were unable to hide the concern in his eyes.

Mistro studied the image in his crystal ball carefully. He wasn't stupid enough to go down there himself.

He recognized the girl: it was his former pupil, though she seemed to have grown greatly in power. Something else seemed to be different about her, as well. He grabbed a deep violet potion from a side table and carefully poured it over the crystal ball. The curves of the glass sparked slightly at its touch.

The image changed to a more purple view, then shaded to something much darker. He nearly gasped as he saw what was living inside her.

"GUARDSSS!"

* * *

'What was keeping that silly-nilly?' thought Cherries. 'Maybe I'll just have to do something to get his attention!'

She smiled evilly at the door guard.

"You know", she said in menacingly casual tone, "I especially enjoy affecting cherries or... cherry-shaped objects."

She glanced at his pants provocatively.

After a moment, it dawned on the guard. He moved his hands to cover himself.

Uttering strange words that seemed to echo throughout the air around the tower, Cherries pointed at the guard. After another moment, he shrieked in pain, doubled over, and collapsed.

Gorm began to inch away nervously.

"Now where are you going, silly goose?"

The barbarian gasped as some invisible force thrust him to the ground, smashing him into the stone workmanship around the Tower's base. He grunted. He was glad that it was only his head that had made impact.

A new feeling came over Cherries- one that enticed her to go further, to cause more pain. It didn't feel like it was coming from the demon though.

"Oh well, whatever..."

Dan Osarchuk

She pulled out her knife and made to eviscerate the barbarian. That he was once her friend made it feel even more delicious... even more... EVIL!

To her surprise, Cherries felt an impact at the back of her head. It made such pretty motes of pink and cherry-blue appear in her eyes. All went dark.

* * *

When she awoke, Cherries was in a room with various books, censors, prisms, and sundry arcane implements. It must be Mistro's study, she realized! She made to exclaim that obvious fact out loud, but realized that her tongue had been removed. She made to check where her tongue had gone and realized that her hands and feet were strapped to the chair she was sitting in.

To her surprise, Mistro and Mistro alone walked in. She had expected some sort of monster or goon to be sent in to quickly dispatch her... or at least for Mistro to look like his brazenly confident self. But the wizard seemed quite reserved instead.

"Ssso, trafficking with Demonsss, are ve?"

Cherries smiled at him with childish innocence,

"Don't be a vool!" Mistro exploded, "You know how thessse thingsss alwaysss turn out!"

Cherries made like she was beginning to cry.

"Now, now, my dear Cherriesss, thisss von't hurt for but a moment..."

He pulled out a wickedly long dagger, nearly 2' in length.

Now Cherries really started crying.

With her eyes closed, she failed to see that Mistro began to look visibly upset, as well. He put the dagger aside and poured a reddish liquid onto her face. Cherries began to choke and cough at first and then started to giggle. While she was distracted further, Mistro began to intone his *own* words of power.

It looked as if Cherries were about to protest, but couldn't stop laughing. After another minute of intonation with her incessant giggling in the background, Mistro smacked her forehead, sending a jolt through her body. Her now maniacal laughter was interrupted with heaving. Mistro quickly grabbed a large glass cylinder, just as Cherries began to vomit up foul black filth. He held his long dagger ready, pointing it at the filth.

Dark black ichor spewed forth, though the odor was one more akin to that which could be smelled during the throws of lovemaking, rather than digestion. A strange sense of lewdness also filled the room, that of uncontrollable lust, to which Mistro found took a great deal of his willpower to resist.

And yet, he was Mistro! Not some stupid peasant!

"How sssstupid vould I be if I resisted the lussst.. or more ssstupidly: made it my massster?!"

The struggle quickly passed; the wizard remained himself, imperious.

As the ichor collected in the jar, the presence it exuded seemed palpable, quite disturbingly so.

When it had finished, Mistro carefully covered the jar with a metal stopper and intoned a protection spell over it. He then wiped Cherries's mouth with uncharacteristic sympathy. Finally, he grabbed another censor, removed her tongue from inside and replaced it back into her mouth.

And only then did he call for an assistant.

"Serving boy, please adminissster to my dear, Cheriesss. AND BE QUICK ABOUT IT!"

158

The blond boy snapped to and began to clean the remaining residue from Cherries's mouth. Continuing to deftly avoid Mistro's random attempts at smacking, he promptly finished up, ducking just in time to avoid a censer being thrown at him.

"Why are you so mean to him?" asked Cherries. She began to play with her newly-attached tongue.

"Because he'sss an idiot," smiled Mistro.

She looked back at him with sad, doe eyes. Mistro shook his head and sighed. He scanned her with his hand, about 3' from her body, stopped for a moment midway through, and then relaxed. He began to release her restraints.

"So I'm fit for duty?" she inquired.

"Perhapsss" Mistro glanced at the entity in the protected glass cylinder. Magic was never an easy thing to trifle with, especially when dealing with demons.

Chapter 20

Harry the Mustachioed Fish

The party stood around the subterranean dock, staring at the aquamarine waters. They now held three new shiny objects: one green jellybean, one blue coin, and one red wolf tooth.

They had regrouped here after their fey encounters. Brymanah, Oborren, and Tepson having survived the Mocking Horse; Kolveig, the wolf. Though the former were quite vocal about their means of defeating the horse, the cleric was silent as to how he had made his own escape.

And even though Kolveig was quiet for a change, Brymanah still growled at the situation. Why couldn't there have been some orcs to fight? Or at least some men? This *mancy*-footing around and completing puzzles riled here to no end. That the stupid sing-songy music started playing again made it even more difficult to *not* strangle Kolveig.

Kolveig's neck stood before her, unprotected, except for some nonsensical male baubles. With one slice of her cutlass, it would all be over. She could even claim insanity- why wouldn't the others believe her? It was Kolveig, after all...

Night Skies Over Valhallow

Before Brymanah's homicidal intent could be realized though, a disturbance occurred in the water. The dark object, seen earlier by Tepson, moved towards the party.

Slowly emerging from the vividly blue waters was a great fish, complete with a mighty, aquatic mustache. Kolveig beamed: some of his favorite leaders had mustaches. Brymanah growled.

"Well, sir," it spoke in a surprisingly genteel accent, "Welcome to my own little slice of Paradise- a tiny world, a small land, a place where we can all smile and be..."

"KILL IT!" Oborren screeched.

Even Brymanah was shocked at the hunter's ferocity. The fish was just beginning its monologue.

The hunter's bolt flew through the air, striking the giant fish's amazingly human-like face. It recoiled as the dart imbedded into its cheek; its eyes narrowed. The great fish growled at the party, teethed clenched. It immediately dove back into the water, but the pool-like clarity of the canal did little to hide its intent: after swimming about a couple dozen feet, it turned and began to head right for the party!

Brymanah lowered into a defensive stance as the fish approached. She eyed the canal waters suspiciously.

Kolveig went for a more diplomatic approach, "Perhaps we can reason with it? It does have a moustache..."

Oborren was now cursing to himself furiously, something about 'stupid fish', as he readied his flail.

And Tepson wisely began to back *away* from the canal altogether, back towards the passage from which they had originally entered the complex.

Suddenly, the great fish leaped out of the waters in a deadly arc set to terminate right on top of Oborren's head. The hunter seemed pleased, a sort of fatalistic rage entering his eyes. He must really not like fish, thought Tepson, especially talking ones.

Brymanah watched the scene as if it were occurring in slow motion. For a split second, she contemplated letting the fish decapitate the foolish man, but then again, she would only be left with Kolveig and the midget for company... He must be saved!

She moved smoothly, turning and slicing with practiced measure, putting her cutlass right through one of the thing's gills. Luckily for Oborren, who seemed to be only able to glare at the fish, Kolveig decided to play his healer's part and pulled him out of the way. And not wanting to be left out, Tepson rushed back towards the group, poking the fish in one of its human-like eyes. He was a biologist after all; he knew how to deal with animals.

The fish flopped on the floor. Saying, "Ow... ow... OW... OOOWWW!!!!", obviously in great pain. Disturbingly human-like blood dripped from its now many wounds. The party backed up to let it have some flopping room- all the party that is, except Oborren. The hunter shrieked in homicidal glee as he lunged at the fish, stabbing with his knife. More wounds bled red as Oborren cut him ferociously; his party members finally pulling him back.

Brymanah couldn't believe what she was going to say, "Maybe we should talk to it? It might tell us something useful."

The party stared at her in disbelief. Being as startled as the rest of them, even Oborren stopped growling and drooling for a moment.

The fish took this opportunity to attempt to reason with the party, "Friends... FRIENDS! Now, we can't have this nonsense going on! I was simply here trying to welcome you as guests into my humble abode... My name is Harry and why can't we all just-"

It was now Tepson who had become enraged, "SHUT UP SHUT UP SHUT UP!" the gnome had grabbed a rock and started bashing Harry in the head.

"I SAY, SIR, WHAT THE HELL ARE YOU DOING?" the fish queried in the midst of the gnome's painful bludgeoning.

Oborren had heard enough. It was one thing for this fish to start talking; it was another for it to curse at one of his party members.

The hunter leaped at Harry, wrapping his flail around the talking fish's tongue, murderous sweat seeping from his brow.

"Let's see you try to say something NOW, FISH!"

Harry actually did try to mumble something (talking fish often forget when it's best to keep their mouths shut), and this time, it was Brymanah who reacted.

Her gleaming cutlass hung menacingly below Harry's neck. The widening of the talking fish's eyes meant that he was finally starting to get the hint...

As the hunter, amazon, and gnome fumed at the fish, Kolveig calmly drew in and began healing its wounds. It felt strange for him being the calm one, the voice of reason. And as an added bonus, the party probably wouldn't notice any of the Karlist side-effects of his healing, such as turning the fish red or redistributing some of the party's wealth...

* * *

Soon, Harry was tied up and Oborren was given the task of threatening him if he got out of line. The hunter seemed well-suited for the task.

"What do these trinkets do?" interrogated Brymanah. The forceful voice of the woman reminded Kolveig of his own beating by amazons just days ago.

Dan Osarchuk

"I SAID…" insisted the amazon when the fish didn't reply, "WHAT DO THESE TRINKETS DO?"

She held the shiny objects that the party had recovered from the various fey realms before the mustachioed fish's eyes. He was surprisingly quiet.

"EEEEOOOOWWWWWAIIIIAAAA…." Oborren began to make an awful sound of rage when the fish continued to refuse the question. It even made the other party members nervous.

This seemed to have the desired effect on Harry. Tepson wisely loosened Oborren's flail from around his tongue.

"I say, I say, I say, sir! I do believe that I haven't felt that tongue-tied since the summer of 194-"

SMACK! Brymanah struck the fish with the side of her cutlass; she turned the sharp end towards his face.

"Well, well, those there trinkets- they be… ummm…."

Oborren stared at him, mouth open, a crazed look in his eyes.

"Keys," finished the fish.

Chapter 21

Into the Bowels of Enak

Mme. Carve glared at the report, attempting to will the results to change. "One can accomplish anything, if you only give it your 187%!" she reminded herself. Apparently though, many of the tutors weren't even giving 85%!

How could this be? I ordered the tutors to attend 177 Mandatory R'ti Schoolhouse Required Meetings this year! And the pupils only got an 84%? PREPOSTEROUS! Perhaps I should have the tutors attend *more* meetings next year?

She attempted to work the problem out using the Mandated Calcula Nova. For some reason, the 30-step mathematical problem that she used (that the *unenlightened* only took 2-steps to solve) wasn't adding up.

No. Something more drastic needed to be done. "I must do something to keep these scum in line!" She glanced at the report again, taking some solace at least in the finely printed words on the pages. Ah, to be done with tutors, she thought. Granted, some were her favorites, her *pet* tutors, but they were fewer now after experiencing a number of her screaming sessions. Some tutors were causing her particular displeasure on a number of occasions though, *especially that Halfdan.* Perhaps some (doctored) Evidence to encourage *Tutor Turn-over* might be in order?

Night Skies Over Valhallow

Ah, to be done with aberrant tutors.... She smiled and gazed lovingly at the plaque on the wall:

> **L**abor for Tutors (ever-increasing)
> **L**oyalty to the Monitors and to R'ti, above all else
> **L**asting Innovation- Everlasting Change

Few knew the *real* significance of what those words meant. At face value, it served well to terrorize and demoralize certain tutors, especially with Mme. Carve herself or one of her Assistants around to back it up with specific threats of *Remediation*. But there was something *more* to it. The many "L"'s made a sound like a purring machine- so holy. And the script itself was not made by any human hands, of course. Oh no, that would be too imperfect. Most fools thought it was made by a well-trained pupil or even a tutor. But that would not please her Master.

The Ancients had come close. He had told her about the near paradise that had unfolded, centuries ago. When tutors in the Old Days were to be partially replaced by automatons. A number of human tutors would remain of course, because then who would be left to blame for failures? And some tutors would even *volunteer* to become more automatonic: they would do anything to please!

But Lights Out put an end to all that. Luckily, her Master had survived. And now he was thriving! She sighed lovingly at the printed report as she thought of his perfection- it even made her recent cold chills subside.

Oh yes, R'ti was certainly a mighty Fell Lord, who continued to receive Carve's adoration, but why stop there? She glanced at the shock-button on her desk: a gift from her newest Master. Carve smiled wickedly as she lightly caressed the button, gazing at the chair across from her... where the resulting shocks would occur.

A bird outside her window drew Carve's attention. The red-crested robin glanced at her curiously before snatching a tender worm-morsel from the grass. Without thought or fear, it fluttered off to fly free. The grassy spot where it had landed remained just out of reach of the Schoolhouse's shadow.

She glanced at the file for Halfdan, that particularly aberrant tutor in her reckoning. He failed to even participate in the Productivity Walk or Clown Tutor Day last year, for Enak's sake! She pulled out a small note from her desk and smiled. Her master would be pleased at her cleverness in eradicating the virus that was Uncooperative Tutors. Perhaps they had failed in the Old Days, but now... they would succeed!

In celebration, she pressed the shock-button, cackling as eldritch lightning sparked and flew- twin bolts, just like her two Fell Lords.

* * *

"Why are you smiling, Mr. Halfdan," one of the pupils queried.

Halfdan often smiled, he had a lot to let go of, especially at the Schoolhouse, but he felt he had to put on a particularly happy air. Mr. Beauly had just entered the room to *Observe Halfdan's Instruction*. He asked the pupils what they were learning.

One of them said, "Nothing!"

All the pupils laughed and jeered at Mr. Halfdan; they knew what was going to happen next! Beauly thanked the pupils and began handing out candied treats. The children began cheering and dancing on the tables. Halfdan watched as his lecture fell apart.

Regaining his composure, Halfdan attempted to get them to return to their seats, when Beauly turned and stared at him. Two Evervigilant Hounds, white shirts blazing, then burst into the room, grabbed Halfdan and carried him away. The hallway spun as the tension from the large men's grappling intensified. He could still hear the pupils laughing and jeering as he was carried away.

He didn't know whether to be concerned or not, until he realized that they were bringing him to the Room of Remediation.

With a synchronized heave-ho, the two Ever-vigilant Hounds tossed Halfdan into the room. He crashed into the edge of the table inside, smashing his knee. The pain brought clarity to his mind, stopping the spinning for a few moments.

The clean, austere room would have been a comfort to his Odinnic proclivities, except for the R'ti propaganda posted over the walls. Noticing the screaming pain in his knee, Halfdan hobbled into a chair and focused on the sensation. It was akin to a burning mixed with an intense vibration, like a high-pitched sound with a touch of nausea added in. He noticed too that his heart was constricted: his *reaction to the sensation*. What was happening could be called an upsetting situation and what he felt could be called agony. That's what his body and mind were experiencing anyway. It helped to know that he was not them; he was simply their witness. It also helped to notice the space both *within* and *around* the sensations.

His pain began to abate, just as the Assistant Monitor entered. The cold look on Beauly's face indicated that he was not here for an idle chat.

"Is it part of R'ti Doctrine to fail to observe one of your pupils, Mr. Halfdan?"

"What are you talking about? I wasn't failing to observe one of my pupils!"

"One of them was weeping in your classroom!"

"Which one?"

Beauly gave the pupil's name. Halfdan was shocked that he was upset- he was a good pupil; he never had any trouble in his lessons before.

170

"I questioned him after you were... *removed*," Beauly added, "he said that something you said to Dakus about an essay on cattle made him very upset."

Halfdan looked at Beauly confused: was he being serious? He still had no idea what the Assistant Monitor was talking about.

"What did I say?" asked Halfdan finally.

"You told Dakus: 'What would you say if his essay had been better.' "

Halfdan was at a loss for words.

Beauly's face hardened, "that's just the type of Hateful attitude we've been hearing about you, Halfdan."

Halfdan continued to stare incredulously. Beauly apparently didn't care that he was attempting to guide Dakus to a More Supportive Outlook of his Classroom Association Peers- one of the many inane Pillars of R'ti Philosophy.

The Assistant in fact seemed to pay no attention to Halfdan's confused look at all. Instead he pulled out a small, clear gem- a judging stone. Such objects were said to determine whether one was guilty of an apparent crime or not.

These days, what few magical items that trickled out of the hands of wizards often ended up in the hands of the elite of a given location. It was no small matter for wizards or other types of magi to craft such wonders. Rumors abounded that even a portion of their own essence ended up in such items, making them quite rare and valuable indeed. That the Assistant Monitor was holding one suggested that he was taking this matter seriously or at least, wanted to appear so. Did the High-Monitors at the County Castle have some sort of spellcaster working for them now?

The Assistant passed the stone under Halfdan's chin and said, "Hatred".

The stone quickly turned amber, darkening almost to a soiled brown color. The Assistant frowned and Halfdan's head spun. Beauly's cold eyes glanced over a chart he held in his hand.

"So we see that you are in fact guilty of Hatred."

Halfdan wondered at what "hatred" really meant to these Cultists; the only thing he hated was the Cult itself. Perhaps Beauly and the other Monitors *just hated Halfdan*?

Beauly then turned to the condemned tutor.

"You have already been warned about showing emotion, Halfdan. This matter will, of course, be referred to the County Castle."

The Assistant grimaced and called for the Hounds. They moved quickly into the room, smacking their fists together in anticipation.

"No. No beating for Mr. Halfdan today. We now have the evidence. It's time to send him to the Gaol."

Halfdan's mind became active with fear once again- he knew what happened to men like him at a place like that.

As the scrawny tutor was hauled away by the Hounds, Beauly sighed and looked back at his desk to scribe another Memorandum of Tutor Failure for Halfdan, hopefully his last. He shook his head though when he realized that most of it had already been written before today's Observation.

* * *

Waiting in the office, Halfdan sat with a 'dunce' cap on his head. A cold presence moved about the room. How ironic, he thought, that once it was the *pupils* who were punished in this manner. It seemed a bitter twist of irony. For a moment, he thought he spotted something flitter in the corner of his eye, but turned and it was gone. He refocused his attention back to his thoughts.

If only this was the sole punishment he would have to endure today. The scriveners went about their business, ignoring Halfdan as he sat in the corner, facing the wall. He was unsure whether they tried to ignore him because he was now Officially Subject to Monitorial Action or because the rumormongers had brought the accusations of Mr. Halfdan's Crimes of Emotional Openness to their ears. It didn't really matter, conceded Halfdan, he guessed that he wouldn't be alive much longer anyway.

The main door's bell chimed. One of the scriveners gazed through the peep hole, nodded, and then unbolted it. It truly was a massive barrier- such security for a place of learning? What had this world come to?

Halfdan remembered to refocus on the moment, as Mme. Carve gregariously greeted the watchmen at the door. They spoke for a few minutes, taking long pauses to turn and glare and point at Halfdan conspiratorially.

"No, but thank you, constable. We'll be dealing with this matter in-house, at least for now."

She stared coldly at Halfdan once more and then smiled cruelly. The watchmen departed. Mme. Carve had something else in mind? What could be worse than the Gaol?

As if reading his mind, Carve answered: "We have something special for you, Mr. Halfdan the Hater. You are supposedly some sort of sage, in addition to being a tutor, are you not? And what better for you to utilize that overly cruel mind of yours than in a very *safe* place?"

* * *

Strange glass bulbs hummed and sputtered, turning on and off in rapid succession, like stars twinkling across an uneasy sky. Halfdan stared at the imitation of the nightly firmament, as the scent of ozone and metal filled the air. Countless wires and

173

terminals could be seen- was it perhaps a place of the Ancients? Halfdan was unsure, for it still hummed with unearthly energy.

As he continued to watch the scene, he noticed his fear rising again. Halfdan slowly became aware that he was also being watched by something *else.*

Suddenly, a strange, monotone voice could be heard at the far side of the room. It boomed loudly, though it was still a distance off.

"I AM ENAK. YOU WILL PROVIDE SERVICE, TUTOR.'

Halfdan stared as a lumbering object, built in some grim pantomime of a man, emerged from behind a large box-like object. Its square head was adorned with blinking lights where eyes and mouth should be. One of its massive arms pointed at Halfdan, who noticed the unpleasant fact that it had metal claws for hands. It stood nearly 8' tall, built of metal and some other substance, perhaps *plast,* and must have been thousands of pounds in weight. Something *else* stared from behind its eyes, something *darker* than simple metal, glass, and plast.

Speechless, Halfdan simply stared back at the horror. The familiar clutching in his chest indicated intense fear now, as well as possibly an impending heart attack. Perhaps the latter would be a less painful fate than what this fiend had in store for him.

The constructed being continued, booming out in a monotone voice as it lumbered forward, "ARE YOU MY QIN?"

Lord help me.

Chapter 22

Journey to the Surface of the Earth

"So how do these damnable things work?" Oborren growled. He still seemed to hold a special ire for Harry as he stared at the 'keys'.

"Well sir, I'm a gonna tell you..."

As music started to play again, the gnome, with an anger that even surprised Oborren, flew into a rage and began pummeling the fish again. It took both the hunter and the amazon to pull him off.

What the gnome and the hunter were experiencing wasn't unheard of. The fey could conjure up a sense of happiness and wonderment, often in children especially. Cheerful singing, presents, and other delights certainly resonated well with the young-at-heart. But in this case, with only angry men and an amazon around, things didn't look very good for Harry.

So the decision was made: do not talk to the fish. Doing so only made some members of the party want to kill him more, so it was agreed that only gestures would be used.

For now, Harry remained tied-up back in the passage with the party. Being a fey fish though, he really didn't need to be in the water to survive. Kolveig was the only one to be trusted to not slay the fish at the first opportunity, so he was given the task of watching him.

After many minutes of repeated pointing and nodding, they finally realized what they needed to do.

In a manner akin to fitting keys into holes, the party members found that they could insert the various items from the three fey realms into small impressions in the walls of the pool from which Harry came. And, with synchronous turns, they heard the sounds of locking mechanisms opening.

Tepson, Oborren, and Brymanah treaded in the warm aquamarine waters as they waited to see what happened next.

Soon, a noticeable, spiral current began to form in the waters. Something seemed to open below the swimming party members and much to the party's chagrin, it began to pull them *down*.

Dumbfounded, Kolveig glanced at Harry and realized that the villain was trying to hold back laughter. His own anger began to rise as the panicked cries of his party members grew louder, only to soon be drowned-out beneath the azure waters. Kolveig pointed his sickle menacingly at one of the fish's eyes, but Harry only shrugged, indicating that he didn't know how to stop the downward pull.

Desperately, Kolveig searched for some way to help his drowning comrades. He noticed the licorice rope still hanging from the subterranean dock. Thinking quickly, he secured it around his waist and dove into the vanishing waters below, uttering a prayer to Karl.

The momentary disorientation subsided as Kolveig realized that the other members were being sucked into a roughly 4' wide aperture at the bottom of the pool. Tepson and Oborren were nowhere to be seen, but Brymanah was not quite through the hole yet. Kolveig reached out his hand and she reluctantly grasped it.

The licorice rope, being quite elastic, then exhibited somewhat of a bungee property as it pulled the duo back up to the surface. They only caught a glance of Harry the Mustachioed fish, now freed and swimming down in the opposite direction, a look of pure malice on his face.

* * *

Soon the pool had drained and the amazon and the cleric, putting their normal bickering aside for the time being, climbed down with the help of the licorice rope once more.

Through the aperture, they could see great treasures below, though the sound of Harry's maniacal laughter emanating up did not make things seem so inviting. They quickly descended further after him, entering an even lower chamber.

Within, they saw a disturbing scene. Harry seemed to have gotten the drop on their hapless comrades, with both Oborren and Tepson tied up. Harry was attempting to push them into some sort of large, metal grinder.

"SO.... I SAY, SIR... YOU'LL MAKE SOME MIGHTY-FINE FISH FOOD... YOU STUPID *^(*&%^&^%%&*$s!"

The fey fish laughed again, not noticing the two individuals creeping up behind him.

WHAM. One strike from the Karlist's hammer was all it took to knock him out.

* * *

When he finally came to, Harry realized that now it was *he* that was being pushed into the fish grinder. His mustachio had been torn off and, if it were possible, Oborren had an even more insane look of hatred on his face as he wore it like a trophy. The bloody impression of where it once lay on the fish's face did little to help with his pleas for mercy.

177

Night Skies Over Valhallow

After the deed was done, the party set aside their feelings of murderous revenge and transitioned to ones of plunder. The amount of treasure amazed the party. Piles of gold and silver coins, gems, jewelry, and even various artifacts- too bad that they were too far below ground to cart it all back up. Still, the party managed to grab whatever they could; stuffing their pockets and packs with as much loot as they could carry.

Even better, it looked like they had found an item that might help them learn more about the Insolitus Novus.

Taking a large vial into his small hand, Tepson reminisced. It was the same one that he had seen right before he was frozen, all those centuries ago- it was unmistakable. The spectral colors of it seemed be gone now, but the bizarrely smiling, cartoon emblem cat on it was still there.

"This is what once held the multicolored light."

The party stared at the gnome. They certainly remembered him as his nigh-invincible chromatic self and even dimly remembered their quest that was the whole reason for them venturing into this place.

"How do you know?" questioned the amazon.

"I saw it before I was frozen."

The other party members rolled their eyes at the little man. Perhaps he really was still mad.

* * *

The decision was made to find another route back to the surface world. Oborren claimed that he felt that it allowed the party to do some additional exploring on their way back, but the real reason was that they were hopelessly lost. Such things were not unusual when spelunking, being bereft of the clarifying gaze of sun, moon, or stars, not to mention the fact that the underrealms could actually *change* their layout from time to time.

So again they wandered, finding yet more esoteric rooms and the occasional creature, always opting for a path that slanted back *up*. Eventually they knew that they were on the right path, as they began to hear strange sounds and the occasional scream. It sounded like goblins.

Activity often seemed to increase the closer one got to the surface, though that usually didn't indicate greater safety.

More signs of habitation grew increasingly evident as the party trod on: refuse, filth, and even graffiti on the walls. It looked strikingly similar to the goblin warren from which they had first descended.

Oborren stared at the writing and examined the filth closely. He found it difficult to concentrate; seeing something as unnatural as a talking fish earlier had greatly unnerved him.

"See anything you want to bring back with you?" teased Kolveig.

Smiling viciously, Oborren nearly grabbed a piece of filth to give the vexing Karlist *something to bring back*, when the whole party froze to the sound of shrieks nearby. Acting quickly, they split to different sides of the passage, attempting to conceal themselves as best they could.

Soon after, two small, bright yellow-skinned humanoids entered the tunnel, unfortunately dressed in little more than smocks. One was slightly larger and wore something of a headpiece. It was tormenting the smaller, apparently less important one. Such evil was quite common amongst goblins.

"You bad! Ha! Me like! Give you to Queen now!" chided the first.

"No! Me no bad! You bad! Me no give me to Queen or to you give now no! Me like Queen!"

In some bizarre manner, the party could understand the goblins. Perhaps they had been underground too long. Still, they had no idea that they would speak so stupidly.

The larger goblin, becoming enraged, grabbed the smaller one by the ear and made to pull it back up the passage. The mewling sound the smaller one made was quickly silenced when a cutlass took the larger one's head off. It rolled onto the floor in a gory display, as the primitive headpiece surprisingly remained on.

Brymanah smiled at the little yellow goblin wickedly, bloodied cutlass in hand. Oborren quickly grappled it before it could run off. The goblin seemed to be getting over the shock at the surprise attack on its tormentor. Oborren decided to encourage its fear to emerge once again.

"So, what's this Queen that your larger friend was talking about?" questioned the hunter.

A quick wave of panic passed over the little goblin's face. It shook its head and held its ears.

"Me no know what you say, human," it claimed.

Tepson took his opportunity to join in the interrogation. He and the goblin were nearly the same height.

"But you're speaking the same language as us, stupid."

Another wave of panic passed over the goblin's face. It then instinctively scratched its large nose, readjusted its smock, and cocked its hips to the side.

It then replied sardonically. "Oh... yes... blah, blah, blah-di-blahdy, blah..."

Brymanah interrupted his feigned inability to communicate by positioning her cutlass directly over its head. She smiled calmly as her strong feminine form towered over the goblin by at least 3 feet. Kolveig assumed that she spared it since it had said that it liked the Queen. Typical Matriarchists!

Some of the remaining blood from the blade dripped down on to the increasingly nervous goblin's head. A small yellow stream began to emit from beneath its smock. Oborren thanked the Gods of the North that he was not standing in its way.

Tepson though, wasn't so lucky and took his opportunity to punch the goblin in the gut. He had no idea how he would get this urine smell off him now- it smelled awful!

Meanwhile, the goblin doubled over from the gnome's punch and made sounds like it was dying. If any of the party fell for its ruse at first, its continued overly dramatic performance quelled any misconception.

Brymanah then took her opportunity to pick the filthy creature up by its neck and stare into its beady eyes.

"You will show us to your queen or I will give you back to the gnome."

For a moment, the goblin seemed to think that the amazon was bluffing. But then it glanced over at Tepson, who glared back at it and smacked his fists together. Even if the amazon was bluffing, the goblin reasoned, the gnome wasn't.

* * *

Their stinky little bright yellow guide tested the party quite a bit, though they refrained from killing it just yet. It still had a purpose to serve and the party had no idea how many more goblins were in its group. Brymanah hoped that a real battle was ahead: she was tired of all these stupid weird rooms and hostage- takings.

181

Night Skies Over Valhallow

Despite Kolveig's protests, Tepson took to wrapping some rope around the creature's neck to keep it from running away. He seemed to be taking a page from the hunter in his rough treatment of the prisoner.

The Karlist was just about to admonish the little man for engaging in Just More Capitalist Slavery when the goblin led them into a large cavern.

The huge place teemed with activity. Multitudes of bright yellow-skinned goblins ran throughout, screaming and laughing insanely, some clambering upon the tall walls on makeshift ladders. Though the spirits fell for most of the party, Brymanah was excited that it appeared some real bloodshed was finally now at hand.

Oborren placed a knowing hand on the amazon's muscular shoulder. She snapped her head back at him, ready to stab him for such a blatant violation of her womynhood, until he pointed calmly at the far end of the cavern.

There the party gasped at a sight with a mix of hope and fear. A great blue color could be seen upon an upper wall. It took them a full moment to realize that it was blue sky: escape was at hand!

Unfortunately though, the party's incredulous excitement was forestalled by many large, winged things fluttering in and out of the exit. Their 4' long insectoid bodies, yellow patterning, and large stingers gave no doubt as to the peril the party would face.

Disappointedly, Brymanah realized that this would not be a *normal* battle after all. And even worse, she now realized what the goblins meant when they had said "queen".

Chapter 23

Around the Bend

The sounds of distant music played in the backyard. It was one of the many pleasant melodies of the late 70's/ early 80's: enchantingly harmonic, simmering with the promise of a magical way of life. It was for this very reason that a very young Halfdan was out wandering. What more wonders could be found around the next bend?

His parents, kind and loving, his world pristine and set well, Halfdan knew that he had his whole life ahead of him. The dreams of that blonde woman (his future wife perhaps, though just a child like him at this stage) had begun and he felt a deep kinship with his family, their friends, and life itself. He felt at home in the world.

What was it that made him want to investigate beyond? At a much older age, he would read from both Robert and Nissar that he had actually come from pure consciousness: he may have actually *chosen to become a person.* And why, as a seemingly happy little person, as young Halfdan seemed to be, did he wish to venture out in search of something more?

It could be said that perspective is everything. In his clearest of minds, Halfdan could recapture the sense of that better world, the world he had lived in as a child. Perhaps someday he would be truly free and recapture that world entirely, or the lack thereof, that condition that even predated his very personhood. It was perhaps this innate sense of gentle reality that led young Halfdan to wonder that if you went around a place a number of times, but didn't come back the same number, you would not be in the same place.

As his loving family ate and chatted, Halfdan, known under a different name in those days, ventured off. There was a childlike excitement in knowing one had a safe place to return to and yet adventuring in search of excitement just beyond. As the scent of barbequed meat and the sound of electric music faded, Halfdan began his walk around his relative's house. He had done this a number of times before; it *was* very exciting. And luckily, he always seemed to come home to where he belonged. Maybe little things were different, but nothing too traumatic.

Traveling around the house once again, he began to notice the changes. The first time: all seemed normal. The second time had minor changes: clouds in the sky, a different song playing on the radio, a change in mood of his family. Still, it could all be chalked up to coincidence.

Halfdan wanted adventure though! So he went around again and again, faster and faster! Three, four, five, six times he ran around the house until finally, he tripped. One of the paving stones on the walkway had become uneven. Or was it *different*? Perhaps he had skirted reality itself? Narrowly avoiding skinning his knee, Halfdan stumbled back to his family.

Some of them were arguing with each other now. That was strange. And what was that smell? It smelled like... like... burning! OUCH! His nose and eyes began to burn slightly ... that was different! Things started to appear blurry as well, his vision was somehow affected. What was more, Halfdan began to notice strange buzzing bugs flying around the barbeque now. Even the music sounded... off. What had happened?

"Dad, I don't feel so good. Can we go home?"

Dan Osarchuk

Halfdan's father looked him over with an analyst's gaze and said that he would have to deal with it for now. Halfdan then looked over at his mother and she looked sad. She was engaged in a discussion about a relative that Halfdan had never heard of before who had died. More clouds began to fill the sky, a strange slender bug landed on his arm, looking like some sort of miniature demon with a long nose and... it bit him!

Everything began to feel sort of dirty- somewhat greasy and unclean. His hands felt sticky. Was he just imagining all these changes or was he really somewhere else?

How could such a seemingly pleasant scene a few minutes earlier change so suddenly? As his young sinuses began to congest and his young eyes grew blurry, he noticed that the whole situation was really much more unpleasant than a few minutes before. The bends! What had he done!?

He felt no magic in this world, and very little love. Nature itself seemed to be vicious and adversarial. He looked at his aunts and uncles, but knew that they wouldn't understand. They were the versions that were *from* this world, so it all seemed normal to them, if not unfortunate. To say anything else would seem crazy! If he had tried to explain what he meant to them, they would just have thought that Halfdan had gone 'around the bend'.... He *had* actually, but not in the way that they thought!

"Enough of this!" Halfdan said to himself.

He often wondered what it would it would have been like if he had stayed in that infernalistic world? Decades of awkwardness, never really fitting in, despite a few years of happiness at University, and then more troubles in his adult life? Having to work at a thankless job, just to put food on the table and a shelter over his head? He might still make some friends, find a little romance, and have wonderful children (since they would have been at least partially from his own world, of course), but he would never be quite able to click with most others. Why? Because it wasn't his world!

His parents yelled for him to come back, but young Halfdan took off around his relative's house, this time in the *opposite* direction. One, two, three, four: he dashed around the house, noticing the changes. He hoped and prayed that he would make it home, back to his *real* world. In his feverish sprinting though, he realized a horrible fact: he had lost count!

Panic overtook the small boy. Tears began to fill his eyes. He sprinted again, making lap after lap around the house, barely aware of his surroundings.

Finally out of breath, he looked around in the meek hope that he had returned home. The sense of magic had returned to him- it now seemed present here. Yet it was altogether *different* than home. Where the party once was, there was now a field of corn. The house was gone, a copse of dwarf pine trees stood there instead. And no music was playing, nor any radio either... or barbeque. In fact, there were no houses, powerlines, cars, people, or anything!

Young Halfdan wandered around this lost land for hours. The plants still made his nose burn and congest, while those strange 'flies' kept buzzing around him. Still, he was too upset to really notice. All he could think about was where was his *real* mommy and daddy?

Luckily for Halfdan, he eventually happened upon a kind family of gatherers who took him in and sheltered him. The people of Claw Island were always very outgoing, no matter what reality one seemed to be in, though they weren't always the most patient. Nevertheless, this family was kind and he lived with them in a quaint cottage in West Seavilla, not too far from where his *real* home would have been, should have been.

As Halfdan grew older, he would venture out with his schoolhouse friends, Oldson and Rucksel, even exploring the very grounds in South Seavilla where his real home would have been. There he would entertain them with his crazy stories of coming from another world. As adolescent friends do, they would jest whenever possible, and simply assumed that was what Halfdan was doing.

"So did you hear what Kerestan said at school?" Oldson questioned. He then made a comical expression, as Halfdan and Rucksel broke out laughing. Oldson and Kerestan had an abstruse relationship that never ceased to entertain them.

Next it was Halfdan's turn to talk about maidens that he wanted to court. He was never very successful in this endeavor, although he always *felt* like he should have been. To get ready to emphasize his points, he leaped on to a hillock and then promptly spilled over as it partially collapsed beneath him. Rucksel and Oldson nearly started crying, they were laughing so hard. Oldson's imitation voices mixed with Rucksel's hilarious chuckles.

An ancient black pine tree swayed in the breeze overhead as the friends laughed. Its branches danced with the nearly-as-tall Norway maples nearby. Light, cirrus clouds floated across the cerulean sky, as the scent of the bay wafted from the south. The sun shimmered down upon the group.

Regaining his composure, Halfdan feebly tried to contain any further laughter. Through the mirth though, he realized that the hillock was covering the foundation of something, the cement-work looked ancient. The three friends worked to clear even more of it away.

Then it hit him: if the foundation of a house once stood there, and that foundation looked a lot like his parent's house, his *real* home, then perhaps this world wasn't too far off the mark after all. Sure, there were bugs, and pollen, and toil, and especially nasty folk, and disinterested maidens, but it did still seem somewhat familiar. What if he hadn't traveled *sideways* when he feverishly

ran around his relative's house the last time all those years ago-
what if he had traveled *forward*?

Later, at University, Halfdan would gain a better understanding
of the past, of the Ancients. He learned how their society had
crumbled, that the power lines went cold, along with many homes,
and many lives. What if that alternate reality party that he had first
stumbled into as a small boy was in the *past* for this world? It
certainly would help him in his studies, for that would mean that
he had been present in this world's Ancient times!

That would explain a lot, for unlike his real home, this current
world seemed generally cursed. It seemed fitting that some
calamity would befall any society in this world, given a long enough
timeline. For sure, there were still good things that happened and
good people to meet, but they could be sporadic at best. Normal for
Halfdan would be extended periods of good times and plenty of
good people. No matter how long he had dwelt in this world, *that
was* what would always seem normal to him, even if it wasn't what
would normally happen. Isn't that strange?

> *Things come and things go*
> *And yet I am remain*
> *To watch them unfold*

What differed from that darker scene with the angry look-alikes
at the party in the past was that the sense of magic *was* present in
the here and now. Perhaps it was because the electric power got
turned off for good? Or was there more of a shift in the ways of the
world itself? It had been centuries since Lights Out anyway,
apparently. God only knew how much could change in that time.
Perhaps it was simply because Halfdan had gotten used to it, that
his heart was more in this world and he therefore felt the magic
here?

* * *

Now stuck in the bowels of the Schoolhouse, at the mercy of some sort of ancient sentient automaton demon-god, it was hard for Halfdan to feel the magic. What surprised him too was that a number of townsfolk were willingly toiling in this mechanical labyrinth. The adults would solder parts, connect wires, bezel vacuum tubes, and transcribe forms written on paper into some sort of 'typing' device- all this with virtually no complaints.

In return, Halfdan surmised that their captor, Enak, would allow them some limited time on a viewing screen called the *Funbox*. Though he wasn't allowed in the room that held it, the toilers who were occasionally let in returned with huge smiles on their faces, looks of euphoric elation. It must have been quite a reward, for Enak seemed to have plenty of humans to toil and their toiling was quite difficult. Halfdan had trouble deciding what was worse: laboring below in this place under a mechanical master or laboring above in the Schoolhouse itself under human masters.

His thoughts were disturbed by the robotic voice of the former, who had just entered the room.

"THIS FORM DOES NOT COMPUTE, QIN, RECTIFY NOW."

Halfdan was at a loss. Not only was he unsure why the robot monstrosity kept referring to him as an Ancient Cathayan state, but he had thought he had filled out the form to increase tutor productivity by 657% correctly.

Enak did not seem convinced. It simply stared at him with its red light bulb eyes, which would seem almost comical if it weren't for the diabolic sentience behind them. It reminded him of a toy he had once had in the pleasant version of his youth in South Seavilla, minus the diabolism of course.

Silently, without comment, one of Enak's huge metal claws moved smoothly towards Halfdan's neck. It seemed that it was now time for him to be *rifted* (i.e. Enak would be creating a permanent rift between Halfdan's neck and head). There were worse ways to go, Halfdan guessed. He would finally get to see if consciousness remained after the body was gone...

And yet, it was not be, at least for now. Walking down one of the spiral staircases that led up to the Schoolhouse, Mme. Carve called out, "Oh Enakky, Carvey's here!"

The fiendish automaton turned from its murderous task and looked at the Head Monitor. Something akin to longing dripped over its features in a substantially disturbing way. Two Ever-vigilant Hounds, perhaps the ones who had first carried Halfdan from his classroom, had an assistant tutor in tow, an older man who was more recently hired. He looked like he had been beaten.

Halfdan couldn't tell if Enak was upsettingly excited to see Mme. Carve or just the prisoner. Neither seemed to be a good proposition.

Chapter 24

The Cult and the Traveler

Oborren couldn't help but smile in the night air. Perhaps venturing underground could allow one to face the dark terrors of the world more easily, but it certainly was stuffy. Here though in George's Forest, the stars were out shining and there was a gentle cool breeze in the air. Ahhhhh, it was good sleeping weather!

It was hard to tell how long they had been underground. And it stood to reason that one could never really determine when and where one would emerge from the underworld exactly, though one could at least *hope* to emerge at least somewhere in the vicinity of where one had first ventured. Still, time and space did get distorted while one was underground, especially when one was gone for as long as he and his party members had been.

There they tramped behind him, apparently in good spirits: Tepson studying the various plants, Kolveig humming gently about crushing the Capitalist Regime, and Brymanah humming gently about crushing Kolveig. That they still carried a substantial amount of treasure only improved morale.

"It looks like things have gotten much wilder, since I've been away!" said Tepson excitedly.

Night Skies Over Valhallow

The rest of the party didn't really know what he meant, but it didn't matter. Gnomes were known for their opinions and usually said silly things anyway.

In fact, it was because of Tepson's very presence that the decision was made *not* to venture through Mauriatown. It wouldn't do to have their new friend taken as an escaped slave, now would it? The gnome trotted happily along, not realizing how dangerous the world had become.

He was interrupted by a brief, but intense twinge of pain in his leg. Tepson was impressed that the party had the intelligence to try for a nighttime escape from the cavern, since wasps were less active then. Still, some *4' long giant yellow jackets* and 3' tall yellow goblins had indeed noticed the party and landed some hits on them.

Luckily, Kolveig's magic appeared to be potent enough to remove most of the wounds. It was strange how such healing would make the party so amiable to redistributing their wealth. Being a scientist, Tepson was uncomfortable with the idea of magic, but still glad to have some gold coin in his pockets and that the giant wasps didn't talk.

It was then that Tepson felt strangely drawn to his pack. Pausing for a moment as the party passed by, he pulled out the flask that once held the Insolitius Novus. Without thinking, he tossed it into the woods. It felt good to be rid of it.

Oborren's thoughts too went back to the encounter with the yellow goblins and the wasps. In keeping with goblin superstition, they most likely worshipped the wasp queen. He smiled wryly, remembered how he had left a special *present* for her.

Suddenly, he noticed a smell of smoke and chanting voices up ahead. This was rarely a good sign. Not surprisingly, his city-slicker comrades had missed it, so Oborren quickly used a hunter's silent gesture for them to stop.

Not knowing the hunter's gesture of course, Kolveig blurted out, "What?" making Oborren wince in irritation. Brymanah showed her greater sense in quickly smacking Kolveig on the side of the head.

"What... is... it...?" she mouthed.

Oborren pointed in the direction of the sounds and soon the rest of the party heard them too, even Kolveig, whose ears were still ringing from Brymanah's smack.

The scent wafted to where the party hunched. It had a fell odor to it, being more akin to burnt mullock than wholesome timber. Strange cat-calls and barks could be heard as well- suggesting that those up ahead may have had more than a few screws loose.

The party inched closer to take in the scene about 200 yards away. It seemed that a number of ruined buildings were positioned to make a rectangular "C" shape, around a central square or green. In that area, a group of humans, perhaps 30 in all, danced around a fire, half-naked. They wore the masks of various animals and monsters.

Something about them made Oborren guess that these were no mere tribesmen, but instead some sort of Cult. Such things were unfortunately all too common in the Vale. Who else would dress up so strangely and not live in the deep wilds? His mind then immediately recalled his hunt of a certain stagman not too long ago and its heartrending conclusion.

Tears began to well up in his eyes; he turned so that his friends could not see. It would be improper of him to show such weakness to others since he was a hunter. And it was a hunter's job to slay, not weep.

Oborren's attention returned to the scene as Kolveig tapped him on the shoulder and pointed to something in the center of the flames. It looked as if the cultists had a captive, a strangely-dressed, pudgy man who looked very afraid. Who could blame him?

Night Skies Over Valhallow

* * *

Wilstrin shouldn't have stayed at the Estate. It never turned out well when he did, no matter which time he did it. It was just his luck too: only hours away now from the Alignment, when the doorway will shift, allowing him passage to the next iteration and hopefully a better one.

The cultist's body odor overpowered him. Why did whackos so rarely wash? Still, he couldn't pick whether that was worse or the ithyphallic drug that the lunatic seemed to be on. At least the madman had pants, even if they were splattered with blood. Of all his visits to the Estate, in so many different iterations, this may have been the worst, of course, since it just might be the one that killed him.

Looking around at the demented cultists screaming and gyrating on the ground, it would appear that he had not found a better place yet. He feebly tried to blow out the flames as the mad folk dragged him ever closer to the bonfire, chanting to someone or something named Ergo.

* * *

The party quickly positioned themselves in preparation for the attack. The double benefit of attacking some cultists and interrogating another stranger seemed to galvanize them into immediate action. They split into each cardinal direction: Brymanah in the north, Kolveig in the south, Oborren in the west, and Tepson in the east. They hunched, weapons ready at the edge of the forest, surrounding the ruins of the estate.

Suddenly, a hush came over cultists. A larger man, eyes bulging and unfortunately completely unclad, strutted into the circle adjacent to the bonfire. The strapping fellow, froth dripping from his mouth, let out an elated moan that silenced any remaining chatters from the assembled lunatics. The party assumed that he was the leader. Pulling his massive shoulders back, the leader began.

"Those who break the sanctity of our holy ground must pay the ultimate price! Ergo, how about you HAVE some death ALREADY?!"

Wilstrin couldn't tell if the cult leader was referring to some damnable patron that he followed or was, in fact, making a terrible grammatical error. He did notice that the meanings of certain words seemed to vary when he went from reality to reality, but this was just too much. Having the meanings of nouns, such as simile and metaphor, change is one thing, but using an adverb incorrectly was just inexcusable.

The towering cult leader did not seem to agree, as he glared into the captive stranger's eyes and smiled. Some froth dripped from the corner of his rictus. The presence of his grimacing assistants didn't help either, especially after they started hooting and howling in anticipation of the stranger's death.

But the sounds of battle interrupted the cultists' glee. From around the circle, four stalwart figures strode in out of the darkness, slashing and felling the poorly armored cultists. It would seem that the cultists were better equipped for capturing a lone, unarmed traveler than fighting a trained war party.

A dark-clad hunter strode into a pair of bald cultists, his quickly flashing flail dispatching one in the jaw and the other across the throat. An olive clad fellow, armed with a hammer and sickle of all things, ducked and swung, taking down a barrel-chested cultist after a bit of an exchange. Stranger yet, a woman (probably) with bulging muscles screamed a war cry that even seemed to set a group of cultists on edge. They soon collapsed, screaming themselves, due to her many cutlass slashes across their bodies. And strangest of all, a little-person with a long beard ran in-between various cultists' legs, smashing them in the crotch with a pickhammer.

Night Skies Over Valhallow

Wilstrin had thought he had seen it all.

* * *

After he was untied, the stranger took a few minutes to thank the party and his lucky stars that he was still alive. That was a close one! Even though those cultists were probably the most blatantly bloodthirsty he had encountered so far, this new group of individuals seemed the most exotic. How could it be that a hunter, a Marxist cleric, an amazon, and a gnome had come together? He might never fully understand. It seemed that each time he returned to the Estate, things got stranger.

As the amazon and the cleric began to argue over the division of the cultists' spoils and of the material wealth of societies, he recalled how it all had started for him. Long ago, he had decided that he had enough of his life. Struggling, he had found the answer, or at least he thought so: to move *between* worlds, to end up somewhere else, hopefully better.

He had started off further 'east' so to speak, in a place that was quite rigid: little magic, little love, all manner of hardship and disease, and a repressive State that had nearly inculcated itself into every aspect of its citizens' lives. Why was it that the world had seemed so impossible? After months or even years of traveling (he had lost count), he could think of nothing other than his goal: how to get to a better place.

It all revolved around the Estate for some reason; at least it did for him. Perhaps other places had the same special quality, to allow passage to another possibility for that place, or in other words, another realm. When the sundial was aligned at the right angle, Wilstrin, or anyone else who entered the cave nearby, would be somewhere else when they reemerged.

Wilstrin struggled with whether to relate that fact to the party. True, they did seem to have their hearts in the right place, since they did rescue him from those horrible savages. On the other hand, he never knew whom he could trust. There was no telling what the laws of reality were in this place, or even the nature of the people who dwelt here. The further 'west' he went, the more extreme things seemed to get.

When he had first left his own world, he was sick of the banality. The only option for him seemed to be to work at a lousy job, to have a boring life, with no sense of magic, no sense of hope or wonder or connection. As he started world-traveling though, he noticed more of a sense of magic and a general relaxing of the people he met. He also noticed that technological availability began to recede as well. But despite the apparently more pleasant and wondrous demeanor of the places he went, greater dangers seemed to lurk there too.

What tied two places together? Was it a thought? Was it a feeling? The sense of déjà vu, so often overlooked, could be the key to it all. For what identified where one really was, but one's perceptions? Some might claim otherwise, but it was ultimately up to one's own observations and decisions about where one really was that would settle the matter.

It was thus that lead Wilstrin to investigate magic. True, it was extremely weak on his homeworld and took years to master even a rudimentary effect, but it at least pointed him towards the direction that he now took.

He attempted all manner of escape- trying to be carried away by tornados, jumping into mirrors, and even yelling that he believed at the top of his lungs each night. Unfortunately though, none of those approaches seemed to work.

Then one fateful day, he snuck away from the tour group at a certain Green Mountain and hid until dark. Conferring with his occult tome, he adjusted the sundial in the main square in front of the Estate to one degree further west. He entered the cave across the Bowling Square and when he came out again, it was different! It worked: the people, the place, the ease of magic, even the very

197

air had changed. Someone seemed to have created themselves quite a doorway.

But it was more than that. It was the feeling of the place. How strange that he had to enter an alternate reality to feel more at home- how ironic! But unfortunately, it would seem that the nastiness of the world he went to became more concentrated. Because even though Wilstrin might run into thugs and gangers in his home world, at least they were human! Here and on other worlds, he encountered very nasty creatures- obviously inhuman ones and worse.

And no matter how much further 'west' he went, the pattern would remain the same: the world would get more magical, some even more animatedly so, but the dangers became more terrifying as well. If he could only find the *right* world for him, then he could be happy. If he could only keep going, then he might be free... and they might even use proper grammar!

He wondered if any of those who had vanished mysteriously from his homeworld had done the same.

* * *

Miles away, the Yellow Goblin High Priest shrieked at the conclusion of the ceremony. The Queen was dead! And it was all the work of stupid humans! OH, how he DESPISED them! Those stupid, oversized pale skins with their miniscule noses and stupidly rigid postures- why couldn't they just admit that were privileged with having to DIE!

He stared at the multitudes of his goblin folk around him. Those invading humans had even tried to make him their prisoner! It was now time for he, Snik Snak the Great, to lead his goblins on the path of carnage and revenge! The few remaining megajacks buzzed overhead in the cavern, yoked by his dark shamanistic spells. They too were without their queen, but they would serve him now, just as the many goblin warriors who were taking up arms.

Dan Osarchuk

"Death to Humans!"

The chase had begun.

Chapter 25

Walstock

A sound at the edge of the camp snapped Oborren awake. Unsurprisingly, his city-slicker comrades were still asleep, probably lost in their own mad dreams, no doubt. Shaking his head, the hunter refocused on the issue at hand: the sound. What was it? He looked around and counted his comrades- one amazon, one Karlist, one gnome who thought he was from the distant past, and... where was that strange fellow they had rescued earlier that evening?

Something else was strange too. A number of the butchered cultist bodies that the party had stacked in the center of the Estate yard had been knocked aside. A sundial beneath was now exposed. Perhaps it was scavengers? And then he realized: it must have been the stranger!

Oborren wished that he had more time to talk with him earlier, but the party had been so busy arguing about how to divide up the loot that it was all he could do to get them to make camp without debating until the next dawn. Even Tepson had been vicious in demanding a piece of jewelry from the fallen Cult Leader. Oborren guessed that the gnome fit right in with the party now.

Night Skies Over Valhallow

And here they were, all seeming to be sleeping soundly, their hidden fire crackling in its pit. Better not wake them, thought Oborren, it was refreshing to see them so quiet.

Stealthfully putting on his gear, Oborren began to look for tracks. He noticed that one pair in particular led from the square back out to a field to the south. He could barely make out a cave entrance there, recessed into only a slight grassy hill. The moon began to rise on the eastern horizon, a shining silver orb, lighting up the cedar forest in a strange, fey light.

Soon Oborren stalked to the cave entrance, taking more time perhaps than he needed to, but as he had learned over the years, one could never be too careful. Who knew what lurked inside?

His suspicions were founded when we spotted the stranger, Wilstrin, venturing back to the cave. He held some exotic tome in his hands, somewhat bloodied and burned, but still recognizable as something of the occult. Thinking quickly, the hunter ducked behind some bushes just outside the cave. Wilstrin approached, apparently oblivious to his waiting acquaintance. He was quite startled when Oborren jumped out and spoke.

"What have you got there?"

"WHAT!! Oh.... nothing..." The stranger struggled to regain his composure.

"Indeed. You know, Wilstrin, it's considered impolite to sneak away from your liberators' camp in the middle of the night and practice the Dark Arts."

Wilstrin was even further taken aback: was Oborren confiding in him or accusing him?

"I... I'm simply going for a walk in order to clear my head."

Oborren smiled, finding no truth in the stranger's story. He deftly swung his flail and took Wilstrin off his feet in one fluid motion.

202

The occult tome flew up in the air and the hunter calmly caught it. He made sure to not even glance at the cover of the book for such things could always be cursed.

Luckily for Wilstrin, he landed flat on his back upon the soft grass. His strange garb settled with him and he reached his pudgy hands out with a look of outrage on his face.

"How dare YOU! That is NOT YOURS TO TAKE!"

Oborren guessed that this book must really have the stranger under his spell, because he was nearly coming to tears as he struggled to arise. With practiced ease, the hunter replaced his flail with his crossbow. The stranger froze as he saw the sharp bolthead pointing directly at his face.

For a moment, no one spoke. Then Oborren ventured a glance down at the book and then returned his gaze back to Wilstrin. He cocked his eyebrows in inquiry.

Taking the hint, Wilstrin explained, still quite emotional, "I NEED that book!"

"Why?"

"It helps me to..." the stranger was unsure if he could trust the hunter. Still, it seemed like he had little choice in the matter now. "...travel."

Oborren smiled again. He hadn't realized how much of a warlock this stranger truly was. Sure, he dressed strangely and looked pudgy, but he could now only wonder at what sort of demons this poor, sad sap might conjure up to go from place to place. And what sort of horrific sacrifices would such demons demand?

Seeing a cruel smile of determination begin to form on Oborren's face, Wilstrin made to run for it. The hunter hesitated for just a moment; he guessed that the stranger might not have been completely corrupted by demons yet. But still, he grudgingly shot the strange fool in the calf.

Wilstrin howled in pain and fear. He certainly didn't seem that tough for a warlock.

* * *

It took surprisingly little debate amongst the party to turn the stranger, whom they had only risked their necks to liberate a few hours before, into the party's captive. Brymanah, of course, felt it only proper to tie up an untested male. Tepson didn't trust the guy, since he claimed to be from an alternate reality, rather than from the past, like Tepson did, which was obviously far more believable. And Kolveig felt that the stranger's garb seemed just too Bourgeois to be trusted.

The party headed south on the Mighty One trail. It never ceased to amaze Oborren how much more quickly one could travel south in the Western Lane. Perhaps it really was true that the Ancients had enchanted it to help in southward travel, just as they had enchanted the Eastern Lane to assist in travel northward. Whatever the case, Oborren was looking forward to dropping off the warlock with the nearest group of witch hunters, claiming his reward from Agnetha in Calvary, and then taking some time to read through Wilstrin's tome- without any witch hunters knowing of course. One had to be well-versed in the ways of the enemy, even if it might risk one's soul.

The pleasant rolling hills and cedar groves soon gave way to the raised entrance to Walstock Road. There, all manner of delicious scents wafted down upon the travelers. As they exited the Mighty One trail, the party resisted the instinctive urge to turn left towards Restaurant Row, the local stretch of themed food houses, and hung right towards the Church of Tyr instead.

Dan Osarchuk

Oborren was impressed by the party's self-control. Perhaps their harrowing adventures had taught them the value of teamwork or, at least, of not arguing whenever they had the chance.

Soon the steepled halls of the church arose before them. Guards stood out front- not guards that one would obviously notice, but Oborren, being a hunter, knew what to look for. These were not some muscle-bound warriors of Thor or even caped knights of Athena. No, the soldiers of Tyr were hunters too, akin to Oborren, but quite secretive and even more fanatical, if that were possible. Their focus was on rooting out and punishing those who practiced the Dark Arts.

The party strode up to the white painted steps of the church as the guards, dressed as common folk, encircled the unknown band of adventurers. The rest of the party soon began to realize what was up, as the apparent commoners began to draw longswords concealed in their packs.

Oborren quickly turned and pointed at Wilstrin. Oborren smiled at the guards. He knew that they couldn't pass up a heretic to burn.

* * *

The scent of Colonel Siegfried's Gnome-whipped Chicken filled the cool, spring air as its intoxicating juices mixed with the aroma of fried, seasoned bread. Even Tepson had to admit that it smelled delicious, despite the obvious persecution of other midg-, *ahem, gnomes*, like him. And between this place, the psychopathic clown proprietor of MacDonaghill's, and the Old-Time Red Head in charge of Cindy's, not much had changed in Walstock. Of course, each was known under different names centuries ago.

What amazed Tepson most though was the way that the people now lived. Gone were the motor cars and flashing lights of his era. Gone were the machined edges to things, as well as the thinking devices that gave such pleasure and such concern. He wasn't sure if he was in the past or in the future. Horse-drawn wagons rolled down the beaten, semi-paved road, as the cloying scent of dung mingled with the crisp burn of wood-fired ovens.

The people now certainly were courteous though, and healthy! Even standing here in Restaurant Row, no one was obese. How could they be? People actually had to *walk* around to get places (or use a less-than-comfortable horse or wagon). And when passing by each other, they *had* to say hello. Because even though it looked like Walstock may have returned to colonial times, the means of justice certainly had become medieval.

There was no blasting music as travelers attempted to vent their imbalances upon passers-by, nor even citizens lost in the staring delusion of a pocket computer. No, for if one were impolite, strange, or unaware when walking passed a person in this New Dark Age, they might take offense. And there were no litigators to use for those who felt wronged anymore. Instead, matters were usually settled by something heavy, sharp, and deadly.

Tepson could certainly see the advantages and disadvantages of this new way of life, as he picked out some hard to identify substance from his mashed potatoes.

The party's attention was soon drawn to a woman who was crying nearby. She was clothed in the compensatory crimson and amber dress for female workers at MacDonaghill's.

"What's wrong?" asked Brymanah.

Oborren sighed heavily. Brymanah quickly realized her mistake.

Almost on cue, Kolveig chimed in as he put a salted biscuit down, "Yes, WHAT IS WRONG? WHAT HAS UPSET YOU, DEAR WORKER?"

The woman ceased her crying for a moment and glanced at the cleric.

206

"My Proprietor has been claiming that the food I've been preparing has been lacking in heat." Tears continued to stream down the woman's eyes. "I've been trying my best to make a living for my small children and today, he said that he won't be needing my services anymore!"

"OH REALLY!" exclaimed Kolveig, as he became increasingly animated, "here we are with just another example of SOME CAPITALIST PIG EXPLOITING THE WORKERS!"

Before the rest of the party could react, the Karlist leapt up and began marching to MacDonaghill's. Soon, he approached the vibrant amber-colored letter 'D' portals that stood around the place. Townsfolk glared at him as he cut in line, making his way into the establishment.

Inside, his senses were assaulted with the aroma of fried potato, roasted cow, sweetened drink, and pretzeled bread. A multitude of workers stood behind a large counter, dressed much as the crying woman that Kolveig had spoken with only a few minutes before.

Continuing to push ahead, Kolveig made his way to the counter, cursing the townsfolk and their Bourgeois ways.

"Yes sir, how may we service you?" said a young lad behind the counter.

Kolveig didn't know whether to laugh or cry at the ridiculous outfit that the lad was made to wear.

"I want to see him!"

"Who?"

"You KNOW who!"

"Roland?"

"OF COURSE! THAT CLOWN HAS A LOT TO ANSWER FOR!" On this last reply, Kolveig's voice echoed throughout the food-hall. All went silent.

Soon a strange laughter could be heard coming from the kitchen. A bizarre man emerged, garishly dressed, complete with make-up of a clown. In one hand, he held a golden walking stick with a bright red handle; in the other, a cup of confectioned cream.

"Hello... SIR..." the clown's voice matched the strangeness of his outfit, "do you have some sort of... COMPLAINT?"

Kolveig glared at the Obvious Capitalist. No, he couldn't hide behind some silly clown make-up! Kolveig could see right through it, and him!

And it would seem that Roland too knew exactly what Kolveig was. As if the small red hammer and sickle pins on the lapels of his olive jacket weren't obvious enough, the much larger, weapon equivalents now in his hands were.

Slipping back into his happy persona, Roland smiled.

"Sir, perhaps you need some... CREAM?"

With that, the clown suddenly flung the contents of his cup right at the Karlist. His bearded face and longjacket became stained white by the sugary affront. Some in the crowd of customers behind him even began to cheer and jeer at the disgraced cleric. Many of the workers stared in bewildered awe.

And just as Kolveig was going to really let him have it with an Official Denunciation, the vicious clown smashed him across the face with his golden cane.

Back at Colonel Siegfried's, Oborren sighed as an obvious brawl broke out inside MacDonaghill's. He was actually a little surprised that it took Kolveig that long to start it.

208

Chapter 26

Of Considerable Unpleasantness & Curses

The prisoner let out a final, hollow moan as Enak removed one of its corrugated, tentacle arms from his chest. What could be called sadistic glee overtook its synthetic features, if it were possible for such a robot head to do so.

During the horrific disemboweling of the assistant tutor, Halfmer, Mme. Carve had seemed to be thrilled as well. The unfortunate assistant must have failed to follow the Edicts of R'ti in some serious way and was now being 'rifted', though carving great 'rifts' in his vital organs was perhaps not the exact meaning of the acronym. Still, he was most certainly being reduced, and force was being applied, so it was not that far off the mark.

Carve also seemed to have some sort of bizarre attraction to the robot Enak and Enak seemed to get some sort of bizarre thrill from watching a defenseless assistant tutor agonize under his unsubtle touch. It was a win-win situation for them both and certainly a triumph in Schoolhouse management. The automaton had even established himself as an alpha male.

What drew Carve so strongly to him? He did have a solidly-built frame, and was a 'brigand-type', so most females would find that appealing. Halfdan had certainly learned that over the years. And

Night Skies Over Valhallow

Enak seemed the perfect "catch" for courtship, to show off to one's friends while on the town perhaps, even if he was evil!

What was it that made certain beings enjoy torturing others in such a way? Humans certainly did. And now Halfdan had just seen this robot do it. And Carve was thrilled! Was it some sort of evolutionary impulse to bond to a strong mate, one who had no qualms about hurting others? Or was it simply pent-up anger that coalesced into bloody wrath? Whatever the cause, it was a cruel world indeed, such that it made Halfdan miss the more idyllic one of his youth.

Enak turned from his now-deceased victim and stared at Halfdan with his lifeless eye-bulbs.

"Two 'Half-'s should now make a whole!" Carve cackled, anticipating Halfdan's imminent demise. Was that lust in her eyes for more carnage... or simply to see the Schoolhouse achieve its Yearly Objectives by assassinating enough tutors... or to merely demonstrate her skills at math?

Halfdan could not take his attention off of the robot's large, blood-stained arms. He wondered: would he die of horror *before* the major internal organ damage? Instead, Enak turned and swept Carve into his arms. As they lumbered away, Halfdan could have sworn that he saw her kissing the automaton.

A steward brought in a water bucket and mop to get ready to clean up the mess. It took a few minutes for Halfdan's body to stop swaying. He grasped the mop handle as he steadied himself.

* * *

A dark presence was all that remained in the work area. The other sycophants had snuck into the viewing room to watch the *Funbox*. They must have assumed that Enak was busy; he was laughing too loudly with Mdme Carve to keep them out. Halfmer's still fresh organs remained on the stone floor, their vital fluids forming a macabre puddle of blood and pus. One would imagine that a steward would need more than a mop and a bucket of water for that. Perhaps that's where he had gone.

Something watched from the shadows. Something Halfdan had not felt since that tutor meeting where the clown band had played- the clown band which he had tried so hard to forget.

Instinctively, Halfdan began to reach for his Odinnic holy symbol, but it had unfortunately been taken from him when he was imprisoned in this place. It didn't pass the muster of the Three L's apparently. As the dark presence moved closer, Halfdan focused within, sensing the space in the moment, watching the fear arise in his mind, the sensations of his body, noticing the one who suffered, the one who was afraid. His fear vanished.

Does the witness ever suffer?

Halfdan had faced such things before. The terror of a ghost was quite unique. Demons would tempt with evil, fey would cause whimsy (sometimes mischievously so), angels would inspire and set right, but the undead would simply *scare*. He had encountered ghosts, both back home on Claw Island and now in the Vale. He found that the only way to rid himself of them was to face them fully, just as one could with all fears, or better yet, notice the *one who was afraid.*

As Halfdan watched through his own porthole eyes, he observed the faint, photo-negative image in the dark presence. It appeared as a teenage boy, a smirking look on his face, deep pools of oblivion eyes. It suddenly reached its spectral hand out of the darkness, thrusting it into Halfdan's face, passing through flesh and bone as if not really there, and yet causing a horrifying, painful chill to the tutor.

Halfdan watched, allowing his body to react. Guided by God, he struck the ghost, using the very mop handle that he was holding, and it miraculously made contact. In seeming surprise, the ghost flew back into one of the bulky computational machines and vanished. He had not needed his holy symbol after all. It seemed that Halfdan had channeled the very power of Gungnir with his own swaying from before.

* * *

Halfdan's eyes began to burn again; at least the mold wasn't as bad down here as in other parts of the building. It could be the mildly toxic exhaust from all the computational machines that inhibited its formation. Seizing the opportunity while Enak and Carve were engaged, he took an opportunity to glance over Enak's files: REASSIGN TUTOR 4031 TO ROOM #303. REASSIGN TUTOR 4032 TO ROOM #507... REASSIGN TUTOR 4033 TO BROOM CLOSET... SOON 657% TUTOR GROWTH PARADIGM WILL BE ACHIEVED... MU HA HA HA....

It gave the semblance of order, while really just causing chaos. It began to dawn on Halfdan that the entire Cult of R'Ti may have emerged from madness just like this. Was Enak its founder? Or was it an even more insane and sadistic individual?

Halfdan's head began to throb: another reminder to *be not the body*. Who knew what made his body so allergic to everything-stress? Mold? A curse? A genetic inability to fully adapt to this particular parallel world that he had mistakenly ventured into as a child? Being locked in a warped labyrinth, ruled by an insane fiend-automaton, who had just horribly slain a co-worker and is now doing Odin-knows-what with one's demented boss was certainly a cause of stress.

Sensation- that's all that pain was really: simply phenomena arising. For some reason, he had certainly endured a lot of it for a large part of his stay in this world- perhaps it was so he could move beyond. Not beyond the pain/ sensation itself, that was in God's hands, but beyond identifying with the *story of the pain*. Because if he didn't identify as the one who was suffering, then who would be left to suffer? And that was truly freedom itself.

212

A pile of ongoing assignments stared at Halfdan. As part of his subterranean punishment, he was to reflect on every lesson he had taught, how each pupil felt every 3/4's of an hour, and how he had failed them. He smiled grimly: what purpose could such work possibly serve in helping pupils to become wiser?

Halfdan realized that he was always allowed to return home. Ironic that he wasn't *actually* a slave, only essentially one. True, he could leave his employ at the Schoolhouse at any time and just not return, but then where would he be? How could he afford anything? Seeing Larnen and Kelne made his life worth living, but he also had to *make* a living. Ironically too was the fact that in order to make a living, he had to do things that seemed to drain the very life out of him. They were more akin to making a dying.

Something dark began to move around Halfdan again. Whether drawn to his darkness or simply being generated by some other agency, it was hard to tell. Lost in his mind, Halfdan began to fall deeper.

He had always found it hard to make friends, but especially so once his built-up confidence since University had evaporated. For here was someone who had spent over a decade with him, but decided that she didn't want to be with him after all. Halfdan didn't blame her for leaving, but the end of his marriage seemed to be irrefutable proof that no one could *really* love him, not romantically, at least.

Any reason could be used to describe Halfdan's 'curse': that he was reaping what he sowed for not being a better husband. That he thought the fairer gender were not fond of him, either because of some obscure Law of Sympathy or that he simply displayed an insufficient mien. That there was something wrong with Halfdan physically... or mentally... or emotionally... or that he was in the wrong world, at the wrong time, and should had never left to go and investigate what was *around the bend*, all those years ago. Or was it all his imagination?

Night Skies Over Valhallow

Any explanation would have fit, because, in the end, who knew *anything* for certain? As Nissar would say, "'I am' is true, all else is inference."

Halfdan could see the evidence, day after day, night after night, no one responding to his postings on the message board tree, sleeping alone in his bed. Yes, some women would occasionally come along and dally with Halfdan for a time, but none lasted more than a few weeks. Perhaps it was better if he just... *died?*

Those things he could observe, but the story he made up about them, that he was *cursed,* perhaps wasn't as true.

It was time to let it go. The darkness receded again.

And that made up Halfdan's mind. He had enough of this damnable place. Enak and Carve were having a great laugh over all the tutors that they would torture. The other workers had corralled themselves in the viewing room. It was amazing what sort of slavery they would go through just for the privilege of being able to stare at some glowing screen. The Ancients probably weren't as foolish.

He glanced around at all the thinking machines, devices, and sundry items around him. Knowing that if he could draw upon his childhood experiences with electricity, he could certainly figure out a way to deal with Enak and his many absurdities now. Then his eyes went to the water bucket. The many recent R'ti-required workshops also came to mind, and to his shock, some seemed actually applicable to his situation now. It was time for Halfdan to act.

I do: Halfdan grabbed the bucket of water. He knew he was supposed to craft a Mission Statement for this part (or was it a Vision Statement?) to make sure the audience was able to show Adequate Annua Incrementum, but since he didn't have an audience (yet), he felt it was forgivable to do it later.

214

Dan Osarchuk

We do: Halfdan then proceeded to barge into the chamber where Mdme Carve and Enak were curled up and throwing darts at the faces of tutors with what seemed to be room numbers they would be assigned to. Halfdan fought back a smile. He knew that smiling was forbidden for a Tutor-Under-Review, but he felt that it didn't matter anymore. As the water bucket flew through the air, it suddenly dawned upon the Head Monitor and the devil robot what was going to happen next. They struggled to move away in time. Halfdan then removed himself from the situation to see what sort of learning would occur.

You do: The lights in the workroom flickered. As the screams of the (hopefully) dying Enak were being drowned out by the outrage of Carve, Halfdan began to venture above ground again. True, he had not really used a great deal of differentiated instruction, nor was he properly able to assess his tutoring objective with a formative assessment, but he did feel that some learning was occurring.

Mdme Carve would certainly regain her composure at some point and be out for revenge. Halfdan had some business to attend to before that happened.

Chapter 27

The Battle of Restaurant Row

"Lay off, Billy!" The large adolescent with a wicked smile seemed undeterred by the pretty brunette's rejections.

"Aw, come on!" Billy chided. Suddenly, a crazed look overcame him. He reached for the girl's neck and began to squeeze with his meaty arms. His eyes grew wide with a murderous lust as she began to shrink in suffocating horror.

"BILLY BERRAY! YOU LET HER GO RIGHT THIS INSTANT!"

WOMHP! A long tutor's ruler smacked him upon the side of the head. It was Mme. Maettrn. His resulting feigned look of outraged innocence did not deter her wrath.

"Time for a paddlin'!" Maettrn announced grimly...

Rubbing his sore hindquarters, Billy fought back tears as he angrily moved to the edge of the Schoolyard. He glanced at his pile of Sir Comkorn books and then back at Mdme Maettrn who was chatting with some other tutors. That bitch will get hers, he thought viciously, they all will! The other pupils stared back at Billy with disgust, almost as if they could read his mind.

He quickly made a rude gesture at them, hopped the fence, and was off. His vengeance was forthcoming.

Night Skies Over Valhallow

* * *

Snik Snak the Great stared at the scene before him with a mixture of irritation and bloody wrath. That stupid sun was still up in the sky, hurting his sensitive goblin eyes. His warriors too showed their irritation by the light, though the megajacks seemed undeterred. That was only natural, Snik Snak pondered, since they guarded their cavern during the day.

"Bwereysundisdbakuweyqwge!" As both the Yellow Goblin High Priest and Chieftain, Snik Snak ordered his forces to begin heroically sneaking up upon the battling humans and begin killing as many as they could! They would pay for what they did to the Queen! He smiled wickedly as he got his own, brutal knife ready for any *sacrifices* that his warriors brought him.

* * *

That Clown was surprisingly nimble for a Capitalist Pig who peddled his Fatty-Sweet Fare upon the Unknowing Proletariat, thought Kolveig. He dodged another swing of the former's golden rod as he countered with his own Marxian hammer. Roland avoided just in time though, his body still pulsating from downing a vat of Highly Sweetened Koka Tea. The beverage's HIGHLY STIMULATING effects were also evident on his speech now.

"YOUSTUPIDCOMMUNISTICAN'TWAITUNTILISMASHYOURBRA INSTOMAKEMYNEXTSECRETSAUCEWITHTHEM!"

The Karlist took this opportunity to try to slash the blathering clown with his sickle, but another customer got in the way. Bedlam continued to unfold in the MacDonaghall's with patron fighting patron and workers attempting to clean up the mess and stay out of the way.

* * *

Oborren disliked battling members of the Watch. He was a hunter, not a murderer. It was his sacred task to slay all the unholy beings that lurked in shadows of the world, all those that didn't look like normal folk.

But recent events had forced him to do that very thing. As he ducked a swing from a Watchman's baton, he cleverly fired a crossbow bolt at a nearby plant pot overhead. Its support cut, it fell on the watchman's head, knocking him out.

Oborren had little time to check on the hapless watchman though when he was struck by a hard, white object flung at him by a bizarre fellow. It appeared to be Colonel Siegfried himself, replete in a white suit, hair, and goatee. And even though his accent was disturbingly similar to the now-deceased Harry the Mustachioed Fish, Oborren retained his composure.

"I say sir, you have confounded me with your indubitable disrespect for the honored ways of Restaurant Row!"

Oborren blocked another hard-boiled egg that was hurled at him by the Colonel as his gnome subordinates began to move in, pitchforks in hand.

Now this sort of fight was just fine with Oborren: these sorts of characters were strange enough for him to have no qualms fighting. He just hoped that they would be brave enough to face such as skilled hunter as himself.

He just hoped that they weren't chicken.

* * *

Only in Walstock, thought Tepson. He didn't know what was stranger: the people's disposition for fighting each other or the bizarre characters that could be found in this town. What had started as a simple brawl between a Karlist cleric and a clown proprietor had somehow degenerated into a block-wide melee between townsfolk. Luckily, they hadn't been using very many medieval weapons yet.

Night Skies Over Valhallow

The Watch had arrived and attempted to bring order, but the scores of fights occurring made such a task impossible. And, as a woman dressed as red-haired Old Time Cindy emerged from the establishment of the same name screaming at some customers who hadn't paid for some of her signature homemade potatoes, he knew that things were reaching their boiling point. There was even some talk amongst the townsfolk who stood watching the fights that the Count might call in the Army to restore the peace.

Tepson's attention was soon drawn to Brymanah, who was watching the fighting with great interest. She yelled her support for any female combatants and coaxed them to be merciless with any males on which they got the upper hand.

Fortune then struck when Tepson noticed a spectator being grabbed from behind a building by a pair of little, bright yellow hands.

Notifying the amazon, the two moved swiftly in to discover a veritable army of yellow goblins concealed behind the buildings. Taking in the scene, his heart sank. Tepson couldn't help but be surprised at how quiet the little monsters were, even with all the dead bodies lying around.

* * *

The Capitalist just couldn't be cornered! Kolveig had managed to disarm Roland by using his sickle to pull away the Clown's rod, after the latter had bumped into an obese patron who was attempting to raid the kitchen. Still, the demented clown moved with a supernatural celerity, despite his unhealthy diet.

"YOU'LLNEVERGETMECOMMUNISTIMICTURATEONYOUANDA LLTHEWORKERSIFNOTALSOTHEIRFOOD!"

Disgusted, the cleric hurled his hammer at the clown's oversized bright orange-colored feet. As he guessed, Roland overcompensated and fell over as he attempted to dodge. Kolveig then took a moment to cast a spell upon the prostrate clown, a spell to Hold him for Official Questioning.

* * *

"I say sir, he'll make a mighty fine work-boy!" exclaimed the Colonel. Apparently Oborren's martial skills were not up to the task of besting Colonel Siegfried and his gnome goons. The demented proprietor had used his signature whip to devastating effect on the hunter, who was now tied up. The Colonel's gnomes stared at him disturbingly. They too were dressed mainly in white, but also wore silly little white hats to demonstrate their subordinate status. They weren't even pointy. Oborren guessed that some slaves remained loyal to their masters after all, even when they could have easily turned on the Colonel.

As the hunter began to ruminate on his future servitude of carrying wood for the Colonel's chicken ovens, a familiar pair soon made their way up the hill. The Colonel had his gnomes stand down. Oborren thought it was because the Colonel felt that Tepson and Brymanah were more of a match for him and his goons than the hunter was. But just as Oborren was about to debate that point, he noticed a horde of stunted, bright yellow-skinned humanoids screaming and charging down the hill from the north. Oborren knew it was time to forge a new alliance of necessity, even if it was with some bastard who sounded like Harry.

Word seemed to get to MacDonaghill's and Cindy's too, for the townsfolk stopped their fighting and glared at the approaching humanoids. Their bandied gaits and cruel glares seemed to make immediate allies of the humans, who had only been beating the tar out of each other a few moments before. It was time for the humans to unite. Was it soon enough?

As if in challenge, some demented goblin priest screeched in his nonsense tongue as hordes of his warped brethren charged into Restaurant Row, hacking and felling those bystanders from before, violating the sanctity of this land of Men with their very presence.

Now freed, Oborren screamed a charge, taking on the unusual role of captain, since they were, of course, fighting creatures that looked different than them. Brymanah and Tepson fell strangely in line too, even supported by the gnome servants of Siegfried, who had been their enemies only moments before. Few things were as compelling as an alien crisis to get people to work together.

Battle was joined, as the ring of good Vale steel struck against twisted Goblin design. The Watch was in it too, though they were only armed for crowd control: the goblins were hard to fight with just billie clubs and padded jackets. The remaining spectators scattered. Oborren hoped that they would call the Army.

Just then, a lucky stab by one of the many goblins struck Oborren in the leg, drawing deep and bloody. He roared as he brought his flail in reply to the foul thing, only to be saved from another strike by a stout wooden cane. The hunter didn't know whether to laugh or sigh when he realized that it was Colonel Siegfried himself who had parried the goblin attack and saved his life.

Soon Brymanah pushed through the goblin ranks, showing a disturbing, but effective aptitude for targeting their masculine parts. Coupled with the fierce war cries of a gnome with a cast-iron chicken spit, the monsters broke and ran. The humans paused for a moment, as they are wont to do, until they saw the bodies of the innocents that the goblins had slain. Blood flowed again as the humans charged in fury.

* * *

Snik Snak stared outraged at the breaking of his army. To the south, the overfed humans were rallying together, driving back his invincible minions. To the east, well-armored humans upon terrifying, tall-legged beasts were marching in. Most of his megajacks had even been shot from the sky by those stupid humans! He passed gas in fury. This could not be! Humans must pay! He turned at one his captives: a middle-aged human female who smelled of cinnamon. He took solace in her muffled screams of terror, as he disrobed and pulled out his wicked knife.

Her eyes grew wide as the demented goblin priest approached. He laughed wickedly as she began to cry, knowing full well what was coming next. Suddenly, a human voice rang out.

"Primitive Oppression of the Workers is still Oppression of the Workers!"

And another voice too rang out, this one apparently under the influence of some sort of ingested stimulant, "YEAHANDYOUBETTERPUTSOMEPANTSONRIGHTNOWYOUCRA ZYGOBLINFREAKWEDONTWANTTOSTAREATYOURFRENCHFR-"

Reacting quickly, the goblin hurled his wicked knife at the bearded human in olive dress. He narrowly parried it with an ornate hammer that he carried. The other human, one with a garishly-painted face and smelled of sweets and oil, rushed forward and swung his cane at the goblin, nearly taking off his head.

The bearded human then rushed forward, taking the opportunity to point his other weapon, a cruel-looking sickle, at a specific spot below Snik Snak's waist.

Perhaps he should have kept his pants on after all.

* * *

Nearly all of the Watch had been called away to deal with a major disturbance at Restaurant Row. Only Captain Tamerland was left to guard the Gaol. As he continued to feed on the 'delicious' suffering of the victims inside, he failed to notice a shadow moving up behind him. Before he could react, a makeshift spear, a holy symbol of Odin was placed directly in front of his face. He flew back in terror, some sort of clear-mindedness of the one holding made it empowered. An aging, short, slender man held the spear at him grimly. Tamerland was frozen in terror.

Night Skies Over Valhallow

"I have some questions for you, Least Offer."

Chapter 28

Halfdan's Improvement Plan

Bright sunlight shined upon the ancient building in town. Motes blazed brilliant yellow and white upon the cracked and aging brick and cement. Hints of grass could even be seen, beginning to turn green at the mention of Spring. A more recent crack in the roof of the building allowed the light to pass through, granting incentive for daytime to penetrate within.

Rows of ancient seats filled the large room with a vaulted ceiling. They all faced in one direction, staring only at a blank space. For all the tales of the Ancients' great escapes into Viewing from Afar, all they were really looking at was nothing. The scent of mold and dust stilled the air, no matter how clean its more recent tenants attempted to make it otherwise. The past could not be so easily cleansed by normal intent.

Bound and gagged, Tamerland the vampiric Least Offer stared at his captor in this place, his deep green eyes burning into him.

How dare he imprison ME, he thought. I am the Jailor! I am the one who throws who I PLEASE into prisons, so that they may rightly SUFFER.

Night Skies Over Valhallow

To make matters worse, something seemed to be shoved between his back and the floor. Despite his superhuman constitution, it bothered him, though he would die before he let his captor see it.

Tamerland steeled himself as that same short, slender, aging man who had captured him last night approached, makeshift spear-symbol of Odin still grasped in his hand. He produced a vial of water and stared at the Least Offer. Still grim, it seemed that the man did not relish his task, unlike Tamerland, who certainly would.

"What is it that dwells in the Schoolhouse," queried the thin man. Halfdan showed that the spear was sharpened, and it was one of *yew, to quiet the ancient dead.* He quickly removed Tamerland's gag with his other hand and pointed the spear at his chest.

"Why should I tell you, scum?" spat the Least Offer.

"For I have a stake at your heart, leech."

At this, the Least Offer only smiled, glaring at the man's face.

The slim man had seen the look many times before in other people's faces: it was defiance. He wrinkled his nose at the lingering stench of this ancient place and at this ancient one's stinking arrogance.

Agony met that defiance, as the thin man poured some of the water onto Tamerland's face. It burned like nothing else, seeming to partially dissolve even what made Tamerland *better* than mortals- hurting him *within his own being.* His screams echoed through the ancient place, resonating against the many seats that faced their direction and the large empty wall behind them. He knew it to be holy water.

"A cleric of Odin, claiming to be holy?" he spat again.

At this the man grimaced and dragged Tamerland a few inches across the floor, dangerously close to a brilliant ray of sunlight.

226

"Perhaps it's best to just leave you here," said the slim man calmly, "in a few more minutes, the sun will be upon you."

Tamerland held back a scream.

"What is it you want to know?" said the vampire, this time with a little less venom in his voice.

"There is far more than you can tell me, though I'll limit my questions to that which you might answer."

The Least Offer looked confused, the man recentered its attention with another dose of holy water. The vampire shrieked.

"What is it that dwells in the Schoolhouse?" the man asked again.

Tamerland held back a snide remark: the holy water might hurt, but exposure to direct sunlight for too long would kill him.

"The unquiet dead," he finally replied.

"Like you?" queried the man.

"Ha! I'm more *alive* then you'll ever be. Why, I can even sense the energy behind your own..... AAAAHHHH!!"

The Least Offer's rant was interrupted by the application of yet more holy water.

"Please limit your responses to the questions posed."

No smile could be detected on the man's face. Had he just made a joke, insulting ME, thought Tamerland?

He was just about to begin another rant when the thin man interrupted. "What else is there? Is the unquiet dead acting alone?"

"Of course not, how could a simple ghost cause all the suffering at the Schoolhouse!?" Tamerland's chuckle began to sound hollow as he noticed that the beam of light on the floor was only an inch away from his cheek. "It's obviously something dev..." The light began to make contact with Tamerland's clothing.

"Looks like you're running out of time, vampire." This time the man smiled.

Tamerland could no longer restrain himself. "You are the one who is running out of time, cur! You're obviously Illegally Occupying this building and Engaging in Inappropriate Contact and Assault on an Officer of the Peace! I look forward to throwing you into the Gaol, where wimpy men like you get to be..."

Tamerland was interrupted again as the thin man's face whipped forward to stare directly into his eyes. He was startled to see no fear in them. The man simply stared at him, his features flat, but there was something else... something in the space *around* the man which scared Tamerland to death, unnerving him to the *core of his being.*

When was the last time he felt fear like that? The beam of light began to touch Tamerland's face now, burning it slowly, causing a light smoke from his right ear and cheek to arise, turning it black. He almost welcomed the pain as it distracted him from the fear.

Tamerland's rage erupted once again. He knew that doom was upon him, that this scum intended him to die. No matter what his fears were, he would let this upstart have it. He pulled his head as far to the side as he could to protect it from the direct light and began.

"I know FAR more than you, mortal. Who are YOU to imprison and question ME? I was interrogating and torturing prisoners before your ancestors even climbed out of the filth of their homelands! Their screams and despair have been sweet melodies to my ears hence!"

The grim man appeared unmoved, yet the space around him intensified. The vampire continued, sweating as much from pain as from fear.

"And I see your mind now too... Halfdan. What fears you have! To make the wrong move at the wrong time? One mistaken word, one mistaken gesture and then... DISASTER! To be punished for decades and longer for one little lapse in judgment. Ha, ha, ha! Those are excellent fears to keep you on edge... FOREVER! I wish I only had a chance to slip some Forbidden Demonic Texts into your home and see what happened to you when the Constables came for you then! My, how little.... Larnen and Kelne would be ashamed at their father being pilloried and then much, much worse in the Gaol for his supposed crime! Ha ha! My, how you would be all alone! Not to watch your children grow up, never to see the stars overhead at night, nor to stand in your Clearing Node, nor to feel the touch of a woman *ever* again, not that it would matter to a freak such as yourself! My... and how you would chastise yourself all for the mistakes you made!"

The vampire continued, apparently reading the cleric's very thoughts.

"Oh, and what is this? Fear of being happy? Ha, ha, HA! Oh that's rich! That's a recipe for eternal fear and suffering now, isn't it? Please do never let your guard down. Oh, it's delicious, Halfdan. Thank you for being so afraid all the time. A delicious meal from a horrible person such as yourself. What was that? You don't think you're horrible? But you are, Halfdan! Why else would you have all these horrible fears?

You know, it's YOUR fault that SHE died!"

The Least Offer stared at Halfdan again. He could tell that the man's mind was becoming active again, taking away his resolve, covering over his presence, causing his eyes to be downcast, tears beginning to form. Even the space around the cleric seemed to diminish. Tamerland kept up his attack.

Night Skies Over Valhallow

"Come now, why don't you release me and I will end your suffering. Don't you want to just die, Halfdan? No one likes you, anyway. Your former wife couldn't stand you and she used to be your best friend! What woman could love such a skinny, aging freak as yourself? You're even a terrible tutor; they all hate you at the Schoolhouse! They even wrote it all down for you to make sure you knew! And you do know you'll make a terrible mistake sooner or later! It's only a matter of time. And then what will become of little Larnen and Kelne?"

That brought Halfdan back to his senses. At the mention of his children, he knew that he had to end this creature. Otherwise, they too might be in peril. He stared back into the eyes of the leech, anger rising.

"Now, now, Halfdan. It is not I who hurt children," the vampire chided. "Why expend the effort? Grown-ups taste so much better, with all their foolish attempts at morality and pointless rage at injustice. Don't you know that this world will simply destroy you sooner or later?"

"But I can succeed at the Schoolhouse," Halfdan said finally.

"Ha! Not with a devil loose. Do you think it's just some stupid shade of a former disgruntled pupil causing all the suffering in the Schoolhouse? Do you even know that you need to destroy its reliquary? Well then, add 'moron' to your list of shortcomings then, Halfdan. It takes something with much more of a punch than a ghost to..." The Least Offer paused, realizing he had accidentally answered Halfdan's original question.

Halfdan smiled. Tears still welled up in his eyes, dripping onto the old wooden floor; for he knew the vampire was right: he was never a perfect tutor, nor a good socialite, nor a sufficient suitor, nor especially wise. He would probably live the rest of his life without the touch of great success or of a true companion again.

But it didn't matter. God would always remain at his side. Always. And Halfdan knew that was enough.

He dragged the Least Offer over to the side again, saving him just as the beam of sunlight moved onto his face.

"Have a change of heart? Ready to be punished, the way you know you should be?" asked Tamerland. His voice shook in anticipation.

"Do you know what this place used to?" said Halfdan, ignoring Tamerland's taunts. "It's where the Ancients used to watch their picture shows. They would laugh, scream, and cry at the pictures, actually getting upset when they mistook them for reality, even as they could easily realize otherwise."

Tamerland was finally silent again. Halfdan continued.

"I sometimes make the same mistake, until I realize that the screen is real; the pictures are not."

With that, Halfdan looked down at the vampire. It simply stared back, confused. For Tamerland, the pictures were all that he had, all that he could ever have. He could no longer grasp the screen, for the mortal that he once was had died a long, long time ago. He was just a story now. The light moved onto Tamerland's face.

Halfdan listened to the Least Offer's death scream, unmoved, and allowed his own mind to drift into silence. In an apparent chain reaction, the vampire's entire body began to combust, his screams echoing through the ancient room, growing louder and more demented, much as the sounds of the ancient picture shows once did too. A potent scent of sulfur began to fill the place with the smoke of his ancient carcass. It seemed to burn away the stench of mildew in the place, bringing welcome destruction to old thoughts and feelings that had lingered far too long: in this place, in the vampire, and in Halfdan.

Night Skies Over Valhallow

The smoke wafted out through the sunlight streaming crack in the roof, casting strange shadows upon the floor where the still shuddering remains of the vampire lay, and upon the Ancient Viewing Screen.

His work done, Halfdan left. As he ascended his ladder to the roof, it occurred to him that perhaps even demons cannot withstand the light of truth. For they, though very dark and disturbing, were just more pictures upon the screen of this life after all.

Chapter 29

The Exorcism of Billy Berray

The clarion trumpet call of the Knights Falcon peeled out across the Row. The battle had reached a pause. Kolveig gritted his teeth. True, the last of those foul yellow goblins were ready to be ridden down, but did it have to be by such an obvious display of Bourgeois power?

Kolveig mustered up enough self-control to refrain from chastising the heavily armored knight beside him. He smiled awkwardly as Captain Sagerein lowered his steel visor over his stern face. Almost on cue, the other mounted warriors rode up beside him, forming a battle line. They maneuvered around the Karlist.

"FOR WALSTOCK!" shouted the captain.

The other knights shouted the same, lowered their lances, and readied the charge. Kolveig never knew that goblins could run so fast, even from Capitalist Dogs.

* * *

The rotten black stench of the Schoolhouse cellar assaulted Halfdan's nostrils. As he descended, the former tutor made sure to avoid the area where he was confined to previously, since he now assumed that Enak was not just some bizarre automaton of the

233

elder days, but was in fact, a true devil. Not a demon, mind you; no- such a being was out for domination and tyranny, rather than just simple wanton sin and destruction.

It all made sense, after a fashion. What better place for a devil to inculcate itself than in a Schoolhouse nowadays? Perhaps the tutors of Old had been too harsh and had attracted it? Doubtful. Most families had practiced physical discipline of naughty children at home for the last few centuries; having it occur at a Schoolhouse would have been nothing special. No, it was most likely the recent trend of torturing tutors that had attracted it.

Halfdan often wondered at how the Ancients had actually done away with physical punishment during the last few decades of their era. Some historians felt that they were able to achieve this through their expertise in Pharmacopeia; others felt that it had never really worked. Whatever the case, most agreed that having a generation of people that relied on narcotics and thinking tech in order to survive contributed to the rapid collapse of the Ancient's World when Lights Out occurred. How could they possibly cope without that society's conveniences?

Halfdan stopped himself as he realized he was lost in thought again. Odinnic teaching advised against such distraction, especially when hunting something this powerful. He needed to remain clear and present.

Releasing the tension that so often comes with thinking, Halfdan's consciousness deepened as he ventured deeper into the cellar. The rank odor shifted to a dustier one as his sinuses attempted to adjust to the place. His lantern light shone upon the many shelves and sundry objects accumulated here over the centuries. So many things held on to- what purpose did they serve, but to clutter?

Absent-mindedly kicking a collection of posters and other gallimaufry on the floor, Halfdan noticed an unusual edge. Moving them further aside, he realized that it was actually a trapdoor. He quickly pulled it up, revealing a yawning hole of cold darkness below. Something *else* was inherent in the darkness too, something *unpleasantly familiar*. If his calculations were correct, he should be directly below the Room of Remediation now.

Halfdan allowed his consciousness to open even further, as he scanned the room that he was still in. Nothing seemed to be out of the ordinary, so he readied for his venture down. He set his makeshift spear aside. Grasping feebly in the shadow, he finally found what felt like a wooden ladder, though he could have sworn it wasn't there when he had first reached for it.

So he began his slow descent, lowering himself into the dark hole. The dusty, musty, cluttered cellar above seemed almost home-like when compared to the unknown abyss into which he now descended. And grasping a lantern while climbing down made such work even more difficult.

Once the light cleared the floor, it began to illume what was below- some sort of strange sub-basement room. Halfdan caught a glimpse of demented, smiling cat pictures scrawled on the wall. And was that a pile of something white? He couldn't get a good look until he reached the floor, which was still a good 20' below.

He continued his descent as the old, wooden ladder creaked. Something seemed to move out of the corner of his eye. He stopped, glanced, but saw nothing. A chill ran down his spine. He waited- hovering in space, feeble lantern light sputtering.

The ladder creaked again, but this time he knew he hadn't moved. The silence below seemed to be waiting, too. His sinuses cleared enough to allow in the stench of old death.

He waited again, breath bated.

Suddenly, as a hideous laughter erupted all around him, the ladder tumbled beneath. His body felt paralyzed as he flew down into the darkness, lantern now illuming piles of Sir Comkorn books and long dead bodies, killed in horrific ways. Halfdan mouthed an Odinnic prayer. As he crashed into the skeleton of some long-dead female tutor, he caught a glimpse of a photo negative-being catching the spinning lantern. He smiled evilly at Halfdan.

At least the ghost had a respect for books.

* * *

"OOOOOOOWWWWWWWW!"

Perhaps the Goblin Chief Snik Snak was finally learning how to speak Amercian, after all.

Oborren had noticed this before in many of the humanoid 'interrogations' he had performed in the past. Poking the little monster with hot, sharp objects in unfortunate places could certainly have the effect of breaking the language barrier. Perhaps the goblin was playing dumb the entire time and actually could speak Amercian? Oborren secretly hoped that wasn't the case, for he was finally getting the hang of torturing....

"Tell me now, sir, is this little bastard telling you anything of merit yet?"

Oborren fought back his irritation at the interruption by Colonel Siegfried. True, True, the man had saved his life only a couple of hours ago, so it could be worse, but few things bothered the hunter more than having one of his 'interrogations' interrupted.

"He might tell me something... if you let me interrogate him!"

The Colonel smiled; he could certainly understand sadism.

Just then Tepson walked in and caught the evil glint in Siegfried's eye. Tepson wondered why the party wasn't torturing the Colonel along with the goblin: he seemed evil enough to warrant it.

Oborren grabbed another hot poker from the nearby fire. He smiled cruelly as he approached and pointed it at the goblin's eye. The formerly proud leader of the goblins let out a terrified shriek.

"Me not know why me invade stupid human town! Me not like humans for obvious reasons!"

This goblin did seem familiar. If he wasn't mistaken, Oborren could have sworn that this was the same goblin that the party had captured prior to entering the goblin cavern. It was hard to tell for certain though- most goblins of the same breed looked alike.

Just as the hunter readied himself to finish off the insolent wretch, a raven flew in through the window and landed on Oborren's shoulder. Ravens were one of Odin's most notable messengers. And, not taking Odin to be one to spare a goblin's life, the hunter mused that it was here for some other purpose.

Sighing in misguided relief, Snik Snak exclaimed, "Oh, thank Great Megajack in Sky for sending large black ugly bird to tell stupid humans to spare me!"

Siegfried and Tepson too stared at the raven on the hunter's shoulder. It seemed to have a deep wisdom and clarity about it, far more than some others currently in the room.

Not realizing how much he was pressing his luck, Snik Snak continued, "Oh, yes! Let us eat big ugly black bird together- it looks delicious! Then you can free Snik Snak and let him return to his cave and we can all be happy friends- yes! Me really like eat big black birds though me much prefer eat stupid hu--, err I mean... dog."

The others tried to ignore the goblin and focus on the raven, feeling the obvious divine presence in the room. It then made a deep croaking sound and flew out the window. Oborren and Tepson, being adventurers, made to follow of course.

"Oh yes! Big ugly dark bird fly away! You let Snik Snak out too and he can help catch it- oh yes! Me real good at catch birds. One time me catch big yellow bird, but it turn out to be megajack baby that sting me... Don't let such delicious bird get away!"

Assuming that the matter was now settled, the goblin began to shift around in his bonds, so as to better have his new friends untie him and assist in the search. Oborren stepped forward and, to Siegfried's and Tepson's surprise, actually slashed through the little monster's bonds, freeing him.

The hunter turned to his startled companions, "Who knows where this raven will lead us, but it will probably be somewhere..." he paused as he made an evil look at the goblin, "...dangerous".

* * *

"Why couldn't Odin have sent a Valkyrie?" muttered Kolveig. "Perhaps I could follow some hot, blonde warrior-woman, but some croaking black bird? Does this really Justify the Ends of Class Struggle?"

Oborren glared at the Karlist for his heresy. Why couldn't he follow a *real* god? But before the hunter could chastise him, Snik Snak's whining drew his attention again.

"Me not know why me not help follow big black bird better without rope on neck!"

Oborren knew better than to encourage him with a reply. Whether it be a Karlist cleric, a deposed yellow goblin chieftain, or a talking fish, he realized that would only make them talk even *more*.

Brymanah settled the matter with a simultaneous slap to both the cleric and the goblin's heads. The raven had now landed on the eave to the Schoolhouse's cellar door.

Great, thought Oborren, what a pleasant place to explore.

Dan Osarchuk

Halfdan came around to a fiery pain in his leg. Perhaps it had broken when he had fallen? What was certain was that the skeleton that he had landed on was broken. He could only imagine at what Billy had done to the poor tutor ages ago... and what he would also do to the former tutor who was at his mercy now.

"So... are... you... here... to... punish... me..., tutor...?" the ghost's voice sounded as a graveyard storm; his eyes shown with bottomless malice.

Halfdan simply stared back. He was ready to die, though in the case of a ghost, it might not really be death he was facing. Whatever the case, if this was what his life's picture showed now, then so be it. He thanked God that he could face the end with a quiet mind. True, he would deeply miss Kelne and Larnen, and really wished he had met that blonde woman and got to tell her how he felt, but still, who could have asked for more?

Undeterred by his calmness, Billy smashed the cleric with his supernatural force. Thrusting him against the far wall, Halfdan was certain that his leg was broken now, if not coming off completely. The sensation was intense, but did it matter? It was just sensation. He remained the observer; the space around the sensation, Halfdan's broken body, and the unquiet spirit of Billy.

Blinking forward with appalling speed, the ghost closed the distance with the cleric again, only to push forward with his ethereal hand, right into Halfdan's chest.

Sounds could be heard overhead. And the cleric felt compelled to let out a loud, "See!", as his heart was being crushed.

Billy's energy flickered for a moment and Halfdan noticed more of the terror overcome his body and mind; terror that he had known long before in Seavilla, a darkness that matched this dim world that he had ventured into, all those decades ago.

Night Skies Over Valhallow

The ghost felt the darkness inside the cleric's heart, too, darkness of love lost, of life denied. Billy's darkness reflected that to an extent, but it was less deep, less true. The ghost's was an evil darkness, born out of spite- not loss, not love.

Billy's form continued to flicker and Halfdan felt his heart stop. Soon he would be with his beloved again in Valhalla, or at least, he hoped that he would, and he thanked God for that.

Chapter 30

All the Tidings We Bring

Oborren rushed forward as Kolveig intoned against the supernatural entity. It vanished easily, its power already weakened by its exchange with the fallen Odinnic. Tepson ran forward and checked the broken man's pulse- nothing.

Snik Snak whined and mewled, but a stern glance from Brymanah silenced the goblin.

She surveyed the area. It didn't take a hunter to know that a ghost couldn't have been killed that easily. Pushing aside the morbid remains of Billy's ancient victims and the bizarre Smiling Cat books, she looked over Halfdan's lifeless form. All but Tepson recognized him from that night in Valhallow, many moons ago.

Hearing the sound of someone yelling "see" a few minutes before had brought the party to the sub-basement quite quickly. They reasoned that it must have been Halfdan.

"Poor sod must have got more than he bargained for," said Kolveig. "Though of course, bargaining is Counter-Revolutionary, because of its Capitalistic..."

Ignoring the cleric, the amazon spied something to the side, near where the dead Odinnic lay. There she uncovered an ancient alcove which housed a similarly ancient thinking machine.

Night Skies Over Valhallow

Rushing over, Tepson couldn't believe what he saw. This thing was almost as old as him! What would such an old computer be doing in the den of some homicidal maniac's ghost? The machine's 'on' button stared back at him.

He pushed it; he couldn't help it, he was a gnome, after all.

The button did not work like he had hoped though. Something prevented it from becoming fully depressed. Tepson quickly opened the back of the computer to investigate. To his shock, the inside was full of a white powder: no wonder the button didn't work.

Oborren moved up and sampled the powder. "Tastes like bone."

"See- it took a man to figure it out!" teased Kolveig.

Brymanah's face turned red in the flickering lamplight. She glared at the Karlist; venom in her eyes, hand on her cutlass.

As the two fell into clamorous debate, the hunter sprinkled holy water into the ancient thinking machine and intoned to the Gods. He hoped that it would lay the remains of Billy Berray to final rest.

Tepson shook his head at the blatant destruction of such a relic, but since he had caught a glimpse of the ghost himself, he felt that maybe such superstition might not be unfounded.

"Let's bring this one back up with us," offered Oborren as he gestured at Halfdan's lifeless body. If he let Kolveig and Brymanah's argument go on much longer, there might be even more corpses to carry up.

"And Kolveig: make sure you reattach his leg first. And somebody torch those books!"

* * *

It was a warm, late spring day. The two lovebirds, now reunited hand-in-hand, strolled through the verdant countryside. He had been away on campaign, his gun arm still aching, though her presence seemed to always ease his pain, no matter how potent.

She smiled lovingly as she gazed at him, her clear blue eyes framed by her dark eyebrows and classic blonde hair. He smiled back, not only was she the epitome of beauty, but she was also the epitome of love and friendship, too. Her clever wit was only surpassed by her sweet and deep, gentle grace. Her very presence was heaven; she was home to him.

He glanced around at the budding leaves of the forest, unsettling memories of his last campaign creeping into his mind, terrible things that he had done for King and Country. But it was all worth it- he was with her again! He made up his mind to retire his commission, to finally marry her and raise a family. The thrill of war was one thing, but it only took him away from her. Why keep doing it?

They embraced; love holding love, one holding the other. Kissing her was akin to becoming one with perfection, where all made sense and all was shining.

She smiled when they were through, offering yet another clever remark, a perfect blend of tease and adoration for one such as he.

Then the shot rang out.

As she lay in his arms dying, he knew that the war had found him here. Just as he had shot others, so now too his love, his true one, had been shot. Right in the belly too, where their new family would have been born. Whether it was some errant hunter or even one seeking revenge upon him, it did not matter: she would be gone from him forever... and it was his fault.

She looked at him knowing that he would never let her go, and that he would thereby suffer eternally, never truly loving another out of devotion to her, his true love. She smiled as she touched his check with her pale hand. He could be so silly sometimes...

So again, Halfdan stood upon Gallow's Hill, noose around his neck.

I know I hung upon a windswept tree...

A gray bearded man with an eyepatch stared back at him, silent.

...nine long nights...

Perhaps this was Valhalla. Was this Odin? Was his lost love a Valkyrie now?

*...Wounded with a spear, dedicated to Odin
Myself to myself...*

He gazed back at his lost love, vowing to always hold her in his loving embrace, always. Always.

... on that tree of which no man knows...

The one eye of the bearded man seemed to answer in silent reply.

...from where its roots run

* * *

"OH MY WONDERFUL TUTORS! WE HAVE A SPECIAL GUEST HERE FOR YOU TODAY!"

The obligatory clown band played with all its usual sinister false-conviviality to announce the speaker in the library. Tutors watched as a large automaton rolled into the room, some looking on in terror, others in resigned acquiescence at yet another Mandatory R'ti Schoolhouse Required Meeting. Still, this was not the usual Guest Speaker, it was Mr. Enak.

"ALL T....TUTORS WHO F....FAILED TO MAKE 187% G...GROWTH THIS Q...QUARTER ARE C....COMPELLED TO RISE." The automaton's booming, monotone voice was interrupted by

244

some stuttering. Perhaps it had been damaged and was malfunctioning somewhat?

Some tutors laughed and others cried as the Assistant Monitors called out the names of various tutors who didn't make the 187%. They stood on either side of the room. Mdme Carve smiled wickedly at the spectacle, savoring the fear in the tutors' eyes. Doing it this way allowed for ALL the tutors to feel the righteous judgment of R'ti!

Carve felt a strange feeling of loss though. There wasn't that usual sense of dark delight in the room for some reason.

As the "Leadership Team" of Mdme Carve, her Assistant Monitors, and Enak chastised those standing with embarrassments and threats, a few tutors noticed a group of adventurers carrying the lifeless body of Mr. Halfdan out of the cellar on a makeshift stretcher. One of them even held a yellow goblin on a leash- not what one would expect to see in the middle of a Required Meeting.

Noticing that her tutor audience was not giving the Chastisement its full attention, Mdme Carve rushed over to see what the disturbance was. Seeing that Halfdan was dead made her quite happy, but otherwise, this Unauthorized Admittance onto Schoolhouse Grounds was unacceptable!

"Oh, Enak! Could you come here a minute?"

Few Mandatory R'ti Schoolhouse Required Meetings were this exciting. For certain, the Monitor Director might occasionally grace the tutors with his presence from time-to-time, but this was far more interesting. The Guest Speaker was now fighting a bunch of Invaders who were carrying the corpse of a former Tutor-Under-Review. And even though Enak still stuttered in his attacks, the party seemed to be no match.

* * *

Night Skies Over Valhallow

Oborren ducked as the automaton's clawed arm swung at him. It had knocked his feeble flail attack aside with ease, but at least he had gotten out of its way. Tepson was not so lucky- the little guy was now caught in the thing's other claw and was being used to club the other party members. He wasn't sure which was more painful: the crushing or the clubbing.

Brymanah let out a war cry, emboldened by the many female tutors who were watching. Even Mdme Carve seemed impressed by the amazon's ferocity, since many Schoolhouses were implicitly matriarchical in nature, if not explicitly so.

"SOMEONE IS SHOWING HER 187%- BUT IN THE WRONG WAY!" Carve's yells got some chuckles from the assembled tutors.

Her attitude soon changed though when the amazon sliced her cutlass into Enak's head, taking one his plastic eyes clean off.

The corpse of Halfdan seemed to stir slightly. Perhaps even his lifeless body recoiled at yet one more Mandatory R'ti Schoolhouse Required Meeting?

The Head Monitor roared in rage as she tackled the amazon, tutors dashing to get out of the way. Brymanah was surprised at the woman's strength, realizing that she must be some sort of cultist. How else could she be so strong?

Seizing the opportunity, Kolveig pulled out his Marxian hammer, ran right passed the disoriented automaton, and stood in front of the remaining tutors. He had the perfect speech prepared for them.

Oborren shook his head in frustration; Enak regained its bearing and lumbered forward with his Tepson-club ready to strike.

As he narrowly avoided being bashed by his gnome friend's body, Oborren considered that it might be time to fall back.

Suddenly Halfdan, apparently now revived, rushed in behind the automaton. He held a steward's broken mop handle as a makeshift spear. With silent intensity, he struck the automaton's back, piercing through and breaking some inner part.

Enak went berserk. Tutors fled in terror as it screamed and flayed its arms in a frenzied, demented manner.

"NO! WRONG COMMAND! FORBIDDEN! NO! OVERRIDE!!!"

Moving in closer, Halfdan dropped his spear and smashed Enak over the head with a large tome. The sound thundered throughout the room, silencing the devil inside.

Oborren's eyes met his in understanding, as the Unabridged Dictionary burst into flame when it made contact with the now exposed circuits of the broken robot's head. What a terrible sacrifice it was, but necessary.

At this, any remaining tutors broke and ran, hoping that they would not be written-up for leaving the Required Meeting before being Officially Dismissed. Hounds of Vigilance began to flood into the room, white tunics gleaming in contrast to the increasingly smoky mess, which was once Enak. Even the obligatory Clown Band made their escape.

With Carve now fleeing after losing the catfight, Brymanah pried Tepson from the robot's finally motionless claw. She was impressed at the gnome's toughness. She then noticed Halfdan standing before her and glanced at him with incredulity. Something in his eyes defied description.

The slender man smiled back, "I was already dead."

Kolveig made his way back to the party too, disappointed that he had lost the chance to give such a captive audience of tutors his Karlist Lesson in Committee Formation.

Night Skies Over Valhallow

The five all gave each other knowing glances as they attempted to slip out of the Schoolhouse before the Watch arrived. It looked like the Mandatory R'ti Schoolhouse Required Meeting was over.

* * *

The party stalked down the hall, trying to conceal their weapons and obviously inappropriate attire. Perhaps if we were wearing clown make-up, we might escape notice, thought Oborren.

Still, the area was in a profound state of confusion: tutors running around screaming, Hounds of Vigilance attempting to keep calm, and even one of the Assistant Monitors spouting R'ti rhetoric in a pointless effort to redirect them all.

Of course, a hunter dressed all in black, an obvious Karlist cleric, a half-dressed amazon, a gnome from the distant past, an Odinnic ex-tutor back from the grave, and a deposed yellow goblin chieftain on a leash found it hard to blend in. A number of the Hounds rushed to confront the party, only to pull back when the latter unsheathed their many weapons again.

Seeing an opening to the exit, the party made a run for it. To the left stood the door to the outside; to the right stood Mdme Carve, a look of resignation on her face. Halfdan couldn't resist. He nodded to his comrades as they dashed out the escape, promising to meet up with him again in Valhallow.

The aging Odinnic stared at the woman who had ruined his life.

"Please allow me to apologize to you, Mr. Halfdan, obviously we were under the control of that hideous automaton, Enak..."

She motioned for him to follow, to continue the discussion in her office. As he did so, he noticed that Carve's two Assistants had just arrived: Beauly and Hollowspoke. The three often worked as a team when they spoke to tutors, or apparently, even ex-tutors such as Halfdan. Perhaps they had some sort of psychic link?

Dan Osarchuk

Halfdan sat in the chair across from Mdme Carve's desk and reminisced. He had been in this office many times before over the years, but under vastly different circumstances, with reasonable and understanding Head Monitors, Assistant Monitors- Monitors who had respected him as a tutor.

The three current Monitors stared back at him in stark contrast, a wicked smile forming on Carve's lips. She stared at what she saw to be a skinny, aging ex-tutor freak; a freak who had attempted to get other tutors to usurp her Enlightened Rulership. A monster that had disrupted one of her precious Mandatory R'ti Schoolhouse Required Meetings and even destroyed the mortal vessel of her precious Master, Enak!

Her finger caressed her shock-button. The cleric stared back at her, unmoved; mind quiet.

She had seen him dead only minutes ago! Perhaps this would REALLY kill him? But then she hesitated. No. Death would be too easy for Halfdan. This ex-tutor freak was what was wrong with Schoolhouses today: a tutor who did not put Scores before Humanity. A tutor who did not bow to her Righteous Tyranny, nor to the Group Conformity that such Tyranny required. A tutor who did not surrender himself entirely to the Most Holy Edicts of R'ti. No wonder they weren't making 187% Annua Incrementum!

No. He should suffer! She nodded to Beauly, who let the Watch in. This time Halfdan would be taken to the Gaol for his crimes. Let's see if he would remain *unmoved* then!

Perhaps the Watch would not understand the Crimes Against R'ti that this former tutor scum had committed, but it was no matter: other crimes could certainly be *described* that the Watch *would* understand. And who would they believe: some pathetic ex-tutor or some Pillars of the Community that were she and her two loyal Assistants?

Halfdan's mind remained quiet as the watchmen escorted him away. In the distance, he could hear the crows cawing. He let go and surrendered to Odin's will, to God's will.

He knew that whatever happened, God would be with him. And he knew too that he was already dead, that whatever seemed to happen to him simply appeared on the screen of life. All else he could let go of. *The question* became clear.

All that was left was I.

And where was the problem in that?